Romancing
the
Cat Burglar

ALSO BY PAMELA GOSSIAUX

Praise for Mrs. Chartwell and the Cat Burglar

A runner-up in the 2018
New York Book Festival

"Mrs. Chartwell and the Cat Burglar is a highly suspenseful, self-described romantic mystery that tugs at your heart and satisfies your intellect.
— John J. Kelly, *Detroit Free Press*

"Mrs. Chartwell and the Cat Burglar is a lovely story and I highly recommend it! It has everything you could wish for: mystery, suspense, romance and a great adventure. I just couldn't put it down!"
— Susan Keefe, *Midwest Book Review*

"Pamela Gossiaux is fast becoming a major player in the realm of writing. She deserves the wards and attention that are bound to come her way!"
— Grady Harp, *Top 100 Amazon* Hall of Fame Reviewer

"The story is well thought out, well written and well worth your time to read."
— William D. Curnutt, *Amazon Vine Voice*

"What a fun read! If you like the feel of movies on TMC you'll like this book. It's a good story spun with great lines and interesting characters."
— Diana Lesire Brandmeyer, *award-winning Christian author*

"It's a cozy, uplifting read for anyone looking for a good story to curl up with. Optional accessories: a cup of something warm and a cat in their lap."
— Xanthe Muller, *Goodreads Reviewer*

"This is a mystery, perhaps a Cozy, but really much more, and is marked by constant cliff hangers and a great ending (that I won't give away)."
— Greg Jolley, author of the *Danser* novels

Romancing

the

Cat Burglar

pamela
gossiaux

Tri-Cat Publishing

Scripture quotations are taken from The Holy Bible, New International Version, copyright 1973, 1978, 1984 by International Bible Society.

Visit the author's website at: www.PamelaGossiaux.com

First Printing, December 2018
Library of Congress Control Number: 2018909937

ISBN 978-0-9987669-4-2 (paperback)
ISBN 978-0-9987669-5-9 (ebook)

Cover Design: Llewellen Designs
Editor: Erin Wolfe, WordWolfe Copy Editing
Formatting: Dallas Hodge, www.ebeetbee.com
Author Photo: Vera Davis Photography

Published in the United States by Tri-Cat Publishing

Tri-Cat Publishing

To Regina, who first introduced me to Paris.
Merci pour les souvenirs, chère amie!

Chapter One

The harness was digging in to Abigail's thigh. She tried adjusting it, but that was hard to do while she was dangling two stories above someone's living room. They had come in through the skylight because Tony had declared the perimeter alarms impenetrable.

She could think of a million things she'd rather be doing right now than breaking in to a home on the west side in an attempt to steal a priceless Picasso.

"This is hurting my leg," Abigail whispered. "The material is all bunched up."

"I told you to wear the pants from the suit I bought for you," Tony whispered back. He was dangling next to her, clad from head to toe in black spandex (*his* pants were probably fine) and digging a can of hairspray out of his backpack.

"They're in the laundry," Abigail whispered. "How long is this going to take?"

"Perfection takes time," Tony whispered back. He sprayed the hairspray in an arc across the air, careful not to get any on the painting. He was looking for laser beams that might trip an alarm. The moisture crystals settled on them down below, highlighting a crisscross pattern a few feet above the living room floor. They were safe up here.

"I have to finish packing," Abigail whispered. "I can't go to Paris with nothing to wear."

Tony capped the hairspray can and looked over at her. "I wouldn't mind," he said, winking at her. "It *is* our honeymoon."

Abigail held back a smile and tried to look irritated, although she didn't know how much he could see of her here in the near dark, especially with her ski mask on. She looked down at the beams as the hairspray dissipated. She wasn't a fan of heights.

"Ready?" Tony said.

She nodded and let up on the latch. Slowly, she lowered herself until she was hanging right in front of the painting. Tony was beside her.

"It's beautiful," he whispered. "Do you have any idea what this is worth on the black market?"

"Do you have any idea how much I don't care?" Abigail said. She pulled her phone out and looked at the time.

Tony spun on the rope so he was facing her. He crossed his arms. "You're *bored!*"

"I'm not *bored*," she hissed. "I just want to get home and finish packing. Can we hurry this up?"

They were right next to each other, but Tony grabbed her rope and pulled her closer. Their faces were nearly touching. "I have an idea," he whispered. He had that familiar, mischievous glint in his eye.

"Oh no."

"*You* can do it this time!"

"Do what?"

"Steal the painting!"

Abigail looked at the priceless work of art. She could imagine her well-manicured fingernails accidently scraping off some of the paint. Even through her gloves. "I'm not touching it."

"Here." Tony opened an app on his phone. "Hold this up and tap on this button. It will scan for an electrical signature to tell you if it's alarmed."

She took it. Anything to hurry this up. Plus, she had to admit, the electronic gadget looked fun to try. She waved it in front of the painting. The app showed a steady red line.

"Nothing," Tony said, shaking his head in disapproval. "Tsk, tsk."

Abigail handed the phone back to Tony, resigned herself to the task, and carefully put one hand on each side of the painting. It was about three feet by four feet, and the frame was thick. She lifted it up.

"It's heavy," she said.

Tony reached over and helped her lift it off the wall. He looked behind it, shook his head, and then put it back.

"Seriously?" he said, looking down. "*You don't have the Picasso alarmed?*"

Abigail looked below to the middle-aged man, who was sitting on the sofa, watching them. His arms were crossed. He shook his head.

"Who needs alarms? You two make enough noise to wake up the entire neighborhood." Jeffrey Steiner, the homeowner, had hired their security company to see if it was possible to steal his beloved Picasso. Apparently, it was.

"You need to have the overhead area secured," Tony said. "I easily got in from your skylight. I'd easily get right back out again with your painting. Take the measurements. It fits through the hole."

Steiner pushed a few buttons on his own phone, and the lights in the house came on. "I've disarmed the beams. You can come down now.

Thank goodness! Abigail's right leg was practically numb. She lowered herself down next to Tony so they were standing in front of Steiner. She pulled her ski mask off and the static made the loose strands of her long red hair cling to her face. She was glad she had worn it in a ponytail.

"I can easily wire overhead," Tony said, pulling off his own mask. His dark, wavy hair seemed to settle right in to place. "And you have another skylight in the bathroom upstairs. I saw it when I was on the roof."

"Nobody is going to crawl through that," Steiner said.

"Don't your children sleep up there?" Tony countered.

Steiner smiled. "You're right. Wire us up tight. I don't want my Picasso *or* my children to go missing."

Abigail coiled up her rope as the men talked. Tony would come back when they returned from Paris to install the new wires. "You'll probably be fine until then," he said. "Your perimeter alarm is impenetrable. Except, of course, for the roof."

Steiner signed the contract. They shook hands, and left.

"That was fun," Abigail said when they were in the car. "Kind of." She was rubbing her leg.

Tony looked at her, his brown eyes twinkling with mischief. "You were *complaining!* I remember when you would have given your right arm to do that a few months ago!"

"I almost gave my right leg tonight."

"I told you to wear the spandex. It's slipperier, and the fabric gives."

Abigail smiled. "Are you a fashion consultant now?"

It was like that, the witty banter they had. She loved it. After a whirlwind marriage five months ago, she still delighted in spending time with him. Tony, a recently reformed cat burglar, had left the life of crime to follow his heart and marry her, a librarian of rare maps and documents. It was at her university library that they had initially met when he descended from her own skylight to steal a map.

Tony pulled up in front of the three-story Victorian house that Abigail had inherited from her aunt. She had filled the home with shelves of books, and when her well-read husband added his collection, they decided to turn one of the guest rooms into a mini-library.

Abigail opened the door and Cocoa, her petite tortoiseshell cat, rubbed against her legs, meowing. "I know, it's late," Abigail said, reaching down to scratch her behind the ears. "It's 11 p.m. Your daddy kept us out past our bedtimes."

Tony laughed. "Mommy just wants to pack. But the plane doesn't leave until tomorrow afternoon."

"But there's so much to do!" Abigail said. "Are *you* packed?"

Tony took her jacket from her and hung it up. Then he turned to her and pulled her into his arms. "All that matters to me is that we're together."

Their faces were close. She could smell his minty breath and his sandalwood aftershave. "And that you have clean underwear," she said.

"They probably have entire stores in Paris dedicated to the sale of underwear," Tony said. "Let's go to bed. It's late, and stealing priceless art wears me out."

Abigail hesitated. She wanted to throw a load of laundry in. And she needed to write out the information about the cat with the vet's phone number. Just in case. Pauline, her friend and co-worker, was coming over to feed Cocoa while they were away.

But Tony leaned in and gave her a gentle kiss on her cheek. His lips were close to her ear, and she could feel his breath. *"Upon thy cheek I lay this zealous kiss, As seal to the indenture of my love."*

And now he was quoting Shakespeare. She tried to place the quote. It was one of the kings. There were so many plays about kings. King Henry. No, King John.

"You're trying to distract me," Abigail whispered.

"She's beautiful, and therefore to be wooed; She is woman, and therefore to be won." Abigail giggled. Tony softly kissed her on the lips.

"Tomorrow we'll be in Paris," he said. "The City of Love."

"The City of Lights," she corrected.

"Love. Light. Same thing."

She hugged him to her. Only a few months ago, she thought she had lost him forever. But he was hers. He was safe. And finally, they would go on their long-awaited honeymoon.

"Okay. But I at least want to throw that one load of laundry in first," she said. "I can dry it in the morning." He reluctantly let her go, and she went downstairs. Their basement had unfinished cement walls and a cold concrete floor. Tony wanted to refinish it this summer.

She was pleased to see that Tony had already sorted the laundry earlier in the day. Most of it was washed, she saw, and folded. She put a load of darks into the washer. She wanted to be sure her favorite pair of jeans was dry so she could wear them on the plane. She thought about Tony, upstairs waiting for her. Their life had settled into a routine these last few weeks. It had been pretty crazy and stressful since they got married. Abigail was up for tenure, which would be decided next month, and she was on probation at her job until after Paris. Tony was the reason she had to prove herself at the maps symposium where she was presenting. Abigail had brought in a rare map collection to the university, only to find out that one of the maps was acquired by the collector illegally. Tony had been the one to steal it several years prior. That's how the collector came to have it.

It had all ended well, or rather, terribly, depending on how you looked at it. The collector, Jean-Pierre Mauvais, had kidnapped Abigail, holding her as ransom to get Tony to do another illegal job for him. She had shot Mauvais (only in the *wrist*, thank God. He was okay now) in order to escape. And at the end of it all, she had to confess to her boss that she had met Tony when he broke in to the library some six weeks before to commit a theft. The past few months had been difficult at work, and the trial with Jean-Pierre Mauvais had left her drained.

It was all a mess, but this trip was her chance to make amends by showcasing their university library to the world and hopefully bringing in some funding. It was also a chance to reconnect with her library director. She owed Ms. Scott for keeping her on even after Abigail had kept Tony's true identity from her.

The fabric of one of her shirts snagged on her wedding ring. She gasped and looked at her hand to be sure the ring was okay. It seemed to be. The emerald was precious to her. She shuddered as she remembered how Jean-Pierre had threatened to take it, even if he had to cut off her finger to get it.

The ring was valuable because of its history. It was a gift given by a famous Italian painter to his lover to seal their illicit relationship. The painter was Tony's great-grandfather, and the child resulting from that relationship was his grandma. It was Tony's goal to learn more about his past while on this trip. His grandma had raised him, and Tony had never known his extended family, which was something he always longed for.

"The most important thing in the world is family and love," Tony often said as he held her in his arms. She knew how much he cherished her. And how much that had cost both of them.

She closed the lid to the washer. As she turned the dial to "on," she thought again of their trip. They would finally have a chance to celebrate their honeymoon. While Paris was a work trip, they had left plenty of time to explore the city. With her romantic husband by her side, she knew it would be amazing.

She smiled and turned off the light in the basement. Cocoa meowed and ran up the stairs ahead of her, eager to go to bed. Abigail would go cuddle up next to her husband, and tomorrow, she would leave for Paris!

She would secure her job and her tenure and work on rebuilding their marriage after all of the stress of the past few months. Maybe now their life could finally settle down.

Chapter Two

Tony had trouble containing his excitement as their plane circled over France. In a very short while, they would land.

"Look!" he said. "Is that the Eiffel Tower?" He had tried to maintain the air of "international mystery thief" to impress Abigail, but he just couldn't hold it in.

"I see it!" She leaned across him to get a better view. "Wow!"

He had flown before. He was pretty sure she had too, but she seemed just as excited as he was. "You've taken some short flights in the States, right?" he asked her.

"The *States?*" she responded, raising an eyebrow.

"That's what we world travelers refer to the US as."

Abigail laughed. "Yes, I've flown to a few workshops about maps, but only short distances. I've done some *state*-hopping."

Tony squinted out the window, trying to see. The sky was pink with the early sun. It was 6 a.m. here. Midnight back home. He had tried to get some sleep on the plane, but neither he nor Abigail had managed much. They watched a movie, ate the cardboard-like dinner, and played a few games of cards. But they didn't get much sleep.

Abigail was winding up her earbuds and putting her tray table up. Tony glanced over at her. He would make this the best trip she had ever taken. He owed it to her. Her life had been pretty quiet before he came in to it. But he brought trouble. His past had caught up with him and nearly gotten her killed.

He didn't like to think about that or about the friendship with George his lies had cost him. His best friend, best man at their wedding, hadn't spoken to him since Tony had confessed to being a criminal, doing jobs in his private time when George

8

thought he was working late. He *was* working, only at stealing, not at something legitimate.

And Jimmy, Abigail's friend and kind-of father figure. He was a cop and had given Abigail away at the wedding, trusting Tony. He repaid Jimmy by nearly getting her killed. Jimmy was still giving Tony the cold shoulder, although his wife, Martha, called regularly.

Tony sighed. He felt Abigail take his hand.

"What's wrong?" she asked.

He turned to her and smiled. Her thick, dark red hair lay in tangles across her shoulders, messy from where she had pulled her earbuds off. "Nothing," he said. "Nothing at all. I'm just so happy to be here. With you."

"Me too."

They hadn't had time for a honeymoon. When they got married, Abigail was working on a project with the map collector Jean-Pierre Mauvais. Tony still couldn't say his name without feeling sick. And Tony had been working community service to make up for his crimes. He was only here in Paris because his lawyer friend, Jonathan Stewart, had gotten him some leave.

So yes. Tony had to make this trip the best Abigail had ever had. She deserved it. Despite everything he had put her through, she still loved him.

After a short while, they landed at Charles de Gaulle airport. It took a while to claim their luggage. Abigail slung her laptop bag over one shoulder and her purse across the other. That left a hand free to pull her suitcase. Tony had his laptop and luggage as well.

"I have the train tickets," he said. It would take them into Paris proper. They were going straight to the hotel and were supposed to meet up with Lulu Scott, the library director, later that day.

The weather was more temperate here in June than back home in Michigan. It was a cool 57 degrees that morning. Tony tried to do the conversion to Celsius in his head but failed. He still couldn't figure that out. Anyway, it was expected to get to 73° Fahrenheit today and be sunny. Perfect.

They boarded the train for the thirty-minute ride into the capital. There were some early morning commuters, all looking fairly sleepy. Tony felt his own eyes starting to close, but he saw a sign warning that thieves worked the train. He made sure to stay awake. In no time, they were there.

"Look!" This time it was Abigail who was excited. "The Eiffel Tower!"

They climbed off the train and looked around them. The city was waking up, and the streets were busy with pedestrians carrying espressos, crusty breads, and pastries.

Tony realized his stomach was growling. "I'm starved."

They needed to find a taxi and get to the hotel. Abigail had her map out. "Let's start walking this way, and we'll eventually run across a taxi."

The crowded sidewalk made Tony nervous. He was always cautious in crowds. He began to steer Abigail clear of the people.

Suddenly someone bumped in to Abigail hard, knocking her against Tony.

"My purse!" Abigail yelled.

Tony saw the thief. He had Abigail's purse in his hand and was running along the sidewalk ahead of them, knocking people out of the way. He was wearing dark trousers and a sweatshirt with the hood pulled up over his head. There was an alleyway about thirty feet up to his right, and Tony knew instinctually that he'd duck down that and be lost. Quickly, he dropped his luggage, handed Abigail his laptop, and took off after the guy.

"Tony, no!" Abigail yelled, but he wasn't stopping until he caught the jerk. He heard Abigail's frantic voice. "Somebody help us! That man stole my purse!"

Then out of nowhere, a woman stepped in front of the fleeing thief and stuck her foot out. It was that simple. Tony saw it as if in slow motion. She turned, stretched her leg out, and tripped the running man, who was looking behind his shoulder at the time to see if there was anybody close on his heels. He had a bandana tied across his face. Only his blue eyes showed.

The man took a head dive, tumbled, and dropped the purse, which slid across the sidewalk. He rolled, got to his feet, and darted, taking the alley ahead of him as Tony suspected he would.

But he left the purse behind.

An older gentleman picked up the purse and handed it to the woman who tripped the thief. She brushed it off and handed it to Tony, who had stopped in front of her.

She looked like she was in her late twenties. Thick brown hair was plaited in a long French braid down her back. She had big, dark brown eyes. She wore a calf-length navy skirt, a white cotton blouse, and a soft leather jacket that hung open in the front.

"Thank you," Tony said, taking the purse. He glanced up ahead. There was no sign of the thief. He had been tall, and slightly built.

"Do you want me to find the police?" she asked in perfect English.

Tony glanced behind him. Abigail was still standing there with the luggage, holding both laptops and looking very shaken.

"Please, come with me," Tony said, and they trotted back to Abigail. He wrapped his wife in a firm, warm hug. "Are you okay?" People had already gone back to their business on the street, as if nothing had happened.

"I'm fine," Abigail said, pulling back and taking her purse. She turned to the woman. "Thank you."

"I could call the police," the woman said. "But the man who stole your purse is long gone, and I didn't get a look at his face. This happens quite a bit along here, unfortunately."

Abigail pulled out her wallet. "Everything seems to be here. Let's not worry about it. But thank you." She held out her hand, and the woman grasped it firmly and shook it. "I'm Abigail."

"I'm Lena," the woman said.

"Tony," he said, shaking her hand. "You're very brave."

Lena laughed, a light, tinkling sound that caused her eyes to light up. "Not at all. Just used to the ways around here. I work as a tour guide."

"A tour guide?" Abigail asked.

"Yes. I'm an art buff, so I give tours of some of the famous painters. I talk about where they worked, their history, stuff like that. Some of them have interesting stories. Monet, Van Gogh, Russo."

"Russo?" Tony repeated. That was his great-grandfather, the man who had painted *Laurel*, which hung in their university's museum back home. It seemed a little too convenient that they had encountered a woman who knew information on his grandfather just minutes after they arrived in Paris. But then again, Russo was famous, and Paris had been his stomping ground. Tony had a habit of being overly-suspicious.

Lena laughed her tinkling laugh again. "Yes. He's my favorite! Are you familiar with him?"

"Somewhat," Tony said, giving Abigail a look. He didn't want her to tell Lena they were related to the painter. He'd like to hear an unbiased version of the history. "Maybe we'll sign up for a tour to learn more."

"Great," Lena said. "How about later today?"

Tony looked at Abigail. They were exhausted and still had to meet with Ms. Scott.

"Do you have anything tomorrow?" Tony asked. Today was Saturday. They were free until Monday.

"Oui! I mean, yes. Tomorrow morning at 10 a.m.? We can meet here or closer to your hotel. Where are you staying?

They decided to meet in front of their hotel. Lena pulled a business card out of her pocket and handed it to them. "Call me if anything changes," she said. "Otherwise I will meet you there. The fee is €40 Euros for a two-hour tour."

"Sounds great," Abigail said.

Something about Lena didn't sit right with Tony, but he couldn't put his finger on it.

Lena hailed them a cab and waved goodbye.

"She was nice," Abigail said.

Tony put his arm protectively around Abigail. "That was quite a welcome to France. Are you okay?"

"I'm fine. Thank you for going after him. But what if he had a gun? I don't want to lose you, Tony. Just be safe."

The cab turned a corner and pulled up to their hotel. It was a beautiful building in the Second Arrondissement near the Seine and the Louvre. The beaux-arts architecture gave it a solid, imposing look, reminding him of some of the buildings in Washington, D.C.

"Let's explore later," Abigail said. She looked exhausted. Tony thought the purse snatching had stressed her more than she let on. He was tired too with the six-hour time difference. Not only had they been up all night, but the past few months had worn them out. It was so good to be away from the publicity of Jean-Pierre Mauvais' trial, as well as the suspicious eyes of Jimmy and Abigail's boss. Of course, he'd have to face Ms. Scott here. But what was difficult in Michigan had to be easier in Paris, right?

They didn't bother to unpack. They both collapsed on the bed and were soon sound asleep.

They awoke to the alarm on Abigail's phone.

After showering and getting something to eat, they walked to the Louvre. A large banner across the door announced the World Maps Symposium, where Abigail would present. Abigail showed her ID, and she and Tony were let in as participants.

"This is *so cool*!" Abigail whispered. "We're like *on staff* at the Louvre!"

"I've always wanted to work here," Tony said. "Can you imagine being surrounded by all of this art?"

"I'll bet their security is top notch," Abigail said.

"Oh, it is," Tony said, a little too matter-of-factly. Abigail glanced at him.

"That's what I've *heard*," Tony said, spreading his hands innocently.

A mustached man led them to a conference room where Ms. Scott was waiting. She had several folders of paperwork with her. Her hair was pulled back in a tight bun, and she had dark red lipstick on, which enhanced the lines around her mouth. She was dressed in a slim black skirt and tailored suit coat over a white blouse. Abigail was just wearing some

13

khakis and a soft pink blouse. She had dressed casually since it wasn't officially a workday. Tony had chosen jeans, which he was beginning to feel was a mistake. But he was just along for the ride.

"Hi, Abigail." Ms. Scott rose and gave her a brief hug. She nodded politely to Tony. Apparently, she still wasn't feeling fondly toward him. He had only seen her twice since the incident with Jean-Pierre. They hadn't talked at the courthouse.

"How was your flight?" Tony asked.

"It was fine." Ms. Scott had come in a day earlier.

"Too bad Pauline couldn't be here," Abigail said of her best friend and co-worker.

After they lost their funding from Jean-Pierre Mauvais, the library couldn't afford to send anybody except for Ms. Scott and Abigail. Abigail took the money out of their savings to surprise Tony with a ticket. She said it was her turn to romance *him* a little bit.

While the two women discussed work, Tony looked around the room. It was too dimly lit for a conference room, and the big wooden table served as more of a centerpiece than a workplace. It had finely carved details around the sides that looked something like half suns and sunbursts. It was oak. Probably worth quite a bit. Tony wondered if they brought collectors in here and bargained for their pieces.

"Right, Tony?" Ms. Scott said.

"Hmmmm?" Tony looked up at her.

"Ms. Scott was just saying that the Louvre is a spectacular place to hold the symposium," Abigail said. "Probably even better than the original venue."

"Right," Tony said.

"The security is better here, for one thing," Ms. Scott said. "The maps that will be on display will be *well protected*." She gave Tony a stern look across the table.

"Yes. I believe so," he said because he wasn't sure what else to say. What was she getting at? "There's no chance of the Mona Lisa being stolen again," he said conversationally. "Did you know that's what made it one of the most recognized paintings in the world? After its theft, which was by a custodian, pictures of it were plastered across the front of newspapers internationally. As the police hunt continued, everyone saw it."

"Sometimes notoriety is brought about for all of the wrong reasons." Ms. Scott said.

Tony glanced at Abigail. She was frowning.

Ms. Scott put down her pencil and gave Tony a solid stare across the table. "We haven't had a chance to really discuss what happened with you," she said. She got up, closed the conference room door, and then sat back down.

Tony swallowed. "What do you mean?" Although he had a pretty good idea.

"You have never apologized for breaking in to my library to steal the map of the city," she said. Nothing like getting to the point.

"Oh," Tony said. He looked at Abigail for some help. She raised an eyebrow.

"Well," he said. "As you know, I was looking for that painting for my grandma. I heard that the city map held the clues to finding it. So, I just figured if I could get it..." He plucked a pencil out of the canister on the table and started twirling it between his fingers. They had fed the story to the press that the city lawyer had found the painting. Not them. He had to keep his stories straight.

"But Jonathan Stewart wound up finding it." He put the pencil down. He looked Ms. Scott directly in the eye. She was right. He never had apologized. "I'm sorry," he said. "You have every right to be angry. But I have changed, and I'm asking you to believe that. Until you trust me again, things will be hard for Abigail."

"Abigail lied to me."

"I—" Abigail started but Tony interrupted her.

"Abigail didn't lie to you. She just didn't tell you the whole story. You asked how we met. She told you she met me when I came into the library for a map. She was protecting *me*, not trying to deceive *you*. I was trying to start over, to begin a new life, and it was hard enough to do without everyone whispering about who I used to be. So I asked her to keep it to herself. Please don't blame her for any of this."

Ms. Scott folded her hands together in front of her. "What about that criminal you both brought in? Abigail could have been killed. *I* could have been killed! I spent a lot of time and money preparing the library for Jean-Pierre Mauvais' collection. You both made me look *like a fool!*" Ms. Scott didn't usually show emotion, but she hissed out those last few words.

This was a discussion that should have taken place weeks ago. *Months* ago. But the trial took over, and between Tony's community service work and his job, he hardly had time to breathe, let alone meet up with Ms. Scott for coffee. But she had a point. He should have taken the time.

"Abigail didn't know Jean-Pierre Mauvais was a thief. You know that. And things would have gone smoothly if he hadn't seen *me*. He had a score to settle with me, and he used Abigail and your library to do that."

"So, it *is* your fault."

"It is." There was so much that was his fault he didn't know where to begin. He wanted to change, but he couldn't seem to leave his past behind. "Yes, it is all my fault."

"No, it's not," Abigail said softly. "I hired Tony to handle the library's security. I knew who he was and that you didn't. Yet I hired him anyway. *Because I trust him,* Ms. Scott. And I want you to trust him too."

Ms. Scott turned her gaze to Abigail. "I'm still working on trusting *you*, Abigail."

The room was quiet. Abigail began to play with the corner of the paper she was writing on. Tony picked his pencil back up.

"What can I do to fix this?" he asked.

"Fix it?" Ms. Scott said.

"Yes. What can I do to be sure that my actions don't impact Abigail's future? Since we're discussing this, tell me how I can fix it."

"There's nothing you can fix that won't take time, Tony," Ms. Scott said, her tone gentler. "Just continue to prove to me that you are indeed reformed and not here to take advantage of the Louvre or the maps that will be on display."

So she was worried he would commit a theft. He closed his eyes briefly and took a deep breath to let the rising anger subside. "Of course." When he opened his eyes again, Ms.

Scott was watching him. "Now if you're finished, I think I'll go look around while you two discuss the workshop." He waited, but Ms. Scott didn't have anything more to say to him. Without looking at Abigail, he pushed back his chair and got up. He quietly closed the conference room door behind him.

He walked a little way down a corridor and stopped at a bench. He sat on it and leaned back against the wall. Paris was supposed to be a way for them to get away from the stress they had been facing these past few months, but it looked like his reputation had followed him. He should have expected it. They both knew this trip had a lot hinging on it for Abigail. And they both knew Ms. Scott was going to be here.

He figured Ms. Scott had come around and that Abigail would get her tenure. Now he wasn't so sure.

He pulled his wallet out of his pocket and took out a folded piece of paper. He unfolded it carefully and read the words. *"You can't go back and change the beginning, but you can start where you are and change the ending."* A quote often attributed to C.S. Lewis. Abigail had written it and put it on the fridge for him. He certainly had a lot of regrets. But she believed in him and saw nothing except a bright future for him. He hoped it was true. He was trying hard to be sure it was.

He sat there for about an hour, watching people walk around the art museum. Finally, Abigail came out. He stood as she approached. "Hey," he said, giving her a big smile.

"I'm sorry about that," Abigail said, hugging him. "Ms. Scott is in a mood."

"You can't blame her. But she'll come around." He would win her over somehow. For Abigail.

"I hope so," Abigail said.

Chapter Three

Abigail was excited. Tony had reservations at the *Jardin des Vers* restaurant, a surprise he had been keeping from Abigail for a few weeks.

"How should I dress?" she asked, because she didn't know anything about the restaurant. She pulled out her phone, which Tony deftly took from her. "No peeking," he said. "Just wear something nice, but not super dressy."

He was putting on his dark blue button-down shirt and was wearing black dress pants.

She pulled a dress out of her suitcase and plugged in the steam iron. "You can't watch," she said. He raised an eyebrow. "I want to surprise you."

He smiled. "I'll go down to the lobby and grab a coffee." He gave her a quick kiss on the cheek and left. Her dress was a dark emerald green, which she knew matched her eyes as well as the gem in her wedding ring. She had brought it specifically for the "romantic dinner" Tony had promised her. *This is it,* she thought, holding the dress up to herself in the long mirror. She couldn't resist twirling—just once though. *This is my honeymoon!*

She steamed the wrinkles out of the dress, freshened up her make-up, and pinned her hair back into a loose chignon. She put in small gold earrings and added a very delicate gold chain around her neck. When she looked in the mirror, she was pleased with what she saw. She switched to a smaller evening bag and went downstairs to find her husband.

Tony was sitting at a bar in the lounge, a cup of coffee in his hand. He smiled when he saw her and stood up.

"Wow! Just when I didn't think you could get more beautiful, here you are proving me wrong!" He pulled her to him for a kiss. "Ready?"

She nodded and took his hand. They went outside, and he hailed a cab.

The drive was beautiful. The city was lit up in the darkness, and the Eiffel Tower was radiant against the night sky. Along the Seine, lampposts cast reflections on the water. People were strolling about, couples holding hands, children running along the sidewalks. It was an enchanting night.

After about ten minutes, the cab stopped in front of the restaurant. From the outside, it looked quaint, with a striped awning and lampposts illuminating an old pair of stone steps up to a wrought-iron door.

Tony paid the driver and told Abigail to wait. He jumped out and ran around to open the door for her.

"My lady," he said, offering his hand.

"Thank you, sir." Out of the corner of her eye, she thought she saw a tall, shadowy figure dart behind a bush. Was it the person who had emerged from the cab behind them? *What on earth?* But the streets of Paris, like most large cities, had all sorts of people, and it was probably a beggar. She looked around to see if she could see anyone else who might have gotten out of the cab behind them. But the driver had already turned on his "available" sign. She dismissed it and quickly forgot about it.

Inside the restaurant, Tony gave their name. The host looked at his book and said in English accented heavily with French, "The Jardin d'été. Fantastic choice, monsieur. The lady will be pleased."

He led them to the back of the restaurant and through a doorway into the one of the most beautiful rooms Abigail had ever seen. The walls were made of colored milk glass, each depicting a saint, poet, or artist created with an inlay of colored glass. Ivy vines of cut green glass wound around each gilded pane and up to the ceiling, giving the room a garden feel. But most dramatic was the domed glass top, which was softly lit with a moon-colored glow. A large, ornate chandelier

19

hung from the center, and small lamps around the room added to the ambience of the evening meal.

"Wow," Abigail said, because it was all she could think of as she took in the sight. It was beautiful beyond words.

The host pulled out her chair for her, and she sat. They were near the middle of the room, so she had a great view of all the decorated glass walls. At the tables around them were mostly couples, as it was obvious this was the romantic place to bring a date. The atmosphere was quiet.

She looked across at Tony as the host handed them their menus. Tony was beaming. "Thank you," she said to her husband.

The waiter came and offered their menu choices to them in English. They ordered crab cakes for an appetizer. Abigail got the shrimp dish in a special sauce over pasta for dinner. Tony went for the steak.

"There's Descartes," Tony said, nodding toward one of the glass walls.

"And Thoreau. Someone from our side of the pond!"

"Joan of Arc," Tony said. "We should take a day trip to Poitiers. We could see the tiny church where she took refuge."

They discussed the figures in the glass, much to Abigail's delight. She loved how well read Tony was. Like her, he devoured information. After they ran out of talk about the images, they made small talk about the trip and what they wanted to do while they were in Paris.

"I have to admit, I am a bit nervous about the presentations," she said.

Tony listened as she described her fears. Most people would have jumped into the conversation to remind her how qualified she was, how knowledgeable. Tony just listened. But only part of her was nervous. The other part of her was thrilled at the opportunity. And she knew she was capable of it.

Their dinner came, and they were busy eating for a while. Abigail's thoughts roamed. She looked around the room again, hardly believing she was here. This night was so perfect.

Abigail forked another shrimp and swirled it around in the incredible white sauce. But as her hand was on the way to her mouth, she paused. Across from her, Tony was gently carving a piece of his steak. His hands were strong, with long slender fingers, and he was very adept with the knife.

She had also watched those hands rapidly type across a computer keyboard, repair the broken molding on their upstairs window, and fold clothes. As she watched him, it suddenly struck her how this little, ordinary task was such a big deal. Because he was *alive*. Because he was here with *her*. And he almost hadn't been. She looked at his hands, and suddenly she longed to reach across the table and touch him.

Hands that had worked so hard for her these past few months. Lifting stone and working in cold, dirty mud during his community service so he could stay out of jail. Giving up a life of pretty lucrative thieving so he could become a man "more worthy of her," as he put it. Hands that worked hours into the night, building a security company so he could help support them. Hands that so tenderly held hers. Hands *she* wanted to be worthy of. He had spent so much time romancing her, proving to her that he loved her—how could she return that? She needed to romance him back.

He raised the piece of meat to his mouth but stopped when he saw her staring at him.

"Your hand is like a holy place that my hand is unworthy to visit," she quoted.

"If you're offended by the touch of my hand, my two lips are standing here like blushing pilgrims, ready to make things better with a kiss."

A slow smile spread across his lips, and he gently put the piece of meat back down on the plate. He lifted the napkin from his lap, set it next to his plate, and then stood. He quietly came across to her side of the table.

"One fairer than my love? The all-seeing sun ne'er saw her match since first the world begun," Tony quoted softly, and leaned down to kiss her on the lips. It was a long, passionate kiss. She felt her hand drop the shrimp to her plate. When he stood, she opened her eyes, and the people around her applauded and whistled. Tony grinned and went back to his seat.

Abigail laughed. She had tried to romance him, but he had once again outdone her.

He put his napkin back on his lap, but his eyes were still on her. The people around them went back to their food and conversation, leaving them in their own little world again.

"What was that about?" Tony asked.

I was just watching you cut your steak—"

"I'm that sexy, huh?"

She laughed again. "No…"

He raised an eyebrow.

"I mean yes! What I mean is I was watching you cut your steak and realizing how much I love you. Your hands…they are so kind to me. You work so hard. You're so adept at everything you do. Your security business, the internet, romance, love, even the menial task of folding laundry. I guess I'm trying to tell you how much I love you."

She was fumbling for words. There was no way to put into language the feeling she had inside her heart for this one man. How much he meant to her, was part of her.

Tony sat watching her, his eyes serious. She was quiet, not knowing what else to say. There was soft music playing in the background, a tune she wasn't familiar with. It felt like the perfect backdrop for their date.

"I fell in love with you the moment I saw you," he said. He leaned forward, keeping his eyes on hers. "I was happy with my life and had never intended to marry. That wasn't even on my radar. But when I dropped in that night and you surprised me by being there, my senses completely left me. I forgot the reason I was there. If I had wanted the map, I would have found a way to get it. But suddenly that wasn't important anymore. And I couldn't get you out of my head after that. You were just so self-assured, smart, and beautiful. I had never met a woman like you. I love how you weren't afraid of me, even though I was dressed all in black and had just descended from your skylight. I love the way you challenged me and threatened me when I told you I was there to steal that map. And I loved how your hair fell around your shoulders that night when I took that pin out of it. Why weren't you afraid of me?"

Abigail folded her hands on the table and leaned in toward him. "I was too busy falling in love. Until that night, I hadn't felt anything for six years. But suddenly, there you were. *You.* Wonderful, amazing *you*, quoting Shakespeare to me and chasing after one of my precious maps."

She leaned back and smiled. "I have to admit, it helped that you had that skin-tight cat-burglar suit on."

Tony smiled and sat back in his chair. "So, it *was* my body you were after."

"Pretty much." She picked up her fork and put the shrimp in her mouth.

He laughed. "I knew it." He went back to cutting his steak.

Abigail sighed happily, chewing her food.

After dinner, they had a cab driver drop them off about a mile from their hotel. The night was mild, and they wanted to walk along the river. Abigail was glad she had brought her shawl and wrapped it around her shoulders. Tony added his warm arm and pulled her in close as they walked side by side down the sidewalk that led back to their hotel.

The light from the lampposts played on the water.

"It's beautiful here," Abigail said.

Tony agreed. "I'm so glad we have tonight."

Ahead of them, a small crowd had gathered around some street musicians. There was a man with an accordion, a woman with a flute, and a violist. An interesting mix.

They were playing something that sounded a little like a waltz.

When they reached them, Tony took Abigail's hand and pulled her up against him. "Dance with me," he said, smiling. She laughed as he swept her around the little area, and soon two other couples joined them. The musicians got caught up in the fun, and the tempo picked up a little bit. When the song ended, Abigail was a little out of breath, and she laid her head against Tony's chest, laughing.

He threw a few coins in the musicians' cases. "Merci!"

Abigail yawned.

"Tired?" he asked.

"Yes. But I don't want this night to end."

"There will be other nights," Tony said. He put his arm around her shoulders and they continued to walk back to their hotel. "And other days. We have an entire week here."

Abigail leaned her head against Tony's shoulder. She couldn't remember ever being happier. But then she felt the hairs on the back of her neck stand on end. She looked behind her. There was someone about thirty yards back. They were wearing a hoodie and staying close to the shadows.

"What is it?" Tony asked.

Abigail looked up at him. "There's someone—" She turned back, and Tony followed her gaze. The sidewalk between them and the musicians was empty. She glanced in the street and only saw cars. It must have been a beggar. Or her imagination.

"I thought I saw someone. Never mind." She felt a chill and pulled her shawl tighter across her shoulders.

The cool night air felt good on her face, if not on her shoulders. She felt Tony's strong arm around her and leaned in to him as they walked. The city lights twinkled in the river below them, and their hotel welcomed them up ahead. She had never been happier.

Chapter Four

The light came in from a crack in the hotel room's curtains, casting a moonlight glow across their bed. Abigail had brought some pretty nightgowns to wear but had ended up in one of his T-shirts tonight. She was snuggled up against him. Her hair was covering some of her face, and he pushed it carefully away from her eyes.

She continued sleeping. He couldn't. His mind was too busy.

He hadn't mentioned it to Abigail, but he had seen someone along the river who seemed to be following them. It was a busy area, with both the tourists and the locals out for a Saturday night. The musicians along the river walk brought in more people, so it was silly of him to pull out someone in particular. Still, the man, or woman, had seemed to be fixated on them. The hooded figure was behind them before they approached the musicians and seemed to be watching Tony and Abigail as they danced. Then it seemed Abigail had felt someone behind her. Even though she had never finished her sentence to him, he knew that's what she was going to say. But when he had turned to look, there was nothing.

Maybe he was just being paranoid. It was a way of life for him because he had spent too many years looking out for both cops and crooks. In his previous profession as a thief, you never knew who was out to double-cross you or arrest you. You always had to watch your back. He was probably just being ridiculous.

He carefully slid his arm out from around Abigail. She stirred but didn't wake up. He climbed out of bed and walked over to the small table in their hotel room. As he did, he caught a glance of himself in the mirror, wearing his heart print boxers. He wasn't at all sure about them. Abigail had come home with them a few days ago for their honeymoon. It wasn't like her, to be so cutesy, but every now and then, she did something like this. He wanted to please her, so he wore them. He just hoped nobody else ever saw him in them. A saying his grandmother often quoted came to mind: *Make sure you have on clean underwear. What if you're in an accident and the ambulance people see them?* Well, they were clean, but he'd be mortified if the ambulance people saw *these*.

He smiled at the thought. That was something else about Abigail. She kept him smiling.

As he sometimes did when he had trouble sleeping, he opened up his laptop. He decided to send an email to his grandma. She had always dreamed of visiting Paris since it was where her parents had met. She wanted to see the places her mom had stayed while going to school here. But she was still very weak from the cancer treatments. She insisted they not worry about her. "I wouldn't go along even if I was healthy," she said. "It's your honeymoon!" He typed her a short email, telling her about some of the things they had seen and what their hotel looked like. He had texted her when they arrived to let her know they got in safely, but she texted back and told him to focus on Abigail this week. He was glad his grandma was tech-savvy.

He thought about emailing George. But how much could one person apologize? George was finished with Tony, and that was something he may just have to accept.

He saw Lena's business card lying on the table. He was looking forward to their tour with Lena, and he went to her website, *Brushstroke Tours*. Catchy name.

It was a simple site, giving her basic information and costs. The website said "they" and "we" but listed no names for guides. There was just one basic phone number. He looked it up, and it was registered to Lena Martin. So it was her personal number. Maybe she owned the business. Or maybe she was a freelancer.

Martin was a very common French surname, much like "Smith" in the United States. He did a search on "Martin" in the Paris phone directory, and there were hundreds just within the city. Lena Martin was listed among them. Same number. No address.

He glanced over at Abigail, who was still sleeping. Because he was bored, he decided to dig a little deeper.

He Googled her. There was no trace of Lena on the Internet other than her phone number. While there were other Lena Martins on Facebook, none of the photos matched the Lena they had met. There was no history of her attending any schools or colleges or having won any awards. And after more searching, there was no record of her listed as owning a tour business.

Lena Martin didn't exist outside of her tour-guide persona.

There were plenty of explanations. She had probably had a bad marriage but still kept her married name. Or maybe she had changed her name legally to escape a bad family experience. She seemed like a nice enough woman.

Tony sighed. He could dig deeper. He had the knowledge and experience to find out who she really was. But he felt ashamed of himself. She had stopped a disaster by downing the thief who stole Abigail's purse. And how was he repaying her? He was already mistrusting her. He blamed his old paranoia. He would quit this nonsense now and go back to bed. Whatever reason Lena had for hiding her real name, it was *her* business. He had promised Abigail he would quit doing illegal things. Hacking in to databases to dig deeper would definitely be illegal.

He quit his applications and closed his laptop, grateful for Google translate. He made sure his laptop was charging and went back to bed. As he crawled in next to Abigail, she stirred and moved closer to him. Her warm body felt reassuring. He put an arm around her and laid his head on the pillow. He thought about the dinner they had at the restaurant. It had turned out perfect, and he was so happy he had pleased Abigail. Soon he was fast asleep.

Chapter Five

Sunday morning, they woke refreshed. They had a very French breakfast at a little pastry shop across the street from their hotel. Abigail was enjoying a chocolate-filled croissant, some sliced pears with cheese, and a latte.

"Let's not tell Lena we're related to Russo," Tony said, biting into an apricot croissant. "I'd like to see what she says about him without any bias. If she knows who we are, she may sugar coat it."

"You think he has skeletons in his closet?" Abigail asked.

"We know he does!" Tony said. "But don't we all? Mmmmmm…this food is amazing!"

She had to agree about the food. She licked the chocolate off her fingers. Outside the window of their bakery, she could see that the people of Paris were wide awake and on the move. Many were dressed up in their Sunday clothes, probably heading to church. The streets were quieter than yesterday, but still, people were out and about.

"I wish I could bake like this," she said.

"I wish you could too."

She glanced up at him.

"I mean…you cook *divinely*. I especially love that boxed chocolate cake you threw together last weekend." He grinned.

"Watch it, Romeo." Abigail looked at her phone. It was nearly 10 a.m. "You ready?"

They met Lena outside of their hotel. She was wearing jeans and a pink cotton T-shirt with a leather jacket over it. Her hair was braided again, with the ponytail hanging halfway down her back. She was pretty, Abigail noticed. Very pretty, with delicate features. She was slightly built, almost a little too thin, and just slightly shorter than Abigail's 5'6". She had a leather satchel thrown over her shoulder.

"Listen," Lena said, holding up a finger to silence them. The air was quiet, and then suddenly, bells rang out, beautiful and crystal clear. "The bells of Notre Dame."

Abigail listened as they chimed, counting to ten. She closed her eyes, letting the morning sunshine warm her face. She couldn't believe she was here, in Paris, with the love of her life.

"I never get tired of hearing them," Lena said. She turned and started to walk along the Seine. "We'll start with Claude Monet. When he first visited the Louvre, he saw painters studying and copying the masters. But Monet decided, instead, to sit by a window and paint what he saw going on *outside*."

Monet was one of Abigail's favorite painters, so she knew a little bit about his style.

"In March of 1861, Monet was drafted into the First Regiment of the African Light Cavalry and served in Algeria for a seven-year period." Lena walked like a teen, turning and talking to them as she walked backward, flipping her braid, always moving. She had a lot of restless energy. "His father was very rich and could have purchased Monet's freedom from the draft, but his stipulation was that his son give up painting, a career choice he despised. Monet refused, so the old man made him stay in the service."

Abigail wondered about that. Passion was a strong force. It made you do crazy and impossible things. She glanced at Tony. *Like marry a man you just met.* She took his hand. He turned and smiled at her.

"I guess it was a mild blessing," Lena said. "He later claimed that the light and vivid colors of North Africa inspired him in his future paintings. He said it was like research. Sadly, he also contracted typhoid fever there. Later, because he was so sick, his aunt got him out of the army early and sent him to art school."

Just across the river was the Musée d'Orsay. Abigail knew it was filled with Impressionist paintings. She and Tony were going to go visit it later this week. Lena stopped on the riverbank and had them sit on a bench. She told them about

29

Van Gogh and which of his paintings hung in the Musée
d'Orsay.

"I love the sunflower painting," Abigail said.

"We'll have to see if it's signed 'to Amy,'" Tony whispered.
Abigail smiled at the Doctor Who reference. Tony was such
a nerd sometimes.

"Next, I'll tell you a little bit about Antonio Russo. Let's
walk this way." Lena turned around and led them north toward
Montmartre and la Basilique du Sacré-Cœur, known in English
as the Basilica of the Sacred Heart. "It's about 2000 meters, a
mile and a quarter, north. Do you mind walking?"

They didn't. The weather was a beautiful seventy-three
degrees, sunny, and no wind. Perfect.

Abigail gasped when she saw the Bibliothèque Nationale
de France. Lena turned at the sound.

"She's a librarian," Tony explained. "A bit of a love affair
with books."

Lena smiled. "I understand! It's beautiful inside. You
definitely need to visit it."

"It's on our list!" Abigail said.

They passed a storefront, and Lena stopped in front of it.

"Here is where Russo's studio was," she said. Now it was
modern set of storefronts that housed a cell phone dealer and
a fast food restaurant. There were some apartments overhead.
"It burned to the ground in the 1940s. At the time, he was
having an affair with a young American woman he called
Laurel." Abigail felt Tony give her hand a little squeeze.

What Lena didn't know was that Abigail was wearing the
exact ring that Antonio had given to Laurel. An emerald set
in gold to symbolize their love. It had been handed down to
Tony's grandma, and he proposed to Abigail with it.

"His wife found out about the affair and torched the
studio," Lena said. "It's a shame how many paintings he lost
in that blaze. Masterpieces we will never see."

"Did any of the pieces survive?" Tony asked.

"Not that we know of. Only those he had sold before the
fire, which are hanging in museums around the world. And
in some private collections."

"Did he ever see Laurel again?" Abigail asked.

"No, and it is said that he never got over her. Sadly, he killed himself shortly after his studio was burned. He lost a lifetime of work. And his one true love."

"What happened to his wife?"

"Gaia? She spent a short amount of time in an insane asylum, but they had a daughter, and she was soon released to go live with her. They didn't have much money. Rumor has it that when Gaia burned down his studio, Antonio gathered up his money and buried it somewhere. Maybe he was planning to go to America to find Laurel. We don't know. But then he killed himself."

"I hadn't heard about the money," Tony said quietly to Abigail. "Interesting. I'll have to tell Grandma."

Lena turned to walk. "We'll go next to where he loved to sit and paint."

Abigail wondered why she didn't mention that the painting of Laurel had been found. Surely, she knew? It was worldwide news, the discovery of the lost painting. If Lena was a Russo fan, she'd know that. Especially considering that as a tour guide, it was her *job* to know.

They continued on north, and Abigail could see the white domes of the church standing strong against the clear blue sky. The Sacré Cœur Basilica, a Roman Catholic church, was located on the butte of Montmartre the highest point in the city.

"It's beautiful," Abigail said.

"The surrounding neighborhood, Montmartre, is where many of the artists come to work," said Lena, "as you'll see when we get closer."

Abigail loved it already. The striped awnings and cobblestone streets added an artsy feeling to the village. This is where Tony had wanted to come, to this place where his great-grandfather had met his great-grandmother. Laurel was an American too, strolling through just like they were now. Then she saw *him*. And love had happened.

There were some painters set up in the area, some on the steps, and some on the sidewalk. Lena stopped at a little section of sidewalk near a corner. "This is where he was sitting when Laurel saw him," she said. "He was painting. She spoke to him, and he quoted a love sonnet to her. Shakespeare."

Abigail glanced at Tony. It wasn't a sonnet.

"Did my heart love till now? Forswear it, sight! For I ne'er saw true beauty till this night," Tony said, his voice low. Those were the words he first wooed Abigail with. The same ones his great-grandfather had spoken to Laurel.

"What?" Lena asked.

"Nothing. Just quoting some Shakespeare," Tony said, squeezing Abigail's hand. "We're on our honeymoon."

"That's sweet," Lena said. "I wonder what happened to Laurel? I always thought Russo should have left his wife and run away with her, but maybe he was trying to do what was right. Especially since he and his wife had a daughter together."

Abigail was thinking they should tell Lena what they knew about the rest of the story. How Laurel had settled in Michigan to have her baby and raise her alone. About how money showed up regularly until Antonio committed suicide. And about the painting, which hung in the university museum near the library where Abigail worked.

But Tony spoke up. "I'm starving."

The smells were wonderful, with the aroma of fresh baked bread, soups, and grilled sandwiches permeating the streets. Even though it had only been about two hours ago that they had breakfast, Abigail found she was ready for more food. It was just so yummy in Paris!

Lena looked at her watch. "I guess it has been two hours," she said. "Time flies!"

"I'm starving!" Tony said. He pulled out some bills and paid her. "Thank you for your time. I really enjoyed the tour." But Lena lingered.

"One of my favorite places to eat is over there," Lena said, pointing. "You should try it."

"It's probably lunch time for you too," Abigail said, looking meaningfully at Tony.

He caught on. "Why don't you join us?" he asked.

"Oh, um, yes, I'd love that!" Lena said.

The restaurant was small, more of a café, and they sat at a table near the window. The door was open to let in the warm, sunny weather, but the seats outside were taken.

They ordered iced teas. Then Lena excused herself to the restroom. They watched her wind her way back through the crowded café.

"Go with her," Tony said.

"Why?" Abigail said. She was browsing the menu.

"Just go. Hurry!"

The urgency in Tony's voice caused her to look up. He had two phones sitting on the table in front of him. He was connecting a wire to his.

"You *lifted her phone?*" Abigail said.

"Borrowed." He winked at her. "Give me five minutes. I'll explain later."

Abigail didn't know why she listened to him, but she had known him long enough to know he always had a reason for what he did. She got up and followed Lena into the restroom, even though it felt very wrong. She knew what he was going to do. He was going to hack in to Lena's phone.

She'd have to hurry and think of a way to stall Lena. She glanced at her watch. Five minutes. It was going to seem like an eternity.

Chapter Six

Tony plugged the wire in to his phone and connected it to Lena's. He opened up an app and typed in some commands to crack the password. The app searched and came back empty. He tried again. *Encrypted.* Her phone didn't just have a simple password like everyone else's did. Why would a tour guide need so much security on her phone? Or was she just paranoid? Like *he* obviously was.

He unhooked the wire and slid her phone under her napkin, so it would look like she had forgotten it. Just in time too. Abigail was coming back with Lena behind her. His wife raised her eyebrows in question, and he nodded.

Lena looked worried as she peeked under her chair. She sat down and immediately picked up her napkin. A look of irritation came over her face. Tony would have expected relief if she didn't have anything to hide.

"Is something wrong?" Tony asked.

"No. Nothing. I thought I lost my phone, but here it is." She gave a little laugh, dismissing it. "I didn't see it under the napkin. I thought I had it in my purse." She stared pointedly at Tony. "But it must have *somehow* gotten on the table."

"Hmmm. I do that. I leave mine places, and then all of a sudden, there it is!" Tony said lightly. He smiled at Lena. She smiled back, but he could see the irritation still in her eyes. He was betting she knew he had picked it out of her purse.

"I think I'll get the Norwegian bagel sandwich," Abigail said.

Tony looked at the menu. "It's in French."

"Don't you have a translator on that fancy phone of yours?" Abigail said, scanning her phone over the menu and showing Tony how it translated the words to English.

"That's cool." *How did he miss that one?* He chose a toasted ham and cheese sandwich on a crusty French roll.

He glanced at Lena as she made her menu choice. She seemed a little shaken, which surprised him. As smooth had she had been so far, he expected more from her. What was her story? He wasn't convinced she was a legitimate tour guide. After his digging last night, he woke up this morning still skeptical. Why didn't she exist on the Internet? He hadn't gone deeper because it felt wrong to do so much research on her. Kind of like how hacking in to her phone was wrong. She had been so nice to them, after all. But he wasn't sure he trusted her. She had wrapped up the purse theft too neatly.

The server came and took their order. Lena ordered for them since neither he nor Abigail spoke any French.

"Your English is as good as your French." Tony said.

"I went to college in America," Lena said. "And I studied English here as a child in primary and secondary school. Unlike Americans, we Europeans are usually multi-lingual. I speak English, François, et un peu de Latin."

"Tony speaks Latin," Abigail said.

"I *read* Latin," Tony corrected her. "I can't really speak it very well."

"Latin?" Lena was surprised. "Usually Americans learn either Spanish or French. Sometimes German."

"Our high school offered it, and my Grandma insisted."

"Maybe she wanted you to become a doctor," Abigail said.

"So, Lena, where did you go to college?" Tony asked.

"NYU."

"New York University?" Abigail said. "What did you study?"

Their sandwiches came. Tony bit into his. It was quite possibly the best sandwich he had ever eaten, besides his grandmother's Italian meatball sandwich.

"Oh, this and that," Lena said. "I went there to study pre-law, and I received an undergraduate degree. But that's not my thing, really. I prefer to be in business for myself."

"Tony has his own business."

Tony wished Abigail wouldn't give up so much information. He didn't like sharing with strangers.

"Oh?" Lena said. "What do you do?"

"I own a security company. A small one. I'm just getting started."

Lena turned to Abigail. "And you're a librarian?"

"Yes."

"Do you ever think of what you would do if you could have more than one career?" Lena said.

Abigail looked dreamily out the window as she chewed a bite of her sandwich. This would be interesting. There was still so much Tony didn't know about her.

"Maybe a veterinarian," Abigail said. "I love animals. Especially cats. I'd also like to be an author. I mean, who doesn't want to write a book? And sometimes I think I'd make a good doctor."

"You'd make an *excellent* doctor," Tony said, a little flirtatiously. She caught the tone in his voice and gave him a slight frown. *Not here.* He hid a grin by taking another bite of his sandwich.

"What about you, Tony?"

"I'd like to be a fireman." That totally wasn't true, but he wasn't playing this game with Lena.

"Really?" Lena looked skeptical.

"I'm pretty athletic."

"And conceited," Abigail said.

"How about you?" Tony wanted to turn the conversation around.

"Me? I'm doing exactly what I want to do," Lena said. "I enjoy wandering around town talking about artists. I guess if I had to pick another career, though, it would be art. I'd love to be an artist and get paid to paint."

"So why don't you?" Abigail said.

"There's no money in it," Lena said.

"But—" Abigail began. Lena cut her off.

"Oh! What about a chef? I absolutely *love* to cook!" Lena said.

"Me too!" Abigail said. "I make this incredible coq au vin!"

"She *does*," Tony said, remembering the delicious chicken dish. Even though he had teased her about the boxed cake, it was true that Abigail was an excellent cook.

"This is perfect!" said Lena, getting excited. "I enrolled in a one-time cooking class. It's right over by the Louvre, so not far from your hotel. It's short⌐—only two hours long. They will teach you to make some of those delicious pastries you can buy in that little café across from your hotel. My friend was going to go with me but she had to cancel, and I still have one ticket. You should go with me, Abigail! It's this afternoon. It'll be so fun!'

"Really?" Abigail said. She looked interested, but then she looked at Tony. "I don't know. It's our honeymoon."

Tony still had doubts about Lena, but they should be fine if it was a public class. He needed to quit looking for trouble where there was none. "Go," Tony said. "It's only a couple of hours, and I can look around on my own. It won't be too shabby if you can learn to bake like that."

They spent the rest of lunch talking about food. Lena apparently was quite the foodie and knew all of the best places to eat in Paris. After they finished, she walked them back to the Louvre, talking about Cézanne, Manet, and Degas. When they stopped just outside of their hotel, it was nearly 3 p.m.

"I should pay you for the extra hours," Tony said.

"Nonsense. It's on me. That wasn't part of what you signed up for. So, the cooking class is from 4-6 p.m.," Lena said. "Give me your phone, and I'll put the address in."

Abigail pulled her phone out and opened up the maps app. She handed the phone to Lena. "I'll meet you there about 3:55."

They parted ways.

"Now you have to change your password," Tony said after Lena was gone.

"What?"

"She just saw you open your phone. She knows your password."

Abigail looked at him. "*Really?* You're that paranoid? She has no interest in my password. Besides, I was facing away from her."

"She could read it backward. It's not hard to do."

"Tony, do you really want to go around being that skeptical of people? Why did you steal her phone, anyway?"

"I *borrowed* it. I wanted to see who she really is. She's not Lena Martin like she says. That person doesn't exist anywhere except as a tour guide in Paris. And her phone is encrypted. Why would anybody want to have that much security on their phone?"

"You do."

He frowned.

"So, what did you find out when you looked at it?"

"Nothing. I can't get in to an encrypted phone in five minutes."

Abigail was silent for a moment. "You promised me you had quit doing things like that."

"I wasn't breaking the law. I was merely looking at her phone." But he knew she was right.

"With your device and some fancy app." Abigail took his phone and opened it up. She knew his passwords, encrypted and all. She looked through his apps. "Which one did you use?"

Tony sighed but pointed. "This one."

She opened it and frowned. "Is it legal?"

"Probably not. I downloaded it off a not-so-legit website. I was using it on a recent job—a *legal* job—and I just sort of kept it. I thought it might come in handy. All it does is break passwords."

"That's all, huh?" She handed him his phone back. "Where's the line?" she asked gently.

"The line?"

"Where do you draw the line between what is okay to do and what isn't?"

"But we had probable cause. I don't trust her."

"Why?"

"Because it was awfully convenient how she stopped the man who snatched your purse. And how she took us to see Russo of all artists, like she knows us. And why didn't she mention that the painting *Laurel* had been found? That was international news! And her tour guide agency doesn't exist. The website phone is her private number."

"She told us she's a freelancer."

"Still."

They stood and looked at each other for a moment. Finally, Tony said, "You just want me to ignore my instincts?"

"No. Instincts are good. But maybe you just need to fumble through like the rest of us."

"Guessing?"

"Yes. Guessing. At least until she does something that we can call her out on." Abigail took his hand. "If you're so worried about her, why did you agree to let me go to this cooking class with her?"

"I'm not *worried* about her. Just a little suspicious." Tony squeezed her hand. "You'll be with people during the class, so you'll be fine. It's not like she's an axe murderer. You're probably right. I'm just being paranoid. She seems perfectly nice."

Abigail leaned in and gave him a kiss. "I love you, you know."

"I love you too."

They went up to their room so Abigail could freshen up before her class.

Chapter Seven

The class took place at a French culinary school called *L'école de la Grosse Oie*. Abigail loved the name. 'Grosse Oie' meant Fat Goose. She had looked it up.

The room was brightly lit, and a long counter ran down the middle of it. Several sinks and ovens lined the walls on both sides of the room. Abigail and Lena shared a cooking area. They would work as partners, as the others were doing.

"I've taken a class with her before," Lena said as they tied their aprons on. "She's really good."

A short, middle-aged woman walked in the room. Her portly figure reminded Abigail of someone's grandma, but as soon as she spoke the impression of sweet grandmotherlyness was quickly dispelled.

"Lave t'es mains!" she shouted, followed by more quickly spoken French. Abigail looked at Lena.

"She says to wash your hands and prepare to get messy. Baking is serious work."

Abigail laughed and joined Lena at their sink, where they used the hand soap and nail brushes provided. Lena was wearing several rings and took them off. She put them on a ring holder next to the sink.

"You should really take your ring off," Lena said. "It'll get messy."

Abigail looked over at the other students, who were rolling up their sleeves and slipping off rings and bracelets.

"I think it'll be okay," she said. She wished she had brought her purse. She could put it in there. The pants she was wearing didn't even have a pocket she could slip it into.

"I doubt it," Lena said. "The flour will cake in it and loosen the stone." She shrugged. "But it's up to you."

"Attention!" said the instructor, who shouted like a drill sergeant. Abigail had to suppress a smile. This was going to be fun. As the instructor started explaining what they were going to do, Abigail looked at what was on their counter. For each student there were carefully measured bowls of flour, salt, butter, and eggs. There were also some apricots, strawberries, and cherries, which she assumed they were going to fold into the dough somehow. She listened as Lena quietly translated.

"To make it fluffy, it takes a lot of kneading and whipping," said Lena. "We'll be getting our hands dirty. You really should take that ring off."

"It's fine." Abigail put some butter in a bowl and used a mixer to whip sugar into it.

Lena laughed, her eyes sparkling, as some sugar flew out on them. "You'll *love* how this is going to taste! And so will your husband! At the end of class, they'll give us a half dozen of each to bring home, so you can take him a treat tonight!"

After each set of directions, the instructor walked around to see how the students were doing. During this time, Lena told Abigail a little bit about her childhood and how much time she had spent baking in her grandmother's kitchen. "It's a family tradition," she said. "You should see what we make at Christmas!" She had a lot of energy, and her enthusiasm for the class was contagious.

It came time to fold the pastries. "I'll let you do it," Lena said. "I've done it before, and this way you'll get the hang of it. A delicate touch is important. The French are very serious about their food."

Abigail looked at her ring again. Maybe it *would* be best to remove it. She slipped it off her finger and put it in the holder by their sink, next to her phone. She plunged her hands into the dough and made it into a ball. Then she set it on a pie board and started to roll it out with the rolling pin. The instructor came over, placed her hands on Abigail's hands, and guided them in a gentle motion back and forth over the dough. "Très bien!" she said, smiling at Abigail. Then she watched as Abigail carefully used the pastry cutter to make

41

squares. These would be folded over into triangles with the fruit inside. Abigail was engrossed in what she was doing, so when the smoke alarm went off, it startled her.

She looked up, thinking someone had started a fire on their stove, but didn't see anything. The lights overhead flashed with the loud, wailing alarm. Her heart was pounding.

"Attention!" the instructor shouted above the noise. "nous devons quitter immédiatement!

"We need to leave now," Lena said, grabbing her elbow. "Look!" She pointed toward the classroom door, and Abigail saw smoke billowing through the hallway. The instructor was shouting some more directions, and panicking students were pouring out of the doorway, leaving their belongings behind and the ovens still on.

"Hurry!" Lena said. She steered Abigail toward the door. The smoke was thick in the hallway, and Abigail knew they had to get out fast. A building could burn quickly.

Then she remembered her ring.

"My ring!" she said, turning around.

"There's no time!" Lena said, but Abigail pulled her arm out of Lena's grasp and ran back to their sink. The ring holder was empty. Lena's rings and bracelets were there, but Abigail's ring was missing.

"It's gone!" she said, looking frantically around. Maybe it dropped? Her phone was there. She grabbed it.

"Allons-y!" the instructor said, clapping her hands at Abigail. The woman was frantically turning off ovens.

"Abigail, let's go!" Lena said. Abigail heard sirens outside on the street below.

"My ring is gone! I think somebody took it!"

"We'll look for it later," Lena said, grabbing her arm. "There's a fire. We have to evacuate *now!*"

Abigail took one last frantic look around and then let herself be pulled away. She was the last student to leave the classroom, with the instructor right behind her.

Outside was total chaos. The entire culinary school had emptied out, and there were over two hundred people standing outside looking up at the building. Smoke was billowing out of a window on the second story, and firefighters were rushing inside.

"I hope they got everybody out," Lena said.

But Abigail wasn't listening. *What had happened to her ring?* Lena had told her to take it off. No, she had *insisted* that she take it off. It had been right there next to Abigail, behind her on the sink. No one else had come over to their cooking area. Abigail did get distracted when the instructor was helping her shape the pastries, but she would have noticed if someone else had come into their area.

She looked at Lena. The girl was standing there next to her, looking up at the building. Her long eyelashes were moist with tears.

"I do hope they got everybody out," Lena repeated.

It didn't seem like the kind of emergency to cry over. They *had* gotten everybody out, and it looked like the firefighters already had everything under control. While there was still a great deal of smoke coming out of the window, Abigail didn't see any fire.

"Lena," she said. Tony hadn't trusted Lena. He was concerned enough to try to hack her phone. *Did Lena steal her ring?*

When Lena didn't respond, Abigail said her name louder. The girl turned to look at Abigail. Just then, Lena's phone rang. She answered it.

"Oh no!" she said. "I'll be right there!" She turned to Abigail, her eyes frantic. "I need to go. Family emergency! If they let you back in, please get my jewelry for me. Merci!" She turned and ran to the street.

"Lena, wait!" Abigail shouted, following her. But Lena had already flagged down a cab. As Lena opened the door, Abigail grabbed her arm.

"What?" Lena said. "I have to go!"

"Did you steal my ring?" As soon as she said the words, she knew how harsh they sounded. She had no grounds on which to believe this woman had stolen her ring. She could have had Abigail's purse earlier today in the restaurant. Why wait and take her ring?

Because it's worth a fortune.

"You're crazy," Lena said. "I invite you to a class with me, and this is what I get?" But there was something in her eyes that made Abigail think she *had* stolen the ring. "Why would I want some family heirloom of yours?"

Family heirloom? Abigail had never told her that. "You *thief!*" Abigail said, but Lena yanked her arm out of Abigail's grasp and slid in the cab. She slammed the door before Abigail could stop her, and the cab sped off.

Abigail turned around, looking for a police officer. There were some up ahead but they were herding people to safety, away from the building. They were all busy.

She turned back to the street, her eyes searching for the cab, but it must have turned a corner. What had been the name of the cab company? Maybe she could call them.

But all she could remember was that the cab had been yellow. She cursed her memory. She'd have to track Lena through her business card. But Tony said that she didn't exist outside of her tour guide company. And that Lena's last name was fake.

Her *ring!* Tony had told her many times not to wear it. It had sentimental value to their family. But it also had monetary value. Because it was the ring that was in the famous Russo painting *Laurel*, it was probably worth hundreds of thousands, if not millions, to the right collector on the black market.

Abigail had her phone. She'd call Tony. He would know what to do.

Chapter Eight

Tony wandered down the streets, taking in the architecture and people. It was a beautiful day, sunny and breezy. He wanted to do a little sightseeing while Abigail was in her cooking class. He turned a corner and saw an interesting building up ahead. It had the same Beaux-Arts architecture as their hotel. He opened the guidebook on his phone and looked it up. The Petit Palais. It was an art museum. It wasn't on the list of places Abigail wanted to visit, so he thought he'd stop in. Maybe one of his great-grandfather's paintings hung in there too.

He bought a ticket, which was half-price since it was so late on a Sunday afternoon. That was fine. He just wanted to browse.

He wandered through most of the first floor, lingering in the Paris 1900s era. It was near there where he saw an area that had been roped off. There was a painting hanging between two others, only this one had a white cloth over it. Tony glanced around and saw a museum guide. He walked over to the woman.

"Parlez-vous Anglais?"

"Yes," she nodded.

"What's that?" he asked, nodding toward the covered-up painting.

"That was left here by the mystery artist," she said, as if he should know what that meant.

"The mystery artist?"

"Two nights ago, someone *broke in to* the Petit Palais," she whispered conspiratorially. "But they didn't steal anything.

They simply drilled a hole in the wall and hung a painting. It's an original."

"Really?" That was weird. But very interesting. "Can I see it?"

She looked around. There was hardly anybody else left on the floor. She glanced at her watch. Tony knew they would be closing soon. "I don't see what it will hurt. There was a picture of it in the newspapers."

She walked over and ducked under the police tape. Tony followed. Carefully, she lifted the sheet off it.

Tony was familiar with fine art. He had stolen plenty of it. This piece was exquisite. It was an oil painting of a bridge across the Seine at night. The pavement was wet, and puddles stood on the sidewalk, suggesting it had just stopped raining. The lighting from the lampposts reflecting on the puddles and the river was beautifully done.

"It's pretty good," Tony said.

"Yes, it is. Our professionals believe it was done by an amateur, though. There are ways to tell, brush strokes and lighting and all. But overall, it's beautiful."

"Did they find the artist?"

"No. Someone hacked in to the security system and turned off the alarms and the cameras. They also knew the guard's rounds, because it was done quickly and quietly. It was either an inside job or done by someone who spends quite a bit of time here. The police have already checked out all of us docents, though."

Tony looked at the painting for a signature. There wasn't one. Instead, there was what looked like a table with two horns coming out of it. No, those weren't horns. Flames, maybe?

"No signature. What does that symbol mean?"

"We're not sure. Our experts recognized it as a symbol representing the goddess Hestia."

"The goddess of hearth, home, and family life. All things warm and fuzzy."

"Yes."

They stared at the painting for a while. A few other people had wandered over and were looking at it.

"It's framed," Tony said. "That costs quite a bit." He inspected the frame closer. "But it's handmade."

"The artist made it," the docent said. "That's what we figure anyway. The artist couldn't take it to a framer because someone would see it and then recognize it in the news. But it's a job very well done."

He pulled his phone out and opened up the camera app. "May I?"

"Sure," the docent said. "It's in the papers."

Tony snapped a photo. It would be fun to show Abigail tonight.

"We're closing now," someone said from behind him.

"Of course," said the docent who was with Tony. She pulled the sheet back over the painting. "Thank you for visiting."

"Thank you." Tony shook her hand and made his way to the exit. He had time to grab something to drink before he had to meet Abigail.

Tony was sitting outside the fast food restaurant at the storefront where Russo's old studio used to reside before the fire. The iced tea he was sipping was delicious. They had put a slice of lime in it. He was used to lemon back home.

He was people watching, one of his favorite activities. There was a mix of tourists and Parisians, and in the half hour that he had been there, two tour guides had stopped at the storefront to share Russo's story with their groups.

Right now, it was quiet on the street. Tony looked up at the apartments above and wondered who lived there. Would they know about the history of this property? Or were they oblivious to the masterpieces that used to be painted here and the love story that took place?

There was a blue door between the cell phone dealer and the restaurant he was at, which he assumed led up to one of the apartments. He thought about knocking on the door. But what would he say? "Did you know my great-grandfather used to live here?"

Why not. He took a last gulp of his tea, which drained the glass, and stood. The door had an address on it, 2B, and a mail slot. He knocked.

He stood there waiting, his hands in his pockets. Nothing happened. No one came. He knocked harder and rang the doorbell. He vaguely heard the chime up above him. Then he heard some footsteps. A young man, probably in his late twenties, opened the door. He was squinting in to the light.

"Did I wake you?" Tony asked. The man's hair was messy.

"Non," He ran a hand through his hair. "Oui." He laughed. "I'm sorry. Yes, but it's okay. I have to get up for work soon anyway."

Tony felt bad he had awakened him but decided to press on.

"I'm a descendant of the artist who used to have a studio here. Do you own this building?"

"Non. Je suis...," then he switched back to English. "I'm just a tenant. You mean Russo?"

"Yes. I was hoping to find out a little bit more about him. Or about the history of this building."

"There are always tourists stopping by here," he said. "I've only lived here for a few months, but you should talk to the owner. He might know some history. He's an older guy, probably in his seventies. He eats dinner here every evening around 6 p.m."

Tony's phone rang. It was Abigail.

"Excuse me a moment. This is my wife." The young man nodded knowingly, as Tony answered it. "Hello, beautiful! What's cookin'?"

"Tony!" Her voice was frantic. "My *ring!* Lena stole my ring! There was a fire, and I turned around and it was gone and—"

"Abigail, slow down!" Tony said. "Are you okay? What fire? Start from the beginning."

He listened as she quickly brought him up to speed on what had just happened.

"And I can't find the cab company's name, and the police are busy!"

"I'll be right there."

48

Tony hung up his phone. "I've got to go," he said. "What's the owner's name?"

"Louis."

"Great. Thanks! Again, I'm sorry for waking you."

Tony took off running for the culinary school.

Tony booted up his laptop. The hotel room was stuffy, and Abigail was leaning over his shoulder. They had come right from the culinary school to the hotel room, and her nervous energy was making him antsy.

"Do you think you can find her?" she asked.

"Maybe. Can you turn up the air conditioner?"

She did and was instantly back. He typed in his passwords and then typed some more, digging deeper into the web. He planned to look in to Lena further than he did last night when he searched under the last name of Martin.

"Why don't you sit down beside me instead of hulking over me?"

"I'm sorry," she said, pulling out the other chair at their little table and sitting beside him. "I just can't believe I *trusted* her! I'm so mad!"

If there was one thing he had learned about his fiery, redheaded wife, it was that she had a temper. Normally, she was sweet and calm, but if someone double-crossed her, she didn't let them off the hook.

He paused, his fingers hovering over the keyboard. By searching for Lena on the dark web, he was using tools that weren't exactly legal. "You know I'm crossing that line."

"I know."

He started with the university that Lena said she attended in America. It took him nearly an hour, but he managed to break their code and hack in to their database of students.

"Let's just hope she's using her real first name."

He searched for her under the years he thought she might have graduated. A Lena Mercier appeared with her student photo beside her. "Gotcha. That was too easy."

Now that he had her real name, he could try to find her in France. He started with legal searches in online phone directories. He Googled her. Nothing. Not even a phone number listed. The French language created more of a barrier than he was used to, so it took him another additional hour to hack in to a government-run medical database.

Her name came up, complete with an address and phone number. He checked it against the phone number on her phone.

"Bingo."

Suddenly a red cartoon creature showed up, a fuzzy monster face with teeth bared. He swore and quickly shut off his computer.

"What?" Abigail asked.

"Somebody put a trace on me. Probably their security company. I broke the connection before they caught me." He leaned back in his chair, exhaling. He was supposed to be over doing this sort of thing. He certainly didn't want to get in trouble in a foreign country.

"Let's go get her," Abigail said, standing.

"Like...how? You think we can just knock on the door and say, 'Hey, we want the ring back?'"

"No. We can break in and search for it. She's not going to *give* it to us."

"I think we should call the police. We can give them her real name now that we have it."

"But you said earlier that you knew her type. That she probably already had it on the black market or had a private buyer already lined up. That's how it works, right? You unload it right away?"

Tony took a deep breath and let it out slowly. "Yes."

"Then if we wait, we'll lose it for sure!"

Abigail was really upset. He turned around so he was looking at her.

"What's really going on?" he asked quietly.

Her angry eyes filled with tears. They had been through a lot. The trial with Mauvais had literally just ended before they came here. That and juggling their jobs had given them very little time to process anything that had happened to them. Or even their marriage.

He pulled her against him, wrapping her in his arms.

"I thought Paris would be a reprieve," she said. Her face was pressing against his chest, muffling her voice. "But I got my purse stolen first thing. And now my ring. And clearly, Ms. Scott is still upset with you. Why isn't God giving us a break? I just want to relax and forget about life for a while. I want a honeymoon." She sniffed. "And I want my ring. *Our* ring. It meant so much to you and your grandma. She saved it for you all those years. And now I've gone and lost it!"

"It's just a ring," Tony said into her hair. "It's okay."

"I am so sorry!" Now she was really crying. "I'm so, so sorry!"

"What matters is that you're safe. That's all I want." Tony said. Yes, he was sad that the ring was gone, but it meant nothing compared to Abigail. He continued to hold her.

After a moment, she pulled back and stood. "I'm through with people taking advantage of me." She walked over to the window and looked out. Her arms were crossed. He could see her shoulders rising and falling with her breathing as she tried to bring her emotions under control. "I understand you not wanting to confront her. But I can't let this go."

He thought about it. Lena would never unload it at a pawnshop. It was worth too much, and he suspected she knew that. She probably had a buyer already lined up before she nabbed the ring. That's the way he would have done it. It was possible, though, that she had stashed the ring somewhere in her apartment until she could meet with him. An exchange like that would take time to arrange.

Maybe they *should* just go over to Lena's apartment. What could it hurt? They could invite themselves in and ask her point blank. He could tell by her eyes if she was lying.

"Okay, let's go," he said, standing up.

"To Lena's?"

"Why not?"

Abigail took a long, deep breath, calming herself. Then she turned to look at him. "Okay. We can just talk to her. What harm can that do?"

Chapter Nine

"Aren't we going in through the window?" Abigail asked.

Tony had opened the door to the stairs leading up to Lena's apartment. He turned and gave her a look.

"I'm sorry." Abigail shook her head. *What had gotten into her?* "We can just pick the lock."

Tony paused on the steps and looked at her again. He raised an eyebrow. *"Look like the innocent flower, but be the serpent under it."*

She couldn't hold back a smile. "I'm kidding. Just keep walking, Romeo."

Lena lived on the third floor, two doors down from the staircase. It was a clean building, but old. Some of the carpet was peeling back in the hallway. They stopped in front of her door. Tony knocked.

"Maybe she's not home," Abigail said after a minute.

"Or maybe she doesn't want us to find her," Tony mumbled.

Abigail looked at her watch. It was a little after 9 p.m. She knocked again, this time louder.

While she waited, Abigail rubbed the spot on her finger where the ring had been. For years after Nick's death, she had worn the wedding ring her first husband gave her. At first, it was out of love and because she still felt connected to him. But eventually, it became part of a disguise she wore to ward off potential suitors. It hadn't worked with Tony, though. He had gotten through her defenses and won her heart. Then he gave her another ring to wear.

To her, the ring symbolized more than their love. It symbolized a turning point in her life, when she realized she *could* love Tony without betraying Nick. Nick was dead, and he would want her to move on with her life. She was sure of that. Six years was long enough to mourn. She still thought of him, but she had learned to let go enough to move forward.

She knew the ring was only a symbol, a material thing that she didn't need to know how much Tony loved her. But it was a symbol all the same. And she wanted it back. A new flash of anger shot through her.

She knocked again, this time even louder. "Lena!"

The door to the apartment next to them opened, and an older woman poked her head out. She said something in French.

"Um...parlez-vous Anglais?" Abigail asked, using some of the basic French she had learned for the trip.

"I heard her go out earlier this evening," the woman said in accented English. "I doubt she is home."

Abigail realized the knocking had been too loud. "I'm sorry. Thank you. Merci."

The woman quietly shut her door.

"Well," Tony said.

They turned and looked at each other. "I'm not picking the lock," Tony said, as if reading her mind.

"Nor would I ask you to."

They heard someone coming up the stairs. Abigail put a finger to her lips. They waited, listening as the footsteps came toward them quickly, lightly running up. A young woman came through the doorway into the hall. It was Lena.

She saw them as soon as they saw her and froze. Then she turned and fled back through the door. Tony went after her with Abigail close behind. They were through the stairwell door quickly, but Lena was nearly down to the second floor. Tony leaped over the stair rail and landed lightly in front of her, a floor down.

"Going somewhere?" he asked quietly.

Abigail stopped a staircase above them. Tony and Lena were right under her.

"Get out of my way," Lena said.

"You're suddenly not the friendly tour guide we spent the day with," Tony said. "Just give me the ring, and we'll leave. No questions asked."

"I don't have the ring," Lena snarled. "Now get out of my way."

Lena was crouched like a cornered animal. Abigail could see her breathing heavily from her spot above them. Suddenly, Lena made a quick move and pulled a knife out of her jacket. She flipped it open and pointed it at Tony. Abigail gasped.

"Whoa," Tony said, putting both hands in the air. "No need for that."

Lena pointed it closer to his face.

"If I wanted to, I could take it from you," he said, keeping his voice low and calm.

"I'd like to see you try," Lena said.

"Tony," Abigail said. "Leave it. Let her go."

Keeping his eyes on Lena, Tony stepped back. Lena moved past him and took off running. Once she was ahead, Tony went after her.

Abigail ran down the steps, her feet pounding loudly in her haste. She burst through the door to the outside. Tony was standing on the sidewalk looking around.

"I lost her," he said.

Abigail grabbed his hand. "It's okay. It's just a ring. Not worth dying over."

He squeezed her hand. "No. It's not."

Abigail wanted so badly to go up to the apartment and break in. She knew Tony could do it. Then they could search for her ring. Lena was scared and wouldn't be back for a long time. She could count on that.

Tony was looking down the street. "She wouldn't keep it in her apartment," he said, as if reading Abigail's mind. "She'd be more careful than that. She's either already sold it, or she has it on her. Or hidden somewhere else. I don't think she's stupid. And I think she knows exactly who we are."

"So what now?" Abigail said.

"Let's put in a police report. Maybe she has a record."

Lena Martin didn't have a police record. Neither did Lena Mercier. The police didn't seem overly concerned about her tour guide business either. There had never been any complaints.

"We have a lot of people who work the streets in different ways," a policeman said, shrugging.

Abigail gave them a description of the ring, including a photo of it she found on her phone from her wedding day. They promised to check in to it and call if they found anything.

"They won't search her apartment without probable cause or some type of proof," Abigail said to Tony.

"Let's stop by to the culinary school, just to be sure it hasn't shown up there," Tony said. "Maybe she got cold feet and put it back.

But the school was locked. It was nearly midnight. "Let's go back to the hotel and get some sleep," Abigail said.

"I wonder what her story is," Tony said.

Abigail wasn't sure she cared what Lena's story was. Did Tony think she was poor and needed the money? It was more than that. This was definitely premeditated. She had planned it all out.

Abigail squared her shoulders.

"I don't know," she said. "But Lena Mercier has messed with the wrong woman."

Chapter Ten

They arrived at the Louvre before it opened. It was the first day of the World Maps Symposium and Abigail was speaking at 1 p.m. on the storage and treatment of rare maps and documents. She was well prepared, and Tony couldn't help noticing that she was looking very nice in her navy skirt and white silk blouse. She was wearing her hair down this morning.

"The only problem with speaking after lunch is everyone will be ready for a nap," she said nervously.

"It'll be fine."

He had on a navy suit with a white shirt on underneath. No tie. He was glad he had spent the extra money on nice shoes back when he had it to spend. He'd have to live all day in these dress shoes. Abigail had told him not to come, that he would be bored. But who could be bored in the Louvre? Besides, what else would he do?

Ms. Scott was standing at the entrance to the auditorium where Abigail would speak.

"Good morning," she said pleasantly. She even smiled at Tony. He smiled back.

Good to see you this morning. You're looking very nice," he said.

She was wearing her usual slim black skirt and white blouse combination, but she had a jacket on over it and a floral scarf tied at her neck.

"Thank you."

Now that the pleasantries were out of the way, Abigail pecked Tony on the cheek. "I have to get to work," she whispered. He nodded.

"I'll be here at 1 p.m. for your talk."

Abigail left to go off and do librarian stuff, and he wandered out into the hall. There was an opening speaker at 9 a.m., and then the first program he thought he would attend was on using historic maps in digital projects. There might be something of interest he could glean from that. This afternoon, after Abigail's talk, he wanted to sit in on the "Legends, Lives, and Lies: A Look into the Mystery of Treasure Maps."

He saw a drinking fountain down the hall and went to get a drink. Two men were standing outside of the restroom doors next to it, talking.

"The mystery artist has struck again!" one said excitedly. He was from England, judging by his accent.

"Really? Where?" said the other man, also with a British accent.

Tony took a longer drink so he could listen.

"At the Musée D'Orsay. They say it was the first time in over a decade someone has broken in to it. They found it near the Monets. He's an exceptionally fine artist."

"Fascinating."

Tony straightened, brushing a few droplets of water from his mouth. He nonchalantly wandered over to the men.

"I overheard you talking," he said. "Was it the mystery artist? Have they determined for sure?"

"Oh yes! They have the whole place roped off!" said the first gentleman who had spoken. "This is the fourth time this has happened."

"Fourth?"

"Yes. I'm sure you heard about the one two days ago, at the Petit Palais."

Tony nodded. That was the one he saw.

The other man chimed in. "Before that, it was the Musée de l'Orangerie and before that, the Musée Carnavelet. It has been all over the news."

"The Carnavelet, where he first struck, has been closed for renovations, so it was easy to get in. Left the painting hanging right in the entrance, he did. In plain sight of the workers who entered the next morning!" The man chuckled. "He seems to be moving up in order from easiest to most difficult. I predict there will be one of this artist's paintings hanging in the Louvre next!"

"Interesting," Tony said. He'd have to go over and check it out. An artist who broke in to museums to *leave* a painting! This was fascinating.

The men excused themselves to go get a seat. Tony wandered in behind them and found a seat near the back of the room.

The opening speaker was interesting and had a great slide show on the history of maps and map making. But Tony's mind kept wandering back to the mystery painting discovered at the Musée d'Orsay. He really wanted to see it. He looked at his watch. He had plenty of time to get there and back before Abigail's presentation.

After the speaker was finished, Tony left the Louvre and took a cab the short distance to the Musée D'Orsay. It was open, and large crowds of people were there visiting.

He'd have to buy a ticket to get in. Abigail would kill him if he looked around without her. She loved impressionism, and this was certainly the museum for it.

He pulled out his phone and converted Euros to US dollars. It was about $16 for a one-day ticket just for the museum.

He was standing in line in the lobby. He looked around. The area to his left was roped off. "Is that where they found the mystery painting?" he asked the person in line in front of him.

"Yes. There's an entire police investigation going on inside there."

There would be no way Tony could get close. He got out of line and walked over to the roped off area.

"Pardon-moi, monsieur," said an officer. He motioned Tony to step back away from the rope.

"Parlez-vous Anglais?" Tony said.

"Oui. I'm sorry, sir. This area is roped off for a reason."

"I'd really like to see that painting of the mystery artist," Tony said. Sometimes honesty was the best policy.

"So would everyone else," the officer smiled. "I'm sorry. That won't be possible."

Tony could see at least two ways past the barrier, but there might not be a need. As policemen were moving aside, he was catching glimpses of it from where he stood.

"Thank you," he said. "Merci."

He stepped back and took out his phone. He opened a telescoping app that allowed his camera to really zoom in on things. He casually lifted it, zoomed, and caught a shot of the painting. He did some rapid shots as people moved, hoping to get a good view of it.

"Monsieur!" a guard walked over to him. "No photos, please."

Tony apologized and put his phone away. He looked wistfully at the crowd of police officers one more time and then turned to go. He wouldn't have to buy a ticket after all. And he needed to get back.

Tony arrived in time for lunch, which was perfect for his rumbling stomach. He had agreed to meet Abigail just outside the lecture hall. He had picked them up some food on his way there.

"I brought you a sandwich," he said.

"I can't eat," she said. "I'm too nervous."

He looked at his watch. "You have to eat something. You have an hour."

"I can't."

She smoothed down her skirt, which didn't need smoothing, and ran her fingers through her hair. She needed distracting. This seemed like a good time to tell her about the mystery artist.

"Here, I have something to show you." He pulled her over to a bench and they sat down. Taking out his phone, he scrolled to the photos of the painting.

"You've been to museums without me?" she said, looking hurt.

"Kind of. But not one you wanted to go to. I didn't even buy a ticket."

She frowned.

"That's not what I mean!" He laughed at the implication. "Yesterday I went to the Petit Palais museum, and they had this area all roped off. Someone had broken in to the museum and hung a painting on the wall!"

"Really?" She took the phone and enlarged the photo. "It's beautiful."

"It is. They're saying it's an amateur artist, but he's pretty good."

"Why do they think it's a he?"

"Aren't all the important things in life done by males?"

He braced for the punch in the arm he knew was coming and laughed again. She was forgetting about her upcoming talk and relaxing.

"Actually, I was thinking maybe the artist is a woman," he said. "Because of the signature."

He enlarged the picture so she could clearly see the bottom right hand corner.

"Fascinating. The symbol for Hestia, the Greek goddess of hearth and home." Abigail looked at Tony. "When she was born, her father Kronos was afraid she was after his power so he swallowed her. She grew up undigested in her father's stomach." Abigail scrunched her nose. "She must have smelled horrible when he finally expelled her."

Tony chuckled. "But he had nothing to fear. She was a peacekeeper and never wanted power. She wanted to tend the hearth and keep a happy home. It was said if the gods wanted a break from fighting, they could sit in peace with Hestia."

"No wonder, after the terrible childhood she had."

"She remained a virgin, poor girl."

"Her choice." Abigail gave Tony a challenging look. "Women don't need a man to make them whole."

Tony feigned hurt. "No?"

Abigail put her arm around his shoulder. "Well, this particular girl does. You are my other half." Then she looked away, thinking. "So why would the artist use her symbol?"

"I don't know but that's why it makes sense to me that the artist is female. Maybe she had a bad childhood? Or maybe she's a homebody?"

"Or maybe she wants the final say. I've heard Hestia referred to as the Last Olympian. What if she is saying when all else is done and gone, she's what's left? Her art is what will stand the test of time?"

Tony smiled and leaned back against the wall behind him. This is what he loved about Abigail; she was so incredibly smart. Well, that and she was drop-dead hot. But no matter. She was onto something.

"And then this morning. "Another mystery painting was found by the mystery artist. This time in the Musée d'Orsay." He brought up the photo he had taken this morning. "I haven't had a chance to look at this one yet."

"There are people in front of it." She flipped to the next photo. "Wait. This one is clearer."

"I had to sneak in a photo. They wouldn't let me near it. It's an active crime scene."

She enlarged the photo. It was an Impressionist-type painting of people picnicking around a pond. There was the Hestia symbol in the corner in place of a signature.

"Maybe we can figure out who it is," Abigail said.

She handed Tony back his phone. He opened up some news stories on the web, and they read about the mystery artist. "They don't really have any idea," he said. "But he or she is capable of hacking in to the systems to turn the cameras and alarms off. Then they come in, hang up their painting, and leave. So far, they've hit the Musée Carnavalet, the Musée de l'Orangerie, the Petit Palais, and now the Musée d'Orsay. They're saying the Louvre is next."

"The Louvre? There's no way anybody could get in here."

Tony shrugged. He took Abigail's sandwich out of the bag and handed it to her. He opened his own wrapper and took a bite.

"What do you mean?" Abigail said, taking a bite out of hers. She was so lost in thought she didn't seem to realize she was eating. Good. She needed some food in her before she went up on stage. He didn't need her passing out in there.

"I've been thinking. Maybe there's some loophole the Louvre security team hasn't thought of yet."

Abigail gave him a look.

"I wouldn't know, not *personally*."

They ate their sandwiches quietly for a few moments. Then Abigail said, "I haven't heard from the police at all today about our ring. I think it's gone."

"I don't think they're doing anything about it," Tony said. "Maybe we should come clean about what it really is and how much it's worth."

"But then the entire city will know."

"An entire city of art collectors."

Abigail nodded. They both sighed. Tony looked at his watch. "You only have fifteen minutes."

"Oh!" she swallowed the last bite of her sandwich and stood. "I'd better go freshen up. I'll see you in there."

She bent and gave him a quick kiss. "Thanks for lunch."

"Good luck!"

Chapter Eleven

Abigail was feeling pretty good about her lecture. It had gone really well and lasted just the right amount of time. Her audience was awake and, more importantly, interested. They had asked several questions. Afterward, a senior map specialist from Great Britain had come up to ask if he could make a trip to the US and personally come look at their storage system. Ms. Scott was thrilled.

The symposium was finished for the day and would resume tomorrow morning. Tony told her that he had particularly enjoyed that last talk, which was on treasure maps. Now, with the time they had off this afternoon, they were exploring the Louvre. They had skipped around, intending to see more of it as the week went by. They saw the Winged Victory of Samothrace, which had brilliant reds in the painting. They had wandered past the Mona Lisa. Now they were in the nineteenth century decorative arts area looking at vases.

The particular vase that had caught Tony's attention was golden with angels standing pressed against the side, doubling as handles. Embedded in the front was some type of turquoise jewel.

"Pretty," Abigail said.

A docent saw their interest and came over to explain its origins. The man launched into a complicated story about who originally made the vase and how the museum ended up with it. When he came to a part about a tragic love and loss, Abigail glanced over to her husband.

Tony was only half listening, Abigail could tell. His eyes were traveling over the vase and the area around it. "Hmmmmm," he said, shaking his head.

"Pardon?" the docent said. "Is there something wrong, monsieur?"

"Well," Tony said, clasping his hands behind his back. "Actually, yes. The security around this particular piece is lacking."

The docent frowned. "Surely not. This is the *Louvre*."

"I'm aware of that," Tony said. "And I don't mean any disrespect. But I work as a security contractor. I own my own business and have done my share of making sure my clients' art was safe. Even a recent Picasso."

"A Picasso?" The docent was impressed.

"Yes. It was nothing. The job, I mean. Not the painting. He hadn't thought of an overhead theft. He had a fantastic, state-of-the art system, but had forgotten one important part." Tony lowered his voice for dramatic effect and leaned in. "And that's where the theft would occur."

"You mean somebody *stole* his *Picasso*?" The docent was aghast.

"Oh no, not under my security," Tony said.

Abigail held back a smile.

"But see here," Tony said, pointing. "These lights. I assume they double as security measures, right? If something breaks the light beam, it triggers an alarm?" His eyes followed the beams up to the ceiling.

"I'm afraid I can't say."

"Of course. But see this gap here?" Tony pointed, and for effect, swooped his hand across a shadowy spot where the light didn't reach. "This is a dead spot. No alarm-triggering light beams here. I could reach in and pull the vase out. It would fit."

The docent considered this for a moment. "But someone would never get it out of the museum. I mean, this is the *Louvre*."

"But just *touching* it would be detrimental," Tony said. "It's an *imperial vase*, after all. What if someone *dropped* it?"

The docent frowned.

"Or," Tony said, walking around the pedestal that it was on. "If I were a thief—and of course I am *not*. But if I *were*, I'd probably reach in from *this* side." He had moved around behind it. "Because the statue of Marcus over there is blocking the view of it from that wall. And the cameras overhead," he pointed to some innocuous-looking lights, "wouldn't catch me if I stood right here in this exact spot. Then I could easily slip it under my coat."

The docent looked around. The only guard in the room was talking to a man and not looking in their direction.

"I don't think so, monsieur."

"Oh, *I* do," Tony said. "Tonight, when you have time, take a look at your security film." He looked at his watch. "It's 3:15 p.m. Scan the room. I can guess you won't see me when I stand right here."

The three of them were silent for a moment, considering. Finally, the docent shook his head. "Very interesting, monsieur. I will mention it to my supervisor later."

Tony pulled out one of his business cards. "If your supervisor has questions, my cell number is on this card. Have him call me."

Tony turned to lead them from the room. He looked over at Abigail and winked. She tried not to laugh.

"Showoff," she said when they were out of the room and away from the docent.

"It's true. They have poor security around that thing. Of course, it's not worth as much as say, the Mona Lisa, but still." He turned to her. "What do you want to do tonight?"

"Well…we probably can't afford another dinner like last night?"

Tony laughed. "No. Not at all."

"Let's find a cozy little Parisian restaurant somewhere, and then walk around afterward."

They decided they would see the Avenue des Champs-Élysées and several of the monuments. "But let's see more of the Louvre first," Abigail said.

Originally built as a castle in the late twelfth and thirteenth centuries under Phillip II, part of the original dungeon remained. Exploring it was fun and the torch-lit area provided enough ambience to make them believe they were walking back in time.

"This is so cool," Abigail said. She remembered reading that the fortress had lost its defensive function in the 1500s due to the urban expansion of the city, and it then became a home to kings. It was expanded several times, resulting in what was now the largest museum in the world.

It was late, and they were ready to leave. As they walked through the lobby, the docent Tony had spoken with earlier flagged them down.

"Monsieur! Before you leave, my supervisor wants to speak with you."

Tony grinned. Abigail rolled her eyes.

An hour later, Tony had a temporary job at the Louvre. He couldn't stop smiling. "You're as happy as a kid in a candy shop," Abigail said, squeezing his hand.

"I can't believe it! And it'll give me something to do while you're working." They were bringing Tony on as a consultant to check out a few weak areas in the Louvre, namely the objects that were of less value. "Now let's go eat."

Ms. Scott stopped them on the way out.

"Abigail, you remember Robert Dunning." There was a middle-aged man standing beside the director. He was wearing a gray suit, which brought out the graying patches in the dark hair at his temples.

She didn't really remember him at all. She recognized the *name* as one of the university library's board members, but she hardly interacted with them back home. She was sure she must have met him the night of her infamous talk on the stolen Vesconte, but she barely registered his face. Her mind had been elsewhere that night. But now that she thought of it, she had seen his face in the courtroom during some of the proceedings.

"Sure," she lied and stuck out her hand. He shook it. What was he doing here, anyway? She looked at Ms. Scott for answers.

"Mr. Dunning is here to enjoy the symposium," Ms. Scott said, but she looked uncomfortable. Ms. Scott was rarely uncomfortable. Abigail wondered what was up.

"How nice," Abigail said. "You remember Tony." Of course, he remembered Tony. The man who had caused so much trouble for the library. Judging by the way his eyes narrowed when he shook Tony's hand, Dunning knew *exactly* who Tony was.

"A pleasure," Tony said, turning on the charm.

"Well, we are off to a dinner," Ms. Scott said. "I'll see you tomorrow, Abigail."

After they were gone, Abigail turned to Tony. "I wonder what that was about. Why is *he* here?"

"I have no idea. But did you see how happy he was to see me?"

Abigail squeezed Tony's hand. "It'll be fine." But she wasn't so sure. Nobody had told her Mr. Dunning would be here. It was just supposed to be her and Ms. Scott. When had he arrived? And why did Ms. Scott look so uncomfortable with the whole situation?

Oh well. She wouldn't let it worry her. If he was here to judge her participation, she was very confident he wouldn't be disappointed. She knew her subject and was well prepared. She could do this with her eyes closed.

They loved the Champs-Élysées. Noted for its upscale luxury shops, they could only window shop, but it was still fun. They saw a window poster advertising an all-night festival on Friday near the Eiffel Tower.

"Oh, we should go!" Abigail said. There promised to be music and performers, as well as food vendors and drinks.

Tony took a picture of the poster with his phone.

On the way to the restaurant, they stopped at the police station to ask about the investigation in to the ring.

"We checked at the culinary school. Nothing," said a chubby, spectacled detective. "The fire was only a few well-placed smoke bombs and somebody pulled the fire alarm. Looks like a prank."

"Did you get them on film?" Tony asked.

"No. The building is old, and there isn't much security. It's just a culinary school." He didn't seem too concerned.

67

"So what's next?" Abigail said.

"We have our eyes on some pawn shops, madam."

Abigail was furious. She could tell they wouldn't put any more effort in to it.

At dinner, for Tony's benefit, she tried to pretend it didn't matter. She smiled, and ate her food, but underneath she was seething.

"What's wrong?"

She looked across the table at him. "They aren't going to do anything about my ring. And I just keep remembering the look Lena gave me when she sped away in the car. After she accidently mentioned it was an heirloom. She knew then that *I* knew, and it was like she was laughing inside. I'm just really mad."

"And it isn't going to turn up in any pawn shops," Tony said. "The police will never find it. Those black market sales are pretty hard to break in to if you don't know about them. Sometimes it's just people on the street exchanging goods and money. There's really no way to trace that."

She toyed with her dessert.

"What do you want to do?" Tony asked.

Abigail swallowed a bite of her chocolate smothered strawberry. Then she looked up at Tony.

"I want to go get it."

Chapter Twelve

"You brought your *tools?*" Abigail asked. They were back at the hotel, and he was digging through his suitcase. It had been too much to bring in the carry-on, which is why he had checked his luggage. Maybe he forgot to mention that to Abigail.

"Well, yeah. How else did you think I was going to do the job at the Louvre?"

"But…"

He pulled his black bag out from inside his bigger suitcase. He hadn't brought anything illegal, of course. Just lock picks, his rope, and a few other instruments he couldn't leave home without. "I honestly thought maybe I could do a few jobs here. *Security* jobs," he added, when she gave him a look. "And now I have one. At the Louvre!"

"Are you going to wear your cat-burglar suit?"

"You wish," he said. He smiled up at her. Abigail had picked up the bad habit of chewing her nails when she was nervous. She was doing that now.

He stood and hefted his bag onto his shoulder. "Are you sure you want to do this?"

"Yes." Her face was set in stone.

"Okay."

It was nearly 10 p.m. when they got to the apartment complex. No one was around, so Tony pulled out one of his tools and ran it up and down Lena's door. It was scanning for heat imprints inside.

"She's not there," he said, clicking it off. "Nobody is."

Then he opened an app on his phone.

"What are you doing?" asked Abigail.

"Scanning for wires, or anything electrical around the door to see if it's alarmed."

"It's an *apartment.*"

"It's *Lena's* apartment. If she has a million-dollar ring in there, she might want to keep people out."

He wasn't sure how he felt about doing this. Part of him had totally justified it because they both knew for certain that Lena had their ring. Tony was pretty certain there were probably other things in the apartment she didn't want the police to see, so if she found them breaking and entering, he doubted that she would call the police on them.

He fiddled with the lock on the door, and it clicked. But when he turned the handle, nothing happened. "There must be a deadbolt," he said, pulling out a small laser gun. He ran it along the doorframe, and it eventually cut through the heavy metal inside. There was the slight smell of things burning.

He glanced at Abigail. Her arms were crossed and there was a look of determination on her face, not fear.

He quietly opened the door. "Let me go in first, just in case."

It was dark. He took out his pen light and swept it around. He didn't see anybody.

"Come on."

Abigail followed him in and closed the door behind her.

Tony walked over to the window and pulled the shade down. It was dark outside, and his light would travel.

There was a table near the door. Abigail turned on the small lamp that sat on it. A soft yellow light filled the room.

Lena's apartment was small and crowded. They were standing in a living room with a kitchenette area off to the left. Only a counter separated the two rooms. Across the room was a bathroom on the left and two other rooms on the right. The door was open on one, and it looked like it might be her bedroom.

Abigail was already opening drawers in the living room desk, shining her own light into them. She ruffled through papers. He was about to hand her some gloves when he noticed she was wearing the soft leather ones he had bought her that winter.

70

"You *brought* those?" he asked.

She gave him a little smile. "A girl needs *her* tools, too."

Tony frowned. "It's summer. Why do you need gloves?"

"I like them."

"Hmmmm."

He would have to discuss this with her later.

They split the room in half, and each went through all of the drawers and cupboards on their side. "I don't think she would hide it some place so obvious," Tony said. He thought of the places he might hide jewelry. He had kept a false bottom in one of his bedroom drawers. He tried the first door on his right. It was locked. He'd pick it in a minute.

He went into the bedroom. There was a dresser, and he started going through it. In the first drawer was a box. He opened it. It contained photos of her childhood. In one of the photos, Lena looked about two years old. She was smiling and standing in between two adults that he assumed were her parents. He fanned through a few more. There were two photos when she was about twelve or thirteen, and she was only with her mother. He didn't find any from her teen years. Nothing here.

The second drawer he opened was her underwear drawer.

"Abigail?" he whispered, shutting the drawer. "You do this one."

She came in the room, but then shined her light up against the opposite wall.

"Look," she said.

A large table near the window held paintbrushes, oils, and canvases. There was an unfinished painting on an easel near the table, with a stool behind it. It was turned so the natural light from the window would let Lena see to paint. From here, Tony couldn't see what it was.

Sitting on the table, framed, was something on letterhead. He shined his light on it. It was a rejection letter from the Columbia School of Art. Why would she frame that?

Abigail shined her light on some paintings that were lined up against the wall near the bed, sitting on the floor. There was a portrait of a woman with blond hair. Another was a still life of a vase of flowers. There was an attempt at modern art.

Not bad, but nothing spectacular. Abigail shined her light on a large object on the other side of the bed that was covered by a white sheet. There were some other ones beside it, also covered. She assumed they were paintings.

Tony walked over to the table to get a better look at the painting on the easel. Before he got there, they heard a click.

"That was the door," Tony said.

They both froze. Tony shook his head. He had gotten careless. One of them should have been standing lookout.

He put a finger to his lips, motioning for Abigail to move toward the closet. Maybe they could hide. They shut off their penlights.

They heard footsteps coming across the old, squeaky floorboards. The footsteps stopped just outside of the bedroom.

"I know it's you, and you won't find the ring," Lena said.

Busted, Tony walked forward to where she could see him in the light from the living room table.

"I knew it was you," Lena said again. She looked a little shaken, but there was steel in her eyes.

"All we want is the ring," Tony said. "We won't press charges or call the police. Just give us the ring back."

Lena laughed. "Do you think I'm crazy?" she said. "You know how much that ring is worth."

"Actually, no, I don't," Tony said. "How much did you get for it?"

Abigail pushed past Tony. "Listen here," she said, getting right up in to Lena's face. "I thought you were my friend."

Tony remembered the knife.

"Abigail," he warned.

But Abigail was just getting warmed up. "I trusted you, and you *lied* to me. You might think it's worth a fortune, but it's worth more than money to me. It has sentimental value because it is a family heirloom, and that is more valuable than money. Or is that something you don't know anything about?"

Tony didn't like the way this was going. Attack was never a plan of his. He always used charm to get what he wanted, and judging by Lena's body language, she was in full defensive mode now. He had to stop Abigail if they were going to get anywhere.

"How dare you!" Lena hissed the words at Abigail. "You and your perfect life! Your stupid librarian career and your wonderful marriage—"

"You don't know the first thing about me *or* my marriage!" Abigail said. "Let me tell you what I've been through in the last—"

Tony stepped between them. "Let's all calm down," he said in the most peaceful voice he could muster. He glanced at both women. Abigail was seething. He looked at Lena. "Can we sit down?"

"Get out," Lena said.

"Lena, please." Tony put a hand gently on Lena's shoulder. She shrugged it off like she had been burned.

"Don't touch me."

Tony glanced at Abigail and then back at Lena. Lena had wrapped her arms around herself and retreated to the corner.

"Get out," she said again.

"Not without my ring," Abigail said quietly.

Tony motioned to the bed. "Abigail, please sit."

Abigail glared at him but did as he asked. He turned to Lena. "We're not going to hurt you," he said quietly to Lena.

Lena glanced at the paintings still covered by sheets. "You have no right to be here," she said.

"We haven't looked at them," Abigail said. "Lena, please give me my ring, and we will leave. We know you have it."

Tony knew he had to get this back under control. He needed to distract Lena, to get the ball back in his court. He casually walked over beside the bed and fingered the sheet over the largest painting. "What *is* this?"

Lena instantly crossed the room to stand in between him and the piece of art.

"It's none of your business." Judging by her reaction, she desperately didn't want them to see it.

He walked over to the desk. "So, you're an artist." He tried to keep his voice casual. He picked up a thick brush and twirled it between his fingers. Putting the brush down, he picked up the framed rejection letter. He turned back to Lena.

"Get out of here!" she hissed between her teeth.

"Let me guess. Rejected by art school, so in scorn, you turned to a life of crime? The world was against you, so you decided to fight back. To make money however you could? You steal at night to fuel your passion by day."

Lena was angry, and the look in her eyes was piercing. He had hit a sore spot. He felt kind of bad, pressing her. She obviously had some rough spots in her life.

"What do *you* know about the world being against you?"

"More than you think."

"I don't have your ring," she said. "And even if I did, I wouldn't give it back to you. I'm going to call the police." She went out into the living room.

Tony met Abigail's eyes. He shook his head.

"No, you won't," he called to Lena. "I have a hunch there are other things in here you'd rather they didn't see."

He and Abigail followed her into the living room. He was right. She hadn't pulled out her cell phone yet.

"I guess it takes a thief to know one," she said.

Tony frowned. "What exactly do you know about me?"

A small, sarcastic smile crossed her lips. "More than you'd like."

"Where's the ring?" Abigail said.

"It's not yours."

"It is too!"

Lena smirked. Tony was using the distraction to scan the room, open a few drawers. He found an address book and leafed through it. A business card fell out.

"Do you think you're Antonio Russo's *only* descendent?" Lena said.

That stopped Tony in his tracks. He came back over so he could face her, look into her eyes. "What do you mean? Is there another one?"

Lena's eyes closed off to him so he couldn't read her. She walked over and opened the door of her apartment. "Leave."

Abigail folded her arms across her chest. Tony knew that gesture, but he reached over and took her arm. "Let's go," he said quietly.

"But—"

"It's not worth it."

They left. Lena shut the door forcefully behind them.

"But my ring!" Abigail said.

Tony kept quiet while they descended the stairs. Once they were out on the sidewalk, he turned to Abigail. "Not here," he said. He flagged down a taxi in the darkness. "I'll explain everything back at the hotel."

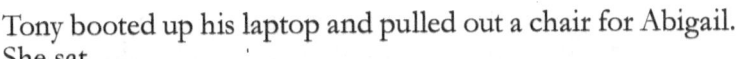

Tony booted up his laptop and pulled out a chair for Abigail. She sat.

"Tell me," she demanded.

He pulled the business card out of his pocket. "I found this in Lena's address book."

Abigail took it and looked at it.

"John Doe." She cracked a smile. "Original."

"He's a dealer in collectibles on the black market. He doesn't go after jewels or art for their monetary value or their beauty. He's more of a sentimental collector. The hairpin that Rita Hayworth wore in her first film. A paintbrush used by Van Gogh. Stuff like that. He's an art historian, so it makes sense that he'd be interested in the ring."

"You think that's who she sold it to?"

"Or is *going* to sell it to," Tony said. "I believe if she had unloaded it already, she'd be gone. I'm sure she'd get a whole lot for it. I really have no idea though. Collectors are peculiar on what they perceive an item's value is."

He sat down at the desk and typed in his passwords. The machine whirled to life. He pulled out his phone and brought up something, which he typed into the computer. The screen changed.

"What's that?" Abigail asked.

"It's allows me to use another server from my computer, so nobody can trace my IP address."

"In other words, it allows you to hack without getting caught."

Tony grinned and looked up at her. "Yep."

He went to the black market auction sites he was familiar with and looked for the ring. Nothing came up. He searched

John Doe's name. "He has nothing for sale, but I can't see if he has bid on anything," Tony said.

He switched sites and sent a protected email to Marvin Tucker, a collector he had worked with in the past. It was 11 p.m. here, 5 p.m. back in the US. Marvin answered his email immediately. Tony smiled. "He probably has John Doe's phone number and residence," Tony told Abigail.

And Marvin did. He texted it to Tony.

"Success."

Tony logged off and shut his computer down.

"You're going to talk to John Doe about the ring?"

"Maybe. Or maybe I'll break in and take a look around. He has a place here in Paris. I assume he's home, or coming home soon, if Lena's going to sell him the ring."

Abigail looked worried. "Tony, I don't think that's a good idea. Maybe you're right. Maybe we should let it go."

"We'll let it go for tonight, that's for sure," Tony said. He got up and put his arms around his wife. He pressed his face into her hair. He loved the lavender scent of her shampoo.

"You have to get up early," he said. "I think we should get to bed."

"How can you sleep now that we think we know who might want the ring? He might have it at this moment!"

Tony pulled back so he could look at her. "If he has it, he'll keep it. I know him. He's a collector, and that's how he thinks. If he doesn't have it, then either Lena still does, or she is selling it to someone else, and those aren't problems we can fix tonight. *What's done cannot be undone. To bed, to bed, to bed!*"

"*Macbeth*," she named the source of the quote, sleepily. "Okay." She wrapped her arms around him. "To bed."

Chapter Thirteen

Tuesday morning came early. As they got ready to leave, Tony couldn't stop grinning. Abigail watched the pure delight on his face as he grabbed his tool bag. He was going in to do some work at the Louvre.

"You're just like a little boy at Christmas with new toys," she said.

His grin widened. "This is going to be so fun!"

Abigail had an easy day today, as she didn't have to present. She was glad she didn't have the additional stress of that. And she was glad Tony had to work. It would keep him from contacting this John Doe guy and keep him out of trouble.

When they got to the Louvre, Tony went off to do his job and Abigail went to the conference area. The room was crowded, but Ms. Scott had saved her a seat near the back.

The first presentation was on the lost art of maps in the digital age. She found it a little sad. The next presentation was drier, and Ms. Scott left to go print out more brochures about their library. She needed them for the lunchtime display booth in the commons area.

Abigail found her mind wandering. The woman in front of her was bored too and had pulled out her cell phone. She was looking at the news. Abigail saw a photo of the mystery artist's painting. It was the one Tony had seen at the Musée d'Orsay.

The one with the mysterious Hestia symbol.

Abigail was sitting in the back, so she didn't see a problem with pulling out her own cell phone. She Googled the symbols for Hestia. *Hearth. Home. Family.* Why would the artist use that? Was he trying to tell people something? Abigail, too, suspected the artist wasn't a "he" but rather a "she." Hestia was a female symbol, and those things were something a woman would be more in tune with. Family, warmth, comfort.

A man would have probably picked a more warrior-type symbol. Right? Or was she being sexist?

She left that page and Googled Lena's tour guide company. The website looked legit. There were even some positive reviews on a few vacation sites.

"Very entertaining. Bright tour guide."

"The history was fascinating. I learned things I hadn't read about in art school."

"Knowledgeable, friendly guide. Priced reasonably."

It seems Lena was good at her job.

So Lena was an artist who loved art history enough that she was making a living telling others about it, while she painted on the side. Or maybe she only *pretended* to love art history so she could make a living and steal from her clients. But Abigail didn't think that was the case.

Lena was passionate. Abigail didn't believe the girl's enthusiasm for the painters she talked about during their tour was fake. She also remembered how Lena's eyes lit up while they were baking. Yes, she might have had an ulterior motive when she met them, which was to steal Abigail's ring. But she knew how to bake, so Abigail felt that was a legitimate session that Lena already had tickets for and not just a set up. It was simply something she was familiar with and decided to use to lure Abigail in.

She had to have a co-conspirator as well. Who had called her at the convenient time of the fire, so she would have an excuse to escape? And who had *started* the fire in the first place? What if the "thief" who had stolen Abigail's purse was the same man? Obviously, the purse snatching was a set-up. Abigail felt a surge of anger inside of her.

There was some applause, and Abigail looked up. The speaker had an image on her Power Point of the statistics of jobs in maps today, versus jobs fifty years ago. It was obviously a dying art, but she was trying to revive it through some social awareness programs. She gave the reasons that maps are still important today, including the imperfection of GPS systems, and the inconsistencies of phone signals.

"What if you are driving on a dirt road in the dark and lose your phone signal? What if your GPS is wrong? I've had Siri take me the wrong way before," the speaker said. Abigail had to agree. She knew Tony loved his tech devices though.

"And kids these days," the speaker continued. She told how kids don't know how to read maps, because they don't have to. "They don't have a visual grid laid out in their heads of where they live. They are growing up not knowing how to give directions, or how to get from point A to point B without their phones."

The next slide was a cartoon drawing of a teenager in his car, with a question mark above his head and a thought bubble showing no bars on his phone. *He's lost.* Abigail smiled.

Lena seemed a little lost. Did she have family? And what did she mean that Tony wasn't Russo's only descendent?

The presentation ended, and Abigail stood up. Ms. Scott came in, looking flushed.

"I just saw your husband dressed in black, scaling down a wall in the artifacts room," Ms. Scott said, putting her hand to her heart. "There for a moment, I thought he was back to his old shenanigans." She gave a nervous little laugh.

"No, no!" Abigail said. "He got a job here."

"I guessed that. I saw two guards with him and some men in business suits. One was taking notes."

Abigail laughed. She would love to see what Tony was up to.

"Are you ready for lunch?" Ms. Scott asked.

They were supposed to meet with some potential donors today. "I'll be there in a minute. You go on ahead."

Abigail sat back down. She wanted to finish the thought that had come to her head a few moments ago. *Lena lost.* Why? And what did her art say about her? It was really pretty good. Had she entered her paintings into any shows? She'd have to ask Tony to search for that tonight.

Lost Lena.

Lost from what? Or just a thief?

Her mind turned back to Ms. Scott. They were here trying to rebuild trust, and Ms. Scott had just had a fright with Tony.

Abigail laughed about that. She had better get back to her and reassure her again. Maybe she'd see Tony on the way. She hurried off to lunch.

She stopped at a restroom. When she came out, standing just down the hall, Dunning was talking to an English gentleman named Michael Benedict. She knew Michael from previous symposiums. He had presented at two that she had presented at, and they had become casual friends. Since he did almost exactly what she did, they sometimes emailed questions to each other about their work.

The two men didn't see her. They were standing close and talking in hushed tones. She wondered what they were up to, and an uncomfortable prickling sensation sent a shiver up the back of her neck. She stepped a little closer and picked up a few words.

"...specialized position..."

"...had thought about moving to the States..." Michael's voice.

"...can talk more later..."

What? Was he offering Michael a *job?* There were no openings at her library. *Currently.*

The two men shook hands, and as Michael turned to leave, he saw Abigail. He froze, looking like a deer caught in headlights. Dunning cleared his throat and adjusted his suit coat. "Ms. Russo," he said, nodding a greeting to her as he walked by.

As soon as he was past, Abigail frowned and immediately went over to Michael.

"I didn't realize you two knew each other," she said sweetly, realizing she should have said "hello" first. She hadn't seen him in person in about two years.

"Um," Michael looked caught. Guilty, in fact.

She might as well get right to the point. "What were you two talking about?"

He swallowed, causing his bowtie to bob. He was a fairly handsome guy, with short, shaggy brown hair, glasses, and a crooked smile. With his British accent, he was quite attractive, but he was so nerdy. His idea of a good time was translating ancient documents and filing.

80

Abigail raised an eyebrow. "Well?"

"He was just introducing himself," he said. His eyes kept darting around. He was unable to meet her gaze. "I understand he's from your library."

"Yes. He's a board member."

Michael looked at his wrist, which didn't have a watch on it. "Wow, I just realized what time it is! I need to meet someone for lunch!" And before she could say anything else, he hurried off.

Abigail watched him scurry down the hall and around the corner, heading toward the lunchroom. She had a growing fear inside her that she knew *exactly* what they were talking about.

Chapter Fourteen

Tony waited for Abigail in the lobby of the Louvre. His shift had ended, and she was due out any time now. It was 2 p.m.

His *shift* had ended. *At the Louvre!* A grin spread across his face at the thought. He was having trouble concealing his smiles and felt that all of this grinning made him appear amateur. But this was his dream job. And today was only Tuesday! He had several more days here before they left. He'd definitely have to ask them for a review on his website for Black Cat Security.

He saw Abigail coming through the double doors across the lobby. She was dressed in light blue today, a soft cotton dress that hung just above her knees. She was wearing some sandals and no nylons. He noticed things like this nowadays. Nylons, bare legs, how her hair was done. He couldn't take his eyes off his wife.

When she saw him, her face lit up and she smiled.

"Hello, beautiful!" he said, pulling her into a hug. He hadn't seen her since this morning, and it seemed like forever.

"Hi, handsome," she said, kissing him.

He took her hand, and they walked out together. She told him about her day. The workshop was going well, and she was pleased with her presentation and work so far. The luncheon she had with Ms. Scott was fruitful, and it looked like they might get more donations for her library. All good stuff.

"And how was *your* day?" she asked.

"I got to break in to the Louvre," he said, grinning yet again.

Abigail laughed. "Your dream job?"

"Yes, indeed! First, I neatly—and quickly, I might add—lifted that vase we were looking at. That was enough for the head of security to hire me for more. So, we walked around, and he asked me to look for other places where one might be able to steal something."

"Did you find any?"

"Of course! There was a case of small statuettes that wasn't alarmed. I fixed that for them."

Abigail hooked her arm in his. "And?"

"And I got to see their *security system!*"

"Is it a good one?"

"The best I've ever seen. If you were going to steal anything from the Louvre, it would have to be an inside job. I'm not even sure *I* could hack in to the computer system from the outside."

"Hmmm."

He loved that she was encouraging him to share his morning.

"Yep. And I get to go back tomorrow," he said.

"Are they paying you?"

"Of *course*, they're paying me!" Tony feigned hurt. "You think someone with my vast experience would work for *free?*"

"*Oh heaven, the vanity of wretched fools!*" Abigail said, laughing.

"Measure for Measure. *Being so great, I have no need to beg.*"

"*Richard II.* I just read it last week."

"We should keep score. Points for correct quotes. If I quote something, and you can't name the source, the point goes to me. But if you correctly name the source, the point goes to you. And vice versa."

"I would win," Abigail said.

"What? Hardly. I have most of Shakespeare memorized."

"Yes, but I'm a librarian. Why stick to Shakespeare? Or would other works scare you off?"

"Ha!" Tony laughed. "*Things done well and with care exempt themselves from fear.*"

Abigail scrunched up her nose. "Ohh. Hmm. A king, maybe? It's always safe to go with one of the kings."

"*Henry III.* Point for me."

"What? I *said* it was a king! You didn't give me a chance!"

"You gotta be fast."

Notre Dame loomed up ahead of them, its beautiful rose window catching the late afternoon sunlight. The medieval Catholic church was one of the biggest and best known in the world. They had read up on it before their trip, and Tony remembered it was built in 1345. That made it well over six hundred years old.

They stopped and stared at it.

Tony saw some steps up the road from them, leading into a park. "Let's go sit," he said.

The steps were made of stone and were the perfect size for sitting. Some trees offered shade from the afternoon sun. From here, they could look across the river at Notre Dame.

"It's beautiful," Abigail said.

Tony nodded. There were really no words to describe it.

"Do you think your great-grandfather attended this church?" she asked.

"I don't know. I'm not sure if he was a Christian or not. Of if he even believed in God. I assume he did. Most people did back in those days."

Abigail squeezed his hand and looked over at him.

"How are *you* and God doing?"

Tony had struggled with God a lot in the past few months. Not in his *belief* in God. He believed He existed. It was more of a trust issue. How much could he rely on God with so many bad things happening? But through the ordeal with Mauvais, and then the trial that followed, he was reassured by Abigail's presence and her own faith in God. She had stuck with Tony. And so had God. He had feared that his past would be too much for both of them, that he didn't deserve their love. But God, like Abigail, had offered Tony a gift. The gift of redemption. The promise of a new life, the forgiveness of a past life and its mistakes, and unconditional love.

Tony met Abigail's eyes. She had come into their relationship with a strong love for God, despite the fact that she felt like God had let her first husband die. Her faith had strengthened Tony's.

"God and I are doing just fine," Tony said.

84

His phone beeped in with a text, breaking up the moment. He ignored it, but it beeped again.

"You had better check that," Abigail said. "The Louvre may need you."

Tony smiled and pulled it out. He saw whom the message was from and shoved it back into his pocket without reading it. Now wasn't the time. He felt a twinge of shame.

"Who's it from?" Abigail said.

He had promised to always be truthful. "Charlotte."

Charlotte was a former client of his, and he had occasionally spent the night with her after an evening of work. That was before he met Abigail. Charlotte was a complicated matter between them. He knew Abigail had been briefly worried about him returning to a past relationship with Charlotte, even though he never would. He didn't love Charlotte. She had just been someone fun to hang out with. He didn't really consider what they had had a "relationship."

"You can read it," Abigail said.

Tony looked at her again and then pulled out the phone. He held it so Abigail could see the screen. Charlotte had recently had a break-in at one of her companies and wanted to hire Tony to beef up security.

"I don't have to take it," he said.

"I'm not threatened by her. Besides, she saved your life on more than one occasion. And mine. If it wasn't for Charlotte, you'd be in jail and I'd be..."

Abigail pulled Tony closer and put her head against his before she finished her sentence. "I'd be without you."

"She's from my past."

"She's also from your present. I actually like her."

Tony kissed Abigail on the top of the head and replied to the text.

Yes! I'm in Paris. ☺ Will text you when I return next week.

He sent it, and Charlotte replied with a smiley. Short and to the point. That's one thing he liked about working with her.

"Speaking of things past and stealing, what are we going to do about my ring?" Abigail asked. "I think we should break in again. It has to be in there. We'll just take it."

Tony looked over at his wife. She was watching some ducks paddle their way down the river. When he had first met her, just a few short months ago, she hadn't been breaking in to apartments or running around with a thief. A *former* thief, he reminded himself.

"Abigail?"

He waited until she looked at him before he spoke again. "Where's that line you were talking about?"

He saw the guilt creep into her eyes.

"I know," she sighed. "It's just…"

He waited, but she didn't finish.

"Just what?"

"It's so easy this way. If we wait for the police, we'll never get our ring back. Your grandma will be devastated. It's obvious they aren't going to do anything about finding it. I suppose we could tell them its real value, but then it would become a huge heist. The whole world would know what my ring is, and I'd never be able to wear it again. But you have your tools here, and you are *so good* at this. We could wait until Lena's gone and sneak in and get it. Unless she has sold it."

"Well, we didn't find it in the short time we were there," Tony said. But that wasn't what was bothering him. "It's not easy to do it this way. There's a cost. Look at what I've lost."

Not to mention that he had been jailed twice and almost didn't get out.

"George," Abigail said. "You've lost George."

"My best friend. And Jimmy no longer trusts me. He's like a father to you, so I know that hurts you. And there's Ms. Scott. I may be 'good' at sneaking in and getting things, but I've lost my integrity. I have to work very hard now to rebuild it. I don't want that to happen to you."

Abigail was silent for a while. Then she looked over at him again, a twinkle in her eye. "It's also kind of fun."

Tony laughed. "Yes. It's a *lot* of fun! Which is why I'm trying to do the same thing now, only on the legitimate side of the law."

The bushes rustled behind them. He felt the hairs on the back of his neck prickle, and he turned around. Tony stood up and saw a tall figure in a black hoodie turn and run. He stood up quickly and took off after slim-framed person. The figure ran up a hill and across a street. A bus drove in between them, slowing Tony down. When he was able to cross the street, the figure was nowhere in sight.

Abigail caught up with him. "Did you see who it was?" she asked.

Tony shook his head. Whoever was following them was quick as a cat.

Chapter Fifteen

Abigail showed up at the Louvre promptly at 8 a.m. Wednesday morning. Ms. Scott was in the auditorium directing a young man with a microphone. "I can't hear you in the back of the room," she said. The young man motioned to the sound guy, who played with some switches. There was shrill feedback and then quiet. He spoke again.

Ms. Scott nodded. "Much better." She turned to Abigail. Without so much as a good morning, she said, "Are you ready for this afternoon?"

Abigail nodded. Today was a big talk, but not as important as Friday's. She was the closing speaker on Friday. That one was her most important presentation, and the library board members and a lot of others were counting on her to make an international impression. They were hoping to increase donations and to win some future grants from her newfound notoriety. Also, there was the small fact that her entire career depended on it. Today's talk would be a piece of cake compared to that one. She was well prepared for both, so she wasn't that nervous.

"Good. I'd like to hear it."

Ms. Scott had requested somebody's office so Abigail could go over today's talk for her. She took down a picture so Abigail could use the back wall for a screen. Then she pulled up a stool and sat on the other side of the room, arms crossed.

Now, Abigail was nervous. She wasn't expecting this.

She booted up her laptop so she could show the Power Point presentation. Her talk was on the history of mapmaking. She had recently worked with a Vesconte map dating back to the 1300s. Vesconte was one of the earliest map designers and was a pioneer in the field of the portolan chart. She was going to use information from that in her talk. It was touchy, though, because the map had been stolen, something she wasn't aware of when she first brought it into her library.

Unfortunately, Tony, in his former life, had been the one to steal it.

So much had happened since then. She sighed, a bit too loudly.

"There's no reason to be nervous," Ms. Scott said, misinterpreting the sigh.

"I'm fine," Abigail said. And really, she was. She *knew* this stuff. She clicked on the first slide and began her presentation.

It lasted exactly thirty minutes. When she finished, she looked expectantly at Ms. Scott.

"Brilliant," Ms. Scott said. "There's nothing I could add to make it better." She continued to sit on the stool though. Abigail closed her laptop and rehung the picture on the wall. When she turned back around, Ms. Scott had a tired look on her face.

"Abigail, it's not up to me whether you keep your job or not," she said. Her voice had lost its usual business-like manner and was gentle.

"What do you mean? You're my boss. The *director* of the library."

"I know. But the board has lost some confidence in me because of the...fiasco."

And there it was. The Vesconte and Mauvais were still haunting Abigail. "It wasn't your fault."

"They think I should have been more on top of things. I should have somehow known that Tony was the thief who broke in to our library last winter. And somehow known that Mauvais dealt in stolen goods."

Abigail leaned back against the desk behind her. She had no idea that Ms. Scott had been in trouble too.

"Why didn't you say something?"

Ms. Scott shook her head. "You had so much going on. I could see how stressed you were with the trial, and you had stuff to work out in your marriage, obviously. I didn't want to add to your burdens."

It wasn't like Ms. Scott to show compassion or emotion. She was usually all business. If she had hidden this information, Abigail wondered what else in her personal life she hid.

"I'm so sorry," Abigail said.

Ms. Scott gave a small smile. "Don't be. It's not your fault. I was angry with you for not telling me the truth about Tony, but I can see why. Love does strange things to people. And it's apparent that you love him."

"I do."

Her director had a faraway look in her eyes. Abigail had never thought of Ms. Scott as having a lover. She had certainly never mentioned one. But maybe in her past?

"Were you ever in love?" Abigail asked quietly, afraid of breaking the spell.

"I was," Ms. Scott said, in a rare moment of vulnerability. "His name was Reggie. I met him here on a work trip some twenty years ago. I thought he loved me…"

She grew quiet, her eyes staring at something from her past that only she could see.

"But then our work got in the way. He promised me it wouldn't. But it did. I was offered the position of rare maps curator at the Louvre that week. I was so thrilled! A job at the Louvre, which would mean a move to the city that was home to the man I loved! It was perfect."

"What happened?"

Ms. Scott looked down at her hands, clasped tightly together on her lap. "He betrayed me. Apparently, he had promised to use his notoriety and money to give it to someone else. He owed someone, I guess. Anyway, he swayed the powers that be to rescind the offer."

How heartbreaking! Abigail had never asked Ms. Scott about her past. What other hurts was she carrying? Maybe this explained why she was so closed off. Grief did that to a person. Abigail knew that personally. "Have you ever seen him again?"

"No. I went home after that. He never contacted me. Never apologized. Never explained. He just said he was in a business I wouldn't understand. Where men trade favors. And it was his turn to give a favor."

"It seems to me like he owes you a favor now."

"I never wish to see him again." The director cleared her throat and turned her eyes to Abigail, indicating the conversation was over. The mood was lost.

"I will do my best to keep you. You're an asset to our library." Ms. Scott uncrossed her arms and got up off the stool. "Now we should get to the auditorium. The presentations are about to begin."

"Ms. Scott?"

The director turned to her.

"What's Robert Dunning doing here?"

Ms. Scott hesitated. When she spoke, her voice was back to its usual business tone. "He's here to observe." Then she turned and left. Abigail's stomach did a flip-flop. Observe what? Or whom? Obviously, it was her.

Abigail took a seat near the back, while Ms. Scott went up to the front row. She thought about what Ms. Scott had just said. Abigail had been trying so hard to make an impression with the director. But it appeared that it wasn't Ms. Scott she had to impress. It was the board members. And now Dunning was *here*. If she didn't procure some accolades and grants, she'd get the boot for sure. Or maybe even if she did.

"What do you think so far?"

Abigail jumped at the voice. A woman who looked to be in her forties sat down beside her and took a sip from a very large coffee.

"The conference? It's great!"

"I'm Julia."

Abigail introduced herself. The opening speaker was interesting and kept Abigail and the woman next to her riveted. After he finished and the applause ended, Julia leaned over to Abigail and whispered, "Have you heard about the mystery artist?"

"Yes! Isn't that fascinating?"

"Who do you think it is?" Julia asked. "My friend thinks it's a famous artist who is trying something different under a pen name, so to speak. Just to see what critics say. But there are easier ways of showing off your art."

"Like an art show, for instance," Abigail said. They laughed.

"So, *I* think it's a disgruntled artist. Someone who was thrown out of an art show, or maybe someone who has parent issues. You know what I mean."

"Parent issues?"

"Yeah. Like his parents forbade him to do art, and now he is stuck in a boring career like hotel management because his parents would only pay for schooling for a 'practical' job. And now here he is. Breaking in to museums."

Abigail laughed again. "Those parent issues will get you."

"Don't I know that," Julia said. "I'm a foster parent. I'm currently juggling six kids. Only three of them are my own."

"Six?"

"Uh-oh. We need to be quiet. The next speaker is up." Julia took another sip of her coffee and settled down in her seat.

But Abigail couldn't pay attention. Something was tickling the back of her mind. Parent issues. A disgruntled artist.

The woman had referred to the artist as a "he," but Abigail still thought it might be a woman. Mostly because of the Hestia symbol in place of the signature.

The artist must be Parisian. They'd have to live in the city because all of the museums were local. None was in London or any other place in Europe. At least, not yet.

She opened up her phone and looked at the photo of the painting from the Petit Palais. She enlarged it.

"What's that?" Julia whispered. She leaned closer to take a peek.

"The painting from the mystery artist that was left at the Petit Palais. My husband saw it."

"May I see?"

Abigail handed her the phone. Julia stared at it for a while. "It's beautiful. What's this?" She enlarged the photo to a certain spot and handed it back to Abigail.

There was a figure standing on the bridge.

"There are others on the bridge, but this one stands out," Julia said. "Look. She has this swirl pattern on her shirt. It's like a wheel. And her umbrella, which is pointed down, looks an awful lot like a sword."

Abigail looked. And while the others had scarves tied on against the recent rain, or hair that was laying down flat, this figure's hair was blowing wildly about. It almost looked like wings.

Julia chuckled. "She almost looks like Nemesis, the Greek goddess of retribution."

Abigail looked at Julia.

"I'm a Greek scholar," she said. "I'm here because of my study in symbology."

"Oh. Wow."

Julia went back to listening to the talk, but Abigail continued to look at the photo. *Nemesis.* When she enlarged the photo, the details were a bit blurry on her phone. She wished she could see the painting up close in real life.

She did a Google search for another image of the mystery artist's paintings. The one that was found in the Musée de l'Orangerie came up. This one was a painting of a carnival with the Eiffel Tower in the background. That meant yet another painting that was set in Paris. She searched through the crowd of people. There! There was the same figure. Hair blowing behind her shoulders. This time she was holding a stick of cotton candy in the air, but it was strangely sword-like. And she had on the same swirly top. Because this was a daytime scene, Abigail could make out the swirl pattern more closely. It looked like a wheel.

"Ohhhh!" Julia whispered, leaning over. "Text that link to me."

She did. Then she searched Google for images of wheels. She found one that matched the image in the painting. It was called the Wheel of Fortune and was a symbol often associated with the Greek goddess Nemesis. Abigail turned to Julia to tell her she was right, but the woman was gone. Probably to use the restroom, judging by how much coffee she had consumed.

Disgruntled artist. Symbols of retribution. Very interesting.

The speaker finished, and they broke for lunch. She was about to call Tony to tell him what she learned when Ms. Scott approached her.

"Abigail, where is your ring?"

"What?"

Abigail looked down at her empty finger. This woman didn't miss a thing. She hadn't mentioned the theft to Ms. Scott because she didn't want to alarm her.

"Um..." She thought about saying she left it in the hotel room but didn't want to lie. She was, after all, trying to rebuild trust.

"It was stolen. I went to a cooking class and took it off to wash my hands. There was a fire, and somebody grabbed it in the confusion."

"Oh my goodness! Did you file a police report?"

"Yes. It isn't doing much good."

"I noticed you weren't wearing it yesterday either."

"No. It happened the first day we were here."

Ms. Scott gave her a look of sympathy. "I'm sorry. I know it was your wedding ring."

Abigail shrugged. What more was there to say?

"Will this interfere with your work?"

"It hasn't so far," Abigail said. It came out a bit more defensively than she planned.

"I'm sorry," Ms. Scott said. "That was impertinent of me."

Abigail rubbed her finger. Tony said he might check some pawnshops today and ask around before he came to work. She wondered what Tony was doing now.

Chapter Sixteen

Tony was sitting in their hotel room, a cup of coffee on the small hotel table. He stretched and cracked his knuckles before getting down to work. Typing in some special passcodes, he logged in to a different browser from his computer, making his searches untraceable. Nobody would be able to read his real IP address now.

His fingers flew over the keyboard as he set himself up to do some searching about Lena under her real name.

After about thirty minutes, he was able to hack in to Lena's financial aid applications. She had been enrolled at a private Christian school until age ten, when her father died. She had received some scholarships to help with tuition. Then, after his death, she had transferred to public school, probably because her mom could no longer pay.

Her senior year, Lena Mercier had applied to three art schools. Two were in the United States, and one was in Paris. She was rejected from one in the United States, and the other two schools didn't offer her financial aid. He assumed she couldn't afford to go. He saw where she applied to undergraduate school for pre-law in the US and got in on a scholarship. So she was telling the truth about that. Her financial records indicated that her family wasn't well off. Not poor, exactly. Lower middle class.

He searched under her father's name. Lena still carried his last name. Her mother had no work skills, and they quickly ended up on welfare. She remarried a year after Lena's father died. This man was named Albert Boucher. He held a job as a foreman in a machine shop. Tony couldn't find anything else on him.

95

He sat there a minute, thinking. How far did he want to go? After a moment's hesitation, he started working on breaking in to Lena's medical records.

She was a healthy kid, but then soon after Boucher came into the picture, she had some accidents. She was brought in to the emergency room for a broken finger. The report said she fell off her bike. Six months later, she was brought in for a black eye and needed four stiches. *Fight at school* was written down as the reason. He didn't see anything else at the hospital, so he went in to the records at her pediatrician's office.

She was seen for well-child visits at age thirteen and fourteen. No apparent problems. After the age of fourteen, there were no other medical records for her. It was like she disappeared.

A pattern was beginning to form in his mind.

Tony closed down her records and did a search on her mom's medical records. As he suspected, Lena's mom was seen in the emergency room five times after she married Boucher. A broken nose. A black eye. A broken rib. All of the accounts listed "accidents" such as fall in the garden or fall off a bike. But Tony knew better. Boucher was abusive.

Angry, he closed down the site and picked up his phone.

"Anders?" he said when his former client answered. "I need you to dig up some information on a guy for me."

He gave him the name and last place of residence and ended the call. Anders had come in handy many times when Tony wanted to know more about someone he would be working with. Tony had great hacking skills, but Anders was better.

So Lena was from an abusive home. After what appeared to be a great early childhood, her mom had married a jerk the second time around. Then Lena tried to get in to art school and couldn't.

He picked up his phone to text Abigail, but then he saw the time. She would probably be in workshops all morning. He didn't want her phone buzzing if Ms. Scott was sitting beside her. Meanwhile, he would let the information he learned about Lena marinate. He was slowly piecing her life together, but there was something he was missing.

He'd see Abigail this afternoon when he went to the Louvre for work. He could tell her what he knew then.

Tony looked at his watch. Maybe he'd go check out the mystery paintings at the Musée Carnavalet and the Musée de l'Orangerie.

The Musée Carnavalet was about two miles southeast along the river, so he flagged down a cab. The building was closed for renovation until the following year, but that didn't matter to him. Less security.

Trucks were parked around the building, and he could hear work going on inside. The front entrance had police tape up, so he figured that was where the painting had been found. The two men he overheard talking had said it was in the lobby, so that made sense.

He ducked under the yellow caution tape and walked up the steps. The door was unlocked, so he went inside. He stood there, hands in his pockets, staring at a piece of impressionism hanging boldly above the reception desk. It had plastic in front of it, and caution tape around it.

"Puis-je vous aider Monsieur?"

He turned to the voice. A man about his own age, wearing a yellow construction hat, had spoken. The man said something else in French.

"Parlez-vous Anglais?" Tony asked.

The man shook his head no.

Tony pointed to the painting. The man nodded. "Artiste mystère."

Tony nodded. "Oui."

Another man came into the lobby. The two briefly spoke in French.

"Sir, I'm afraid you must leave," he said to Tony in English. "This is a crime scene. And we need to get our work done."

"Of course. I only wanted to take a look at it," Tony said. "When did it show up here?"

"Last weekend."

"It's beautiful."

"Oui."

It was a picture of some plein air artists painting outside on a sunny day. Sunlight filtered through the trees, creating a pretty display of light, which the mystery artist did a great job of rendering. Their easels were set up on the cobblestone streets. Most of them were painting portraits. There was a pretty little blond girl seated by the central figure. She had a flower in her hair. There were cafes in the background with striped awnings. It seemed like a happy picture.

"Is that Montmartre?" Tony asked.

"Oui. Now you must leave."

"Yes. I'm going." He pulled out his phone and took a picture. Better to ask forgiveness than permission. "Thank you. Merci."

Both men nodded and watched Tony until he was out the door.

He walked across the street and found a place to sit on some concrete planters under a shade tree. The wind rustled the leaves as he opened up the photo. In the corner was the telltale signature of the Hestia symbol.

He wanted to go check out the painting at the Musée de l'Orangerie next.

His phone rang. Maybe it was Abigail. He couldn't wait to tell her about the paintings.

It was Anders.

"I have the info you wanted. He's a nasty man."

"Dude, it's like 4 a.m. there," Tony said.

"I don't sleep. Anyway, this guy has a bad habit. Lots of them, really, but judging from his internet activity, his biggest hobby is meeting up with women in unsavory places."

Tony nodded. "I see."

"He's ex-Army. The French Army. Special Forces. Has a history of hitting people and was dishonorably discharged. And his last wife? Died four years ago from injuries to her ribs and head. The accident report says 'fell off ladder,' but I'm thinking that isn't the case."

Lena's mom.

"It also looks like he has a daughter. He filed a missing person's report on her shortly after the mother died. She would have been about thirteen then. Dana Boucher. The police have never found her. I'm thinking he offed her too."

Tony sighed and rubbed his forehead.

"Tony?"

"Yeah, Anders, I'm still here. That's some rough stuff."

"I know. Stay away from him. He's mean."

"Of course."

Anders gave him Boucher's newest contact info anyway, and Tony ended the call. Now he knew what Lena was running from.

Tony wondered if Boucher would have the family's records. Surely, there was a birth certificate in the home some place. And what had happened to the other daughter?

Had Lena lost both her mother and her half-sister to that man's brutal temper?

There was only one way to find out. Tony opened up the maps app on his phone and found a route to Albert Boucher's apartment. It wasn't far from here.

But right now, it was time to go to work. He flagged down a cab. He had just enough time to stop in to the hotel and change before he went to the Louvre. He bought a burger from the hotel restaurant on the way back out and ate it as he walked to the Louvre.

He saw Abigail in the lobby. She was waiting for him.

"Guess what!" She ran over to embrace him. He gave her a kiss.

"What?"

"The mystery paintings! There's a figure that is in each of the paintings."

"Really?"

She had her phone out and was opening up a photo. She enlarged it. "Here. What do you see that's different?"

He saw it immediately. A figure of a woman standing on the bridge. He enlarged the photo and saw the hair was blown back like wings. There was a certain swirl pattern. It reminded him of something he had read about somewhere along the way, but he couldn't put his finger on it.

"*An angel; or if not, an earthly paragon,*" Tony quoted quietly.

"Not an angel. Definitely not a paragon. Nemesis."

"Nemesis? The Greek Goddess?"

"Yes. Look." Abigail opened her browser and showed him some symbols. The wheel pattern matched the swirls on the figure's shirt in both paintings "And it's on the picture that was in the Musée de l'Orangerie too," Abigail said. She brought up a photo from a news story and enlarged it. "The woman with the cotton candy. Look at her hair."

"Wow," he said.

"Yeah."

"So, somebody who is looking for revenge," Abigail said. "Or retribution."

"I think you're onto something."

Ms. Scott came into the room. "You about ready, Abigail?"

She closed her phone. "Yes. I'll be right there."

"I have news too," Tony said. "Probably too much to tell you now, but I found out a lot of things about Lena."

"Like what?"

"Like she had a great childhood until about the age of ten, and then it all went downhill."

"I'm intrigued."

"I'll tell you later."

Abigail gave him a quick kiss. "There's a lot riding on this talk."

"You'll do fine. You're smarter than everybody else in that room. Remember that."

She nodded, swallowed hard, and followed Ms. Scott into the auditorium. He walked in and picked a seat near the front.

"Tony," Ms. Scott said, coming over to him. "I'm so glad to see you are doing well. I saw the Louvre has hired you to do some of their security."

"Yes." He wondered where this was going. He silently reminded himself that not every conversation was one where Ms. Scott was questioning his integrity.

"That's great. I think they picked the right man. They spoke to me earlier for a reference. I told them you were good." She smiled and left to take a seat across the aisle from him.

That surprised Tony. Sometimes you never could tell about people. Maybe Ms. Scott was warming up to him after all.

He saw a familiar-looking man come into the room and sit down next to Ms. Scott. She nodded briefly at him. Then Abigail stepped up on the stage and took the podium. Tony prayed silently that Ms. Scott's heart would be softened so Abigail could impress her.

Chapter Seventeen

Dunning was sitting in the front row. Abigail felt a mixture of nerves and anger stir inside of her. How dare he fly all the way to Paris just to judge her? That's what it felt like anyway.

To make matters worse, she saw Michael Benedict slip in and sit beside him just as she was about to start.

Well, whatever. She wasn't going to let either of them upset her. She was above that.

She picked up her mic and switched on her Power Point. The first screen came up and her title, "The History of Cartography," blazed out. Simple enough.

She began talking about the earliest forms of mapmaking. Most exciting, she thought, was her story about Anatolia and the nine-foot painting they found on a wall there. It depicted a town plan, complete with buildings and a volcano.

"It's estimated to have been made around 6300 B.C.," she told her audience. "It is believed to be the first real map."

She then talked about papyrus, an early Egyptian material used for map-making. Her library was capable of storing something that old, and in fact, had a few. She had designed the preservation system herself. She'd have to make sure Dunning knew about *that*. Maybe she should throw it into the lecture.

No. Best to stick to the script. So far, Dunning seemed interested.

Not that she cared. Oh, but she did. Who was she fooling? She looked at Tony. He smiled encouragingly.

The next section was on the portolan chart. Here was where she would discuss the Vesconte. She brought up the map they had in the library. Yes, it was originally stolen by her husband, but it was a good picture and an excellent example.

And Ms. Scott had heard her talk and hadn't said to take it out. Maybe Dunning wouldn't recognize it.

She glanced at him as she brought up the photo. His eyes narrowed, and he crossed his arms. She continued on in a very professional manner, discussing Pietro Vesconte and his contributions to their craft. She saw Dunning lean over and say something to Michael. They both snickered. Ms. Scott glared at the men, and Dunning turned his attention back to Abigail.

The jerk.

She plowed on, gratefully moving forward in time. When she finished, she was pleased with her presentation. The audience seemed to be too. Dunning sat with his arms crossed, not applauding with everyone else. Michael started to clap, but when he noticed Dunning wasn't, he stopped.

Ms. Scott clapped very loudly.

Abigail sighed and packed up. The next speaker was ready to begin. She went down and sat next to Tony.

"Who's the jerk in the front row?" he whispered.

"I'll tell you later."

Tony looked at his watch. "I need to get to work."

"I know. Thanks for coming." She leaned over and kissed his cheek.

"You did a great job! The Vesconte section was my favorite."

"Et tu, Brute?"

Tony smiled. He was trying to be funny. She laughed at his little joke, determined not to let Dunning ruin her day. She was good at what she did, she reminded herself for the thousandth time.

After this speaker, there was a break. Abigail decided to go to the restroom. She could also use a drink of water.

Dunning stopped her in the hall. "So, your hubby came to see the talk with his map in it, huh?" He grinned.

"Ha, ha," Abigail said. She looked lingeringly at the water fountain.

"I can't believe you put the stolen Vesconte in there."

"Nobody recognized it. Except for you. I know that map well—"

"I'm sure you do."

"—and it was great example. Ms. Scott didn't have a problem with it."

"You're walking a fine line, Russo," he said.

He turned and went toward the cafeteria. Abigail sighed and went to get her drink of water.

Chapter Eighteen

The security room at the Louvre was a fascinating place to be. A half-dozen computers hummed, sending information to a wall full of screens. There were cameras in each room, as well as along the outside perimeter. It was a well-oiled machine.

"Kid with sticky hands in Room 3," Alphonso said to him. Tony looked at the screen he was indicating. It literally was a kid with sticky hands. He looked about three years old. He had just finished a pastry, which he was not supposed to be eating in that room, and was looking for a place to wipe his hands.

His mother saw him and pulled a wet wipe out of her purse. But he was heading for an antique tapestry.

Alphonso called it in on his mic. The guard in the room intercepted. They watched as the guard spoke with the mother. There were smiles and nods. She took her tyke's hand and led him in the direction of the restroom.

Tony chuckled. "Is this typical?"

"Oh yes," Alphonso said. "You have no idea. Last week, we had a man who wore one of those drink hats in. You know, the kind where you put your beverage in your hat and a straw hangs down to your mouth? I have no idea how he got it past the front. But he kept taking sips of it. Not very discreetly. He refused to empty the can, saying it was some sort of expensive beer. We had to remove him."

"Tourists," Tony said with disgust.

"Yep."

They let Tony play with the computers a little bit to learn the ropes. Then Alphonso said he needed to take a bathroom break. "Think you can take the helm?"

"I'd love to," Tony said. There were four other men in the room in case the museum was overtaken by toddlers with sticky hands. He figured he could handle it.

It wasn't exciting work, really. He just had to sit there and watch the cameras. He scanned the room where the workshop was taking place and saw Abigail sitting in the back of the room, listening intently to whatever the speaker was saying. She had done a terrific job on her talks this week. He knew she would nail Friday's talk as well.

Alphonso came back. "Thanks. Looks like you're free to go for the day. Our manager got called home. His wife is sick. But he wants you back in tomorrow."

Tony nodded and stood. That meant he had two hours before Abigail was finished. That was plenty of time to check up on Boucher. Instead of putting his tools in the locker the Louvre had provided him, he kept the bag with him.

He hurried outside and hailed a cab.

Boucher lived just on the outskirts of Paris, in a lower rent district. He had moved here last year from the suburb where Lena had attended school. Tony wondered what brought him to Paris. It was a longer drive for him to work than where he previously lived.

Tony instructed the cab driver to drop him off a block from Boucher's apartment. He wanted to check it out before he was seen.

It was a four-story building. Boucher was on the second floor. Tony sat outside on a bench and dialed Boucher's cell number. Tony's phone was encrypted and his ID untraceable, so he didn't worry about Boucher tracing the call.

"Hello?" The voice was deep. There was a whirl of machines in the background. Boucher was at work. Tony hung up.

He took the stairs, digging his lock picks out of his bag. When he reached Boucher's apartment, he did a body heat scan through the door, just in case. The apartment was empty. The lock was easy to pick, and there was no deadbolt.

Tony pulled his gloves on and entered. He quietly closed the door.

The apartment was messy. He walked into the living room. A coffee table sat to his right in front of a sagging, stained couch. Both were littered with porn magazines. An empty pizza box sat beside the television remote. A can of beer was tipped over. There hadn't been much liquid left in it, but what was there had soaked in to one of the magazines on the table.

There was a counter dividing the living room from the kitchen. The stove was greasy and dirty. The refrigerator had finger smudges that looked like jelly and grease.

Tony stopped and scanned the room. Where would a man like Boucher keep records? He walked back through a short hall. There was a bathroom and two bedrooms. One was where Boucher slept. The bed was unmade, and it smelled of old sheets and unwashed clothes.

The other room had cardboard boxes stacked in it. Bingo.

He opened a few. He was surprised to find books in two of them. Thrillers, but still. Did Boucher actually *read*? One contained some kitchenware items that still needed to be unpacked. The fourth box had papers in it.

He sat down and leafed through them. They were in French, of course. He opened his phone and found the translation app that Abigail had used in the restaurant. It took a moment to download. The internet was slow here.

While waiting for it, Tony continued to look through the box. Nothing showed up that looked like Lena's family history. He was looking for birth certificates, adoption papers, anything he could find out about her mom and grandma.

He opened a fifth box. More papers. Like the last box, there was no order. Things had been thrown in haphazardly. If Boucher had been here six months, when was he planning on unpacking?

Near the bottom, he found a birth certificate in an official-looking envelope. Dana Ilene Boucher. Albert's daughter. The mother was the same as Lena's. According to the date of birth, the girl would be seventeen now. He found some more papers underneath and pulled them out. Another official document that Boucher had signed.

The app was downloaded, so he opened it and scanned the print. It was a missing person's report. Boucher filed it three years ago when Dana went missing.

Or when he killed her.

Tony dug deeper. He needed to know who Lena really was. There was just something about her, and her comment about Russo's other heir made him wonder.

Instead, he found discharge papers on Boucher. The man had spent four years in the French army. Special Forces. Dishonorably discharged for hitting a superior. There was a photo of Boucher, a square head on a beefy neck. Muscular, at least in his younger days when this photo was taken. Not a terribly ugly man, but he was definitely scary.

He looked at his watch. He had been here nearly a half hour. He called Boucher again. This time, when the man answered, it sounded like he was in his car.

Crap.

Tony took photos of the birth certificate and missing person's report and quickly closed up the boxes. In his haste, he dumped over an old, dead plant that had been sitting in the corner behind him.

Crap again.

He tried to clean it up, but the dirt rubbed in the carpet. He scooted a box over the mess. Maybe Boucher wouldn't notice.

He got up and quickly made his way to the door. He went through, locking it behind him. Slinging his bag over his shoulder, he started to descend the stairs. A huge man was coming up toward him. It was Boucher.

Tony nodded. As they passed, their coats brushed. At the top of the stairs, Boucher turned and watched him go down.

He said something in French.

Tony stopped and turned. He gave Boucher what he hoped was a confused smile. "I don't speak French."

"Who are you?" Boucher easily switched to English. "I haven't seen you around here before."

"I was looking for a girl I met at a club this weekend. I think she gave me a false address." Tony laughed and shrugged.

"What's her name?"

"I think that may have been false too. Cathy."

Boucher frowned. After a moment, he said, "You must be terrible in bed."

"Or maybe it was the cheap dinner I bought her."

Boucher smiled and walked back down the stairs toward Tony. He reached into his pocket, and for a moment, Tony thought he might have a gun. But he pulled out an ink pen.

"Here's a great place to meet girls," he said. He scribbled a number down and folded the paper in half. He reached over and put it in Tony's shirt pocket. He gave the pocket a firm slap with his palm.

"Paris is the city of love. Enjoy."

Boucher turned and went back upstairs to let himself in to his apartment.

Tony let out a breath. "City of Light," he mumbled and walked back down to the street. He hailed a cab. As he glanced back up to the apartment, he saw Boucher watching him from a window. The curtain was pulled aside. He was staring out of it with dark, beady eyes.

Tony's phone rang, and he jumped. It was Abigail.

"Where are you?"

"I'm uh..." He looked up at the cab driver. He didn't want to say much in front of the man. "I'm on my way back. I'll be there in a few minutes. Love you."

He hung up before she could ask any more questions. He'd have a lot of explaining to do when he saw her.

Which made him think of the paper that Boucher had put in his pocket. He pulled it out, and the pen was still clipped to it. The paper had the name of a club and a phone number scribbled on it. Tony looked it up on his phone. It was a strip joint.

"Idiot," he muttered to himself. He needed to get a life. What was so darn important about finding Lena's family records anyway? Was he so desperate for family that he was willing to risk everything?

The cab pulled up in front of the Louvre. Tony paid and got out. He had planned a fun evening for them, and he hoped this didn't ruin it. He'd see what kind of a mood Abigail was in and decide when to tell her he had just gone snooping. Illegally.

And then he'd apologize and promise never to do it again.

Chapter Nineteen

Abigail was glad to be finished for the day. The pressure she was now feeling about her job was enormous. She kind of wished Ms. Scott hadn't said anything about the board members being the ones to make the final decision. *Ms. Scott* knew how hard Abigail worked. She saw her daily and knew how devoted and passionate she was about her job. But the board members? Well, the last time *they* all saw her work, she had a panic attack in the middle of a huge presentation and bolted out of the room. She wound up stopping a thief and nearly died in the process, but still. She had made quite an impression on them, and she was sure it wasn't the good kind. This week was her chance to impress Dunning, at least. She was afraid she had failed so far.

Tony was waiting for her outside. He was sitting on a park bench near the entrance to the Louvre.

He stood when he saw her. A protective wave of love washed over her at the sight of him. She'd do anything to stay with him, even if knowing Tony meant losing her job.

"Hi, beautiful!" He kissed her.

"Hi, Romeo." She laid her forehead against his shoulder for a moment, drinking in his warmth and his sandalwood scent.

"I have a fun surprise for you," he said.

She lifted her head and looked in his eyes. "Another surprise?"

"There's someone I want you to meet." He took her hand. "We're going out to dinner. Only this time, it's fast food. American."

She scrunched up her nose.

Tony laughed. "Okay. We don't have to *eat* there. But there's someone there who we both want to meet."

As they walked toward the spot where Russo's studio had been, he told her everything he had found out about Lena. Apparently, he had done a little online hacking this morning.

"So, you think she is a victim of abuse?" Abigail said.

"I know it. I mean, what else could it be?"

Abigail was quiet for a moment, thinking. "That's a lot of emergency room visits. And after her medical records ended, I'll bet the abuse continued."

"I had the same thought," Tony said. "That poor girl."

Abigail couldn't imagine anyone who would want to hurt a child. What made a person so evil? That would certainly explain why Lena was so guarded.

She shuddered at the thought. There had to be a way they could help her. But there was nothing she could do about it now. She'd think more about it later. She turned her attention to the surprise ahead.

"So where are we going?"

Tony explained to her about how he had talked to a tenant in the storefront that used to be his Russo's art studio. The tenant told him to come back to find the old man.

"He said the man eats dinner at the fast food joint around this time every night. And he always sits at a certain table. I guess when you own the building, there are perks." Tony laughed.

"And heart disease." Abigail said.

When they reached the building, there were about a dozen people sitting around the outdoor tables eating.

"Do you know what he looks like?" Abigail asked. Several of them were families with small kids.

"Who are you looking for, son?"

They turned to the voice. There was an old man sitting at a table near the back, under a veranda and out of the evening sun. He was eating a cheeseburger.

"Quite possibly *you*, if you're the owner of this building" Tony said. He walked over to the old man. "Antonio Russo was my great-grandfather."

A smile spread across the old man's weathered face. The wrinkles around his vivid blue eyes creased, forming deep crow's feet in his papery skin. "So you've come home," he said. He had a heavy French accent. He nodded toward a chair, motioning for Tony and Abigail to sit down. He took another bite of his cheeseburger.

"Something like that," Tony said. He pulled out a chair for Abigail and then sat in one next to her. "My name is Tony."

"Louis." The old man held out his hand and shook Tony's. "And who is this lovely young lady?"

"My wife, Abigail."

Abigail reached across the table and shook his hand. "Nice to meet you, sir."

"Nice to meet you too, Abigail." He looked like he was in his seventies, about the same age as Tony's grandma.

Abigail glanced at Tony. His eyes were sparkling.

"Russo," the old man mused. "You said he was your great-grandfather. With which woman? He met a lovely American girl here."

"Laurel," Tony said. "She's my great-grandmother."

"Laurel." The man got a faraway look in his eyes. "But that wasn't her real name. Her name was Margaret, and she was lovely. My mother knew her."

"Your mother *knew* her?" Abigail asked. She felt her heart rate quicken. They had stumbled upon a wealth of information if this man knew Russo's history personally!

"Yes. They went to the université together. Margaret was charming, very friendly. Somewhere, I have a photo of the two of them together, my mom and Margaret. If you're in town a while, I'll try to find it to show you."

"We're here until Saturday," Abigail said. She couldn't wait to tell Tony's grandma.

"Very good." The man dipped a French fry in ketchup and munched it. Tony was eager for more information.

"Do you own this building?"

"Yes." He nodded his head, chewing. "I own the building. Now that I've leased part of it to a fast food restaurant, I'm gaining weight." He patted his belly, which seemed far from plump. "You Americans eat fattening food."

Abigail smiled. "Yes, we do."

"So, you're from Margaret's line," the old man repeated, looking at Tony.

"Yes, his daughter with his wife died childless," Tony said.

"Nonsense. There was a child. She was born when the daughter was sixteen after a high school liaison. Secretly given up for adoption. You won't find it in any of the histories. Only the natives around here know."

"A daughter?" Tony looked at Abigail. She squeezed his hand. That meant he really might have other relatives out there. Lena was right.

"How can I find her?" Tony asked.

"No one has ever found her," the man said. "She remains elusive. Maybe she doesn't want to be known, but I would think with Russo's famous name, one of her offspring would come out and maybe try to get a book deal or something. You know how money hungry the youth are these days."

"Or maybe she doesn't know who her real parents are. Since she was given up for adoption."

"There's that. And she would be close to seventy. She could be dead." He finished up his cheeseburger. He took a long time chewing the last bite and then carefully wiped his lips with the paper napkin. "These things are good, I have to admit." He stood, gathering up his trash.

"If you can come back in a few days, I'll have the photograph for you," he said. "How about Saturday? Same time?"

That was the day their plane left for their return trip home, but it was later in the evening. They'd have time, but Abigail wanted to talk to him more before then. She had so many questions! And she was sure Tony did too.

"Can we meet you sooner? Buy you dinner maybe?" she asked.

"I'm leaving tonight for a short trip with my wife," he said. "To Genevieve. The gardens are lovely this time of year. It will have to be Saturday."

"That'll work," Tony said. He stood and shook hands with the man. "See you then."

They sat there a while, mulling over what he said.

"This is so exciting!" Abigail said after a moment.

Tony smiled, but he seemed deep in thought. He was playing with the paper from a straw, folding it between his fingers. She wondered why he didn't seem more interested.

"What are you thinking about?" Abigail asked.

Tony's gaze slowly returned to her. "I'm wondering who Lena really is."

"As in...?"

"As in...is she a descendent of Russo? She knows a lot about the history."

"So do a lot of Russo fans."

"I know. But then she tracked us down."

"For the ring."

"Maybe. Probably."

Tony sighed heavily. He reached across the table and took Abigail's hand.

"I broke in to Albert Boucher's apartment this afternoon," he said quietly.

She was silent for a moment. He had been working at the Louvre. She had *seen* him. When had he had time for that?

"When?"

"I got off my shift at the Louvre early. I wanted to look for information on Lena's grandma..."

Abigail felt a trickle of anger rise up in her. She tried to push it down. "Did you find them?"

"No. But I found the birth certificate for Dana Boucher. Lena has a half-sister. She went missing four years ago. And Lena's mom is dead."

"Oh no." Abigail thought about that. Lena's mom was dead. And her little sister? "Do you think the girl is dead too?"

"That's what I suspect. He probably beat her to death. Or worse. Who knows where the body is."

No wonder Lena had changed her name. Boucher was a dangerous man. Abigail looked over at her husband. She waited until he met her eyes before she spoke.

"Tony, you promised."

"I know. But I had to find out. And I was careful. It'll be okay. But I'm sorry. I acted impulsively, and it was stupid. I realized it in the cab on the ride back to the Louvre. It won't happen again."

She squeezed his hand. Her emotions were fighting. Fear that he could have been hurt. And anger at what he had done.

"This is a foreign country. If you get caught breaking and entering, you don't have Jimmy here to bail you out."

Tony nodded and dropped his eyes back to the paper he was folding. Her fear that she could lose him was making her angry. But what could she say? She had wanted to break into Lena's apartment and had tried to talk him in to doing it.

Could it be the line blurred for her too? Was it okay to break the law if it was justified?

No. Jimmy would say no.

She brought his hand to her lips and kissed it.

"It's okay. Let's move forward." She pushed back her chair and got up. She saw Tony's shoulders relax. He had been worried about her reaction. But at least he wasn't keeping things from her. "You must be starving. Let's find some place decent to eat."

They walked slowly back toward their hotel, holding hands. Abigail's mind was churning, trying to figure out how to find more information about Russo's daughter's child, who would be Tony's grandmother's half-niece! That was a mouthful.

"There have to be adoption papers," she said. "You know. Somewhere in the system."

"Only if it was a legal adoption."

"We could go to a records department tomorrow and look for the birth record for Russo's grandchild," she said. "Like a city hall. Is that where they keep those things over here?"

"They'd be sealed. They would never let us see them."

"Or you could hack in," Abigail said, teasing.

He laughed. "What? I would never do that! Besides, there probably isn't an electronic record." His face clouded. "Most places keep sealed paper copies to avoid hackers. Adoption records are impossible to open. The children can't even do it."

Abigail turned to him. "How do you know all of this?"

Tony was quiet for a moment before he spoke. "I talked to people in the records department when my grandma took me in. She was talking about moving, and I was afraid my dad wouldn't be able to find me. You know, if he got sober again."

She stopped. "Tony." He turned to look at her. She took both of his hands in hers. His father had died an alcoholic, lost to grief after Tony's mother died of cancer. "Your grandmother would never have kept you from your dad if he showed up."

"I know that now," Tony said. "But I didn't know it then. I was just a stupid kid."

She leaned forward and kissed him gently on the forehead. "I doubt you were ever stupid."

They resumed walking. She had underestimated how important finding family was to Tony. He went around with a light-hearted attitude, acting as if things didn't bother him, but obviously they did. And finding his lost relatives was important. She'd have to think of a way to make that happen.

Chapter Twenty

Tony was so glad that Abigail hadn't been too upset about his break-in to Boucher's place. And he had to rule out breaking in to the records department to peek at Lena's adoption papers and to look for Russo's grandchild, even though he was tempted.

They walked in silence for a while.

"We'll just *ask* Lena," he said finally. "She's the talkative sort."

Abigail laughed, but her mind seemed somewhere else. He had asked her about her day earlier, and she said it went well. But something was troubling her. He had been worried about telling her he had broken in to Boucher's apartment. Then later he was so enthralled with Louis' story, that he had forgotten she had her own problems.

"What's bothering you?" Tony asked softly.

She smiled. "You know me too well. After only a few months of marriage. How can that be?"

He put his arm around her shoulder as they walked. "Love does that."

She sighed and leaned in to his arm. "Ms. Scott told me today that it's not really up to her if I keep my job. It's up to the board members."

"What?" He felt a surge of protective anger, followed by a stab of guilt. That seemed to be the norm when he thought about how her relationship with him had hurt her job. "But they aren't even here to see your presentations. And they don't work with you!"

"The worst part is that one of them *is* here. Robert Dunning. He was the guy who was sitting in the front row.

He's a board member and not a particularly pleasant man. Today, I saw him talking to Michael Benedict. Michael does exactly what I do, only for a university library near London."

She let the thought hang in the air.

"You think Dunning's looking for your replacement."

"Yes."

Tony stopped walking and turned toward her. He gently put his hands on her shoulders and looked her in the eyes.

"You are the most incredible, intelligent person I've ever met," he said. "There's no way they could ever find anyone even half as good at your job as you are. Or as passionate. He may be looking, but he's not going to find someone he likes better."

Abigail gave him a soft smile. "I'm afraid he might. And if he does? Well, he does. I don't have any regrets."

The sun was setting. Its rays were turning her red hair to the color of fire. For the thousandth time, Tony wondered how God figured he deserved her. She was his everything.

He placed a gentle, lingering kiss on her lips. He felt her arms come around his waist and draw him in to her, and he got that flutter in his chest that only she could give him. Happiness. Completeness. When they pulled away, she was still smiling.

"I love you," he said.

"I love you too."

He took her hand and gave it a soft squeeze. They continued walking.

"It'll be okay," he promised.

"I know. As long as I have you."

The sidewalk they were on wound into a park. A few evening runners were out. An elderly man passed them, walking his little white dog. Tony was starting to think about food when he saw a familiar figure sitting on a park bench ahead of them. She was wearing a hooded sweatshirt, but her shape was recognizable, and he knew her shoes.

"Lena," he said.

"Where?" Abigail glanced at him and then followed his gaze ahead. "Oh."

The hooded head turned. They saw her face, confirming it was her. She watched them and sat quietly as they approached her, as if she had been waiting for them.

"Have a seat," she said, when they reached the bench.

Tony looked over at Abigail, who nodded. They sat, one on each side of Lena. Other than the runners, who were now way down the sidewalk, no one else was around. The trees offered them some privacy, as did the progressing darkness.

Lena pulled her hood back off her head. "I have a proposal for you," she said.

Tony leaned casually against the back of the bench and folded his hands in his lap. "I'm listening."

"You want your ring back. I want something else. Something that, you, Tony can provide. I'm willing to do a trade."

"Hmm. And just what is it that I can provide you with?" Tony asked.

"Your expertise. I want to break in to the Louvre."

Tony was so surprised that he laughed aloud. But Lena didn't laugh.

He turned to look at her. "You're serious."

"Of course."

He looked around, suddenly feeling a little paranoid. They seemed to be alone in the park, but Tony kept his voice low. "That's just stupid. Nobody can break in to that place. It would take a genius."

"Which is why I need you."

Tony looked across Lena to Abigail. His wife was frowning, but when she spoke, her voice was quiet.

"When we were in your apartment, you said 'It takes a thief to know a thief,'" Abigail said to Lena. "What exactly do you know about us? About Tony?"

Lena was quiet for a moment, thinking. Finally, she took a deep breath. "You know I'm an art buff and know quite a bit about Antonio Russo. So it would only make sense that I followed the story about *Laurel* being discovered in the United States. People have been looking for that painting for decades."

Tony nodded. The story had been widely publicized.

"And you're a Russo," Lena said.

"I changed my name," he said simply. "I'm really a Venezio."

"Through your father's side. Your mother is from Russo's lineage."

"So you know who I am."

"Yes."

"You *arranged* to meet us," Abigail said. "The purse snatching. That was a setup, wasn't it?"

Lena didn't acknowledge or deny the accusation. Instead, she answered with her own question to Tony.

"You're a pretty good con yourself, aren't you? I did some research on you, Tony. You're not *just* a Russo. You're an excellent thief. And I need for you to show me how to get into the Louvre."

"It's impossible," he said. "And besides, I don't do that anymore."

Abigail wasn't done with her interrogation. "You knew we were coming to Paris. How?"

Lena looked at her. "I did a bit of electronic spying. Some computer hacking. I knew there was a world maps symposium here and that because of your job, it was likely that you'd be invited to present. That was confirmed when you purchased your plane tickets."

"I did that on my phone," Tony said. "How on earth did you get in to my phone?"

"It was your financial records that I got in to."

"What?"

How smart *was* this woman? Tony had hacked in to plenty of people's phones and computer systems in his life, but nobody had ever hacked in to *his* stuff. Nobody. At least until now. He was blaming the bank's poor security for that one. He'd have to look in to that. "You hacked in to our *bank account?*"

"Yes. You two don't have much money."

Abigail gave a snort of laughter.

"Anyway, I need your help. You now have a job at the museum that I want to break in to, which is a marvelous coincidence that I had *no idea* would happen. The fates are on my side." Lena smiled. "If you tell me a little bit about which security systems they use, I can take care of the hacking part to turn them off. Then you can tell me the best way to go in. You don't have to be involved when I go into the Louvre. That way you can keep your precious new name clean. That's all I want from you. *Information*. And in exchange, I'll give you the ring back ."

"You still have it?" Abigail said, her eyes lighting up with hope.

"No. I sold it. But I know who has it. And he'll hang on to it."

Tony almost said the name aloud. Part of him wanted to show her that he was just as smart as she was, that he had already figured out that John Doe had the ring. But he didn't want to give away all the cards in his hand.

He had to admit, he was intrigued about breaking in to the Louvre. As a thief, he had always dreamed of a big heist, and the Louvre had been on his bucket list.

But he didn't do that anymore. Mostly. And besides, it was impossible. He knew this because, well, he might have looked in to it a few times through the years. When he was bored.

"It's impossible," he said for the second time.

"Let me get this straight," Abigail said. "You're holding our ring hostage because you want our help. If you get our help, we get the ring back, only you don't actually have it in your possession anymore."

"How much did you get for it?" Tony asked. He couldn't help it.

"I don't discuss prices," she said.

He glanced over at Abigail, who was frowning at *him* now.

"Aren't you curious?" Tony asked his wife.

"My plan changed a bit," Lena admitted. "Originally, I was only after the ring. But when Tony got this job at the Louvre, well, the plan came together."

Something still didn't fit. Was she going after a bigger find? "Why do you want to break in to the Louvre?" Tony asked her.

Lena gave a coy smile. "That's my business."

"You're making it mine if I help you."

She turned to him. "So you will?"

122

"Tony?" Abigail's voice cut through his thoughts. He looked across Lena to Abigail, giving his wife a look that he hoped said, "Let me play this out." Abigail could read him like a book, he was sure of it. He wanted to find out what Lena wanted.

"Tell me what you're after," Tony asked Lena. "A painting? A vase? Because I know one that isn't secured very well."

"I could make a lot more money on the black market with something out of the Louvre than I ever could with your ring. Ne c'est pas?"

"True," Tony agreed. "And there are some exhibits that aren't secured as well as others. I'm working on fixing that. I could leave a few strings unattached, so to speak."

"Tony." Abigail's voice had an edge of anger to it. Apparently, she *wasn't* reading him like a book.

"Or not," he said.

Lena ignored that. "You're in town until Saturday night. Meet me on Friday at the Petite Café on Rouge Street. 10 a.m. I'll have your ring for you, if you have the information I asked you for."

Lena pulled her hood back up and stood. "Avoir." She walked off into the darkness, disappearing behind some bushes.

"What on *earth?*" Abigail said, after they were sure she was out of earshot.

"What? I was only getting her to talk..."

"No. I mean, what on earth could she want that would fetch her more money than the ring?"

"Oh, there's plenty. There's the—"

Abigail cut him off. "The ring is already *hers*. She has the cash. Why would she risk what she already *has* for something much more dangerous?"

Abigail had a point. What could she want so badly from the Louvre that she would risk a lifetime in prison for? She'd have to wait months, maybe years, before she unloaded it on the black market. Word would get out, and the stolen item would be plastered everywhere, with a huge reward attached to it.

Tony sighed and stood up. This was all too much for him. And he was starving. He thought much better on a full stomach.

"Let's go get something to eat," he said. "There's nothing more we can do tonight. And you have a board member to impress tomorrow."

Abigail stood with him and put her hand in his. Together, they continued down the path toward their hotel and a restaurant.

There was only one thing left to do. Tony would have to break in to John Doe's house and take his ring back before Lena did.

Chapter Twenty-One

Abigail was tired. She hadn't slept much last night. Her mind kept going over something Lena had said that was tickling a memory at the back of her mind. There was something, and she hadn't been able to put it together.

When she did sleep, fitful dreams about Dunning kept waking her up. In her dreams, he was watching her, pointing his finger at her, yelling at her. She kept getting into trouble, but she never knew what for.

She stood at the entrance to the commons room and watched people milling about their booths. Soon the talks would start. Tony was in the building somewhere, beefing up the security to some of the exhibits.

"Abigail," Ms. Scott said behind her. Abigail jumped. "What are your plans for tonight?"

"Um, I don't think we have any," she said. But there was so much they wanted to do. Tour the Musée d'Orsay. Go up in the Eiffel Tower. It was already Thursday. They were running out of time.

"Good. I'd like to take you and Tony to dinner. My treat," Ms. Scott said.

"Okay. Wow! That would be great!" Abigail forced a smile. Ms. Scott nodded and went toward the auditorium. Abigail texted Tony.

Dinner with Ms. Scott tonight. Let's tour the Musée d'Orsay this afternoon. I can miss some of the presentations.

She received a text back right away. **Okay. Rappelling down the north wall right now. Having fun but should probably get both hands back on the rope!** ☺

She smiled and put her phone away. She picked a seat near the back of the auditorium. The first talk was on colors used on ancient maps and how certain inks lasted longer than others did. She knew this stuff.

So what was Lena after? Was it just one thing or a lot of them? She was an art history buff, so maybe something by one of the great artists? As a painter herself, she would know what paintings were the most valuable, profitable for selling and—

Wait a minute. Lena. An artist herself.

Abigail knew there was something she was missing. Lena had been rejected from art school, yet she still had the passion. That was proven by the paintings in her apartment. She had several finished ones as well as the paintings covered with sheets.

Lena had really panicked when Tony fingered that one sheet. Most artists didn't want anyone to see their unfished work. Abigail understood that. But there was more to it than that. Lena had overreacted. She had been *terrified* of them seeing it. Of course, she had just had her apartment broken in to, but still.

"Enjoying this?"

Abigail jumped. It was Julia, who slid in the seat beside her. She had a giant coffee in her hand again.

"Not really," Abigail whispered. "I know most of this stuff. This is a dry one."

"Bummer."

But now her train of thought was broken. She couldn't put her finger on the thought that had been tickling her mind. She focused on the speaker again but was restless. She pulled out her phone and brought up the painting by the mystery artist. The one of the river with the woman standing on the bridge, her hair blowing out, the umbrella in her hand like a sword. Like Nemesis. Retribution.

Suddenly it clicked.

Lena, a disgruntled artist, didn't want to break in to the Louvre to take something out. She wanted to break in to the Louvre to put something *in!*

Abigail jumped up so quickly she scared Julia, who nearly spilled her coffee.

"Sorry!" Abigail whispered. "Gotta pee!" And she walked quickly and quietly from the room to find Tony.

It took her a good ten minutes of wandering, but she found him on the second floor near the Flemish paintings. He was explaining to a man how the thin glass window on the case of some nearby figurines wasn't enough to stop someone. It was easy to pick the lock and slide it open. She watched as Tony demonstrated.

Abigail stood in the shadows, waiting for them to finish.

"Okay, well, get to it then," the man said and left the room so Tony could work.

"Hey!" Abigail said, walking up to him.

"Hi, beautiful! I thought you were listening to lectures."

"They were boring. But guess what I figured out!!"

She paused, letting the tension build. Tony wasn't the only one who knew how to play his audience.

He raised an eyebrow in question.

"Lena is the mystery artist!" Abigail said, in what she realized was too loud of a whisper. She looked around, but they were alone.

"Lena? How do you figure that?"

She explained it to him. "She got rejected from art school. She comes from an unhappy home life. She wants retribution! Her signature is the Hestia symbol because she longs for family and a home. *She* is Nemesis, the figure in the painting, wanting to get back at all of the people who have hurt her. Specifically, the art world. I'd imagine that art is her escape—*was* her escape—until she wasn't allowed to fulfill that dream by doing it professionally. So she's getting her art out for the world to see any way she can."

Tony's eyes had lit up right away, and he was practically dancing with excitement.

Abigail continued. "She wants in to the Louvre so she can *leave* a painting, not *steal* one. And I'm betting the big one in her room, covered with a sheet, is the one she wants to put in the Louvre."

"Brilliant!" He grabbed both sides of her face between his hands and kissed her full on the lips. "You are *brilliant!*"

"All we have to do is break back in to her apartment and uncover the painting to be sure. Then we can call the cops. The painting in her apartment will match the others. I'm sure of it. When she gets arrested for that, we can get our ring back. Because we'll have proof that she's a thief, capable of stealing stuff."

"We'll do it tonight," Tony said.

"After dinner with Ms. Scott."

"Yeah, what's that about?" Tony asked.

"I don't know. I think she's feeling bad about my job and Dunning being here. She really didn't say, but if I'd have to guess, that would be it."

She leaned in and gave Tony a kiss on the cheek. "I'll see you this afternoon."

"I'll buy us some tickets online for the Musée d'Orsay. And I want to see the Eiffel tower too."

"Sounds like fun!"

Abigail left him to do his work and hurried back toward the talks. The boring one had ended and everyone inside was clapping. *Almost* everyone. She found Robert Dunning outside the room talking to Michael. She ducked around the corner and tried to listen.

"So, lunch today it is," Dunning was saying. "My treat!"

The two men shook hands. As they turned to part ways, they saw her. Dunning gave a small smile, and Michael once again looked like a deer caught in the headlights. Guilty. Of something.

Of trying to take her job, she'd bet.

She brushed past them and into the room to find a seat for the next talk. This one would be on paper quality and how to reduce the loss of integrity in older documents. She didn't want to miss it.

Despite the fact that Michael and Mr. Dunning had had lunch together, Abigail managed to enjoy her afternoon with Tony. Today's after-lunch lectures were of no interest to her and no relevance to anything they did at their own library, so Ms. Scott had promised her the afternoon off when they were originally planning their itinerary.

Paris was busy. The lines to go up into the Eiffel tower were long and sold out. Tony bought them tickets for Friday and put them in his wallet. They'd go up Friday night before the festival got fully under way. She knew he didn't like crowds.

"At least I bought the Musée d'Orsay tickets ahead of time," he said, giving her a rueful smile.

The museum was just as wonderful as she expected. They both really enjoyed the Antonio Russo display. She had never seen such a large collection of his work. His paintings were beautiful. There was a plaque telling of the recent acquisition of the *Laurel* to their very own art museum at the university back home. It was exciting to read, and there was an accompanying photo of the painting. As per the story they had fed the press, the painting had been found by a Mr. Jonathan Stewart. Their own names weren't mentioned, thank goodness.

For dinner, they met Ms. Scott at a mid-sized Parisian restaurant not far from the Louvre. It was in the medium price range but had nice atmosphere and linen napkins. Abigail ordered the coq au vin so she could compare it to the version she made at home. She noticed they offered a dark chocolate cake for dessert. She was probably going to gain a thousand pounds on this trip.

After they placed their orders, Ms. Scott took a sip of her iced tea and cleared her throat.

"I want to apologize," she said.

Abigail glanced at Tony. She hadn't expected this at all. "For what?"

"I have behaved badly. You both lied to me, kept things from me, and I was hurt. I have reacted personally and not professionally. Abigail, I've come to like you over the years we've worked together. I have grown...fond...of you. And quite frankly, it came as a surprise to me that you would keep such important information from me."

"I'm so sorry," Abigail began, but Ms. Scott raised a hand to silence her.

"No. I'm the one apologizing tonight. It's true I had a right to be upset. But you apologized several times and tried to make amends. Then you went through that horrible trial with Mr. Mauvais. And your husband here has been raked over the coals publically."

Abigail didn't mention that Tony's revelation as a thief might have been publically humiliating, but it had helped his security company take off. Oddly, people figured if he could get *in to* places, he would know how to keep people *out*. Which was true.

"I was thinking of how this had hurt *me*, both personally and in my career. The board, as I told you, holds me to blame for some of this." Ms. Scott took another sip of her tea. "But you have been through so much, my dear. I have been unkind and short with you at work, and it should not have gone on this long. So I am asking for your forgiveness."

Abigail felt tears in her eyes. She blinked rapidly to keep them from spilling down her cheeks. "Of course," she said.

"And professionally, you are an excellent worker. You're very knowledgeable about your craft. One of the best in the world, I think. If it were up to me, I would keep you on."

Abigail swallowed. "They're not…keeping me on?"

Ms. Scott met her eyes. "I have no idea. Dunning isn't sharing information with me. But if I were you, I'd start networking. Just in case."

Abigail looked down at the napkin in her lap. She unfolded it and then folded it again. Working at the university library was the only job she had known since college. What would she do if she lost it? "Oh," she said quietly. She was about to ask about Michael Benedict.

But Ms. Scott had turned to Tony.

"And you, Tony. I owe you an apology as well. I have held a grudge against you and have had trouble trusting you. But it's apparent you have changed, and that you meant no ill harm to anyone that night you broke in to my library."

Ms. Scott always referred to it as *her* library. Abigail smiled.

"You have turned your talents around," Ms. Scott continued. "Here you are, providing security for the *Louvre*, of all places! How wonderful! If *they* trust you, then surely, I should too. And I do. I just let my personal feelings get in the way of logic."

Ms. Scott took yet another sip of her tea. Clearly, personal talk made her uncomfortable. "I just wanted to say that I am proud of both of you. You've been through a lot and come out better people because of it. And Abigail, if you do lose your job—and I will fight hard to keep you—you can depend on me to write you a glowing letter of recommendation."

Abigail looked over at Tony, who was smiling at Ms. Scott. "Lulu," he said, and Abigail cringed. No one called her that. "There's nothing to forgive. But if it's forgiveness you are looking for, you have it. I appreciate all you've done for my wife. And thank you so much for being in her corner."

Tony's eyes were sparkling, and he raised his glass to Ms. Scott. She lifted hers, and Abigail joined them. "To a brighter future, together, at the library!" Tony said.

Abigail saw the color rise in Ms. Scott's cheeks. Tony had a way about him, a way that drew people to him. She looked at her husband and back at Ms. Scott. They may have lost a lot these past few months, but she realized how rich she was to have both of these people in her life.

Thank you, God, she thought. And raised her glass again.

Now if only she *deserved* the trust Ms. Scott had in her. She felt a small stab of guilt. Tonight, they were going to break in to Lena's apartment to see if their theory about Lena being the mystery artist was right. Then she'd never do anything else illegal again.

Ever.

Chapter Twenty-Two

"I've just about got it," Tony whispered. Lena had replaced the dead bolt, but he was lasering through it again. No one was home. At least he hadn't been able to detect any body heat from his scans of the main living area.

"We're in," he said, holding the door open for Abigail. It was midnight. None of the neighbors seemed to be up.

They worked their way quickly back to the bedroom. Tony paused at the closed door off the living room. Still locked. He'd have to open it on his way out.

When he got into the bedroom, Abigail was holding her penlight up and had a hand on the sheet. "Ready for the unveiling?" she asked.

Tony nodded, and she lifted the sheet off with a flourish. Underneath was a large oil painting, about four feet by three feet. It was incredible. The scene was of a sidewalk at night, wet from a recent rain. The colors of the lights displayed across the puddles and cement were beautiful. There were two people walking down it, their backs turned to the viewer. They were holding hands. One was a woman with dark, flowing hair, swirling out from her shoulders. She was carrying an umbrella, which was closed and pointing down. With her was the blond girl.

And in the bottom right-hand corner was the Hestia symbol. The same one that was on the other mystery paintings.

"It's beautiful," Abigail breathed.

"There's Nemesis," Tony said, shining his penlight on the woman with flowing hair.

"What are you doing!?"

Tony and Abigail both jumped at Lena's loud shriek. Abigail dropped her penlight. She bent to pick it up. Lena hurried over to them and quickly put the sheet back over the painting. Her breath was coming fast. Her eyes were big. She was scared.

"You have no right—" she said.

"You're doing it all wrong," Tony said calmly, trying to diffuse the situation.

"I—how—what are you talking about?" Lena couldn't seem to think straight. Her hands were shaking. She glanced quickly behind her toward the living room, still scared, and wrapped her arms tightly around herself.

"You're doing it all wrong," Tony repeated. "The order. You should have started with the biggest museum first. Instead, you did the Musée Carnavalet first. Then the Musée de l'Orangerie. Then the Petit Palais. That painting is my favorite, by the way. And you hit the Musée d'Orsay. The Louvre folks are *expecting* you now. They're waiting for you. Classic rookie mistake."

He shook his head. He smiled, trying with his tone and body language to put Lena at ease, talking thief to thief. It wasn't working.

He heard the door open, the locked one that was off the living room.

"Lena?" It was a female voice.

"Get back in there. Keep the door locked!" Lena said, her voice firm. "I'm fine."

The door closed, and Tony heard a click. "Who's that?"

"None of your business," Lena said. She bit her lower lip and looked like she was about to cry.

"You can't get in to the Louvre. It's impossible," Tony said.

"Then help me."

"You know I can't do that," Tony said. "But what I *can* do is call the police right now and show them this painting. They'll figure the rest out on their own."

"You would turn me in?"

"You'll get in to some trouble, yes. But I'm actually doing you a favor. If you break in to the Louvre, you'll get caught in the act and go to jail for life."

"*You* didn't. Didn't go to jail for life. And you got caught."

There was silence in the room. Tony looked over at Abigail and took a deep breath, letting it out slowly. "No. I didn't go to jail. I had someone in my corner."

He knew that wasn't the case for Lena. Lena didn't have anyone in her corner. She had lived a life of abuse with that jerk, Boucher. And from what he could piece together, escaping away to art school hadn't turned out well either. It did seem the world had turned on her.

"Lena?" Abigail said, her voice soft.

The young woman turned to Abigail, her arms still tightly wrapped around her. "Just give us the ring back, and we'll leave. We promise. That's all we want from you."

But Tony knew that wouldn't happen. Because then Lena would be left with nothing. And Lena wasn't going to go down without a fight. People like her never did.

He walked into the living room. She had left her phone on the counter. He quickly pocketed it. Then he tried the closed door.

"Stay away from there!" Lena said, coming out of the bedroom at a run. She flung herself in between Tony and the door. Whoever was behind that door, Lena was wildly protective of her.

Tony turned to Abigail. "Let's go," he said quietly. Then to Lena, he said, "We'll see you tomorrow at the cafe." He gave her a brief nod and left. Abigail followed him out.

"We're leaving?" Abigail asked after the door closed behind them.

"Yes."

"Because we feel sorry for her?"

"Yes."

They walked down the stairs and out into the cold night. Tony put his hand in his pocket and felt for the phone. He wrapped his fingers around its cold frame.

"And because I have an idea."

Back at their hotel, he pulled out his own phone and hooked the two together like he had in the restaurant.

"Oh no," Abigail sighed. "Not again."

"Just watch."

It took some time, but by including some decoding software from his laptop, he managed to break in to her phone.

He went to her texts and matched a number up with the phone on John Doe's business card.

"Bingo!" he said.

Abigail was sitting with him. Together they read the latest texts. Lena had set up a time two days ago to sell him the ring. The day after their meeting, John Doe had texted with a simple "Thank you."

"So he has it," Tony said. "I'll just go in and get it tomorrow. And we'll be through with this nonsense."

Neither of them felt like calling the cops and revealing Lena as the mystery artist. She had enough trouble in her life. She wasn't hurting anyone. And they certainly didn't want to get tangled up in another court trial.

"Just go in and get it," Abigail repeated what he said. "Tony, it's only a ring. Let's just call it a loss. It's one thing to break in to Lena's apartment. But I'm pretty sure this John Doe guy has a lot more security."

Tony yawned and stretched. "He'll let me in. I know him from...my previous work. We'll talk about it more tomorrow. It's 2 a.m., and you need some rest. You're the closing speaker tomorrow. Dunning will be there. You need all of your wits about you."

She reluctantly agreed.

They went right to bed. He could tell by her breathing that she lay there a long time before sleep finally overcame her. When she finally went to sleep, he crept out of bed and opened his computer. He had to find a way into John Doe's house. Just in case he wasn't invited to tea.

Chapter Twenty-Three

Friday morning came too soon. Abigail was tired. Again. She yawned, stretched, and took a sip of the large coffee that Tony bought her at the café across from their hotel. Then he had walked her to work, told her he'd be back for her talk this evening, and left.

But drinking the coffee was probably a bad idea. The butterflies in her stomach were a testament to that. She was nervous about a lot of things. Dunning, for one. She wondered what he and Michael had talked about at their lunch yesterday. And she was nervous about her talk. While she was well prepared for it, she knew that Dunning would be watching. Then there was a luncheon with a wealthy potential donor, Elijah Coopersmith, to woo him for grant money. Would she get it?

But worse than that, she had a feeling that Tony was going to try to break in to John Doe's house this morning. In broad daylight. When she asked him, he winked at her and said, "Don't fret." Then he quoted some Shakespeare from a love sonnet and kissed her, trying to distract her. When she persisted, he had said, "I'll see how the morning goes. Maybe he's home, and when I knock on the door, we can have a nice chat."

She didn't want him chatting with some thief who had God only knows what in his house. Guns? Dogs? Henchmen?

Henchmen? Her mind was running away with her.

But then again, she had some past trust issues with Tony. He tended to get impulsive and just *do* things. Like breaking in to Boucher's apartment.

But he was just as trustworthy as she was. He hadn't done anything worse during this vacation than she had been doing.

She found the nearest trash can and tossed the cup of coffee in it. She didn't need anything else jangling her nerves today.

You'd think she'd be used to stress by now. Her life had been a series of surprise events, running like a movie of the week, ever since...well...

Ever since she had met Tony.

"Abigail!"

She jumped and turned at the voice.

"There you are!" It was Ms. Scott. She hurried up to Abigail. "I've saved us a seat next to Coopersmith. Maybe you can sit by him and make some brilliant comments during this lecture."

Brilliant comments? Poor Ms. Scott. Was this her desperate attempt for Abigail to win over this man and his grant money? At least her boss was trying to keep her on.

The morning talks were interesting enough. Abigail wasn't too worried about the luncheon. Coopersmith had donated to their library before, and she felt that he would again. She had talked to him a few times on the phone before the symposium, and she was the one who arranged to meet him today for lunch. She felt she had it in the bag.

They met at one of the round tables in the dining area at the Louvre because there was no time to go out. They worked their way through the line, picking up the sandwiches and bags of chips that were provided for the presenters.

Abigail was heading to their table with her food. Ms. Scott was already seated. Suddenly, Dunning and Michael Benedict approached her with a smile. They sat next to her.

Abigail wasn't expecting them to be in on the conversation today with Coopersmith. She glanced at Ms. Scott as she sat down. Ms. Scott gave her a sympathetic smile. Apparently, this wasn't planned.

"A fine day today!" Mr. Coopersmith was all smiles under his handlebar moustache as he approached their table and sat down. "I believe I have fallen in love with Paris once again! It has been at least four years since I was last here. I'll have to make it less time between trips. What a marvelous city!" He unfolded his paper napkin and put it on his lap.

After some pleasant chitchat, Ms. Scott approached the topic of the grant money. "You have been so generous in the past," she said. "Abigail has some wonderful ideas of how we can use your grant money to purchase some additional storage. We have been promised some amazing maps and documents from a Bulgarian museum which recently went bankrupt. If we can fund the storage, we can get them. They would be an incredible addition to our already world-renowned collection."

"Our maps are already bringing in scholars from around the world who want to study early map making," Abigail said. "And who want to research historical events related to these maps. As you know, we have one that was hand-drawn by Napoleon. We have one of the best and most diversified map collections in the world. The Bulgarian maps would add significant value to our collection."

"Unless, of course, one of them is stolen," Mr. Coopersmith said, laughing. It was a joke, but not a very funny one. Dunning burst out into laughter too, and Michael followed with his own nasally laugh.

"Oh, Mr. Coopersmith, you're a funny man!" Dunning said. "But we have moved on from that unfortunate incident."

"*International* incident," said Mr. Coopersmith, wiping some crumbs from his mouth. He placed the napkin back on his lap and looked at Abigail. "Ms. Russo, you do bring some notoriety to your library! The wrong kind, perhaps, but I must say, you are certainly world-renowned now!"

There followed another round of laughter. Abigail was getting angrier by the minute. She had to get this under control. She had a whole spiel prepared to give him.

"I think what you'll find—" she began, but Dunning cut her off.

"Mr. Benedict here has come up with quite the plan for your money," Dunning said. "He and I were just talking over lunch yesterday, and I'm sure you'll be quite impressed with his ideas."

"I didn't realize Michael worked for your library," Mr. Coopersmith said.

"Oh, he doesn't. At least not yet." Dunning cut a look at Abigail and then returned his gaze to Coopersmith. "I was thinking we might see if we can add him on."

Add him on? Abigail was seething. But Michael cleared his throat and launched into a plan to use the grant money for funding public awareness about the necessity of preserving historical documents. Which was *exactly* what she was going to get at after she explained the public awareness campaign they *already had in place.*

"We started a public awareness campaign this spring with the addition of the Napoleon map," Abigail said, but Dunning cut her off again.

"Ms. Russo. Mr. Benedict is already on top of that. Let him continue."

Abigail was ready to stand up and leave, but she knew she had to see this out. How dare Robert Dunning show up and usurp her luncheon!

Michael went on in that long way he has, giving statistics and numerous examples. But Coopersmith seemed drawn in. Abigail tried to interrupt a few more times, but Dunning shut her down. Ms. Scott looked terribly uncomfortable. Abigail felt a stab of pity for her. Dunning was part of the board, the people who made the decisions about *all* of their jobs, including Ms. Scott's.

Lunch was over, and it was time to get back to the talks. Mr. Dunning stood and shook hands heartily with Mr. Coopersmith. Michael Benedict shook his hand too. "It's nice to meet you, my dear fellow," Coopersmith said to Michael. "I look forward to seeing what more you can do for this library!"

"He doesn't work there," Abigail broke in.

"But I am so impressed!" He turned to Dunning. "I'll tell you what. If you bring this young man on, I can promise you'll I'll write you a big check." Mr. Coopersmith took a last sip of his tea. "I'll see you all around!" He gave quick handshakes to Abigail and Ms. Scott and left.

Ms. Scott hung back with Abigail until the men had left the room.

"I'm so sorry," she said. "I had no idea."

"I know you didn't," Abigail said. She was angry. "Looks like Dunning already has his mind made up."

Ms. Scott shook her head. "I'm not sure if there's anything I can do to stop it. Not now that we have a promise of funds if we bring Michael on. He wouldn't be an addition. We just can't justify the extra staff. He would be a replacement. Someone would have to go."

"Yes," Abigail said. "And I know exactly who that someone would be."

Chapter Twenty-Four

John Doe wasn't home. Or at least no one was answering the door. He lived in a small but opulent home in central Paris, with upscale restaurants and an excellent bakery within walking distance. Tony knew the latter was true because he had stopped on his way and bought a cinnamon bun. Now his fingers were sticky.

He wiped them the best he could on his napkin. The front porch, where he was standing, was facing a busy street. There were too many people around for him to pick the lock. And there were probably security cameras in the shops across the street, and also hidden on Doe's front porch. They would capture anything he did on film.

He was turning to go when the front door opened. A very elderly gentleman poked his head out.

"Puis-je vous aider monsieur?"

Tony turned back. "Parlez-vous Anglais?"

"Yes, sir. I speak English quite well," the man said. "How may I help you?"

He was very old. From the way he was dressed, in a black and white uniform, Tony guessed he was a butler.

"I'm here to speak to…" he was about to say "John Doe," but realized suddenly that wasn't his real name. Darn! He hadn't done his research. He took a stab at it anyway. "John Doe."

The old man looked taken aback. He lowered his voice to a whisper. "Why don't you come inside, sir?"

He turned and shuffled ahead, leaving the door open. Tony went inside and shut the door. He followed the butler's slow progress across the entryway and into a study. No wonder it took him so long to answer the door.

"Would you like some tea?" the old man asked.

"No, thank you."

"My name is Hobbes." He didn't declare if that was his last name or his first. Hobbes sat down on a fading turquoise wingback chair. He motioned to a matching chair across from him. Tony sat.

The room was decorated with pinstripe wallpaper, white with thin pink-colored lines running from floor to ceiling. Abigail would probably call them salmon. The chairs matched a turquoise-checked sofa across from them. A crystal chandelier hung above them. The room's decor was different, but quite eye-catching.

"Mr. Doe is not at home," Hobbes said.

"Oh. When will he return?"

"He has been away on a business trip since last week. He's due to arrive this afternoon. Is there something I can help you with?"

Tony was taking in the room and the house. There was a bowl of crystal balls of different colors on the table in front of them. Shelves lined the wall to his right and were filled with a mixture of books, porcelain figurines of various animals, and framed photos. There were so many baubles and collectibles around the room that it would be impossible to easily find the ring. And each bookcase looked like it could contain hidden panels. He suspected the entire house was this way, from what he could see of the room beyond this one. He would hate to dust this place.

"I want to inquire with him about an item," Tony said.

"He will be happy to do that online." The old man pulled out a business card just like the one Tony had taken from Lena's apartment. "You can reach him at this email address."

"Thank you," Tony said. "But I already have one of those. I was really hoping to see him in person."

"That's impossible now, but I can set up an appointment for when he returns and has rested."

Tony thought about that. They were leaving tomorrow night to go back home.

He didn't have that kind of time.

He didn't like to show his entire hand of cards, but he had to work fast. Taking a gamble, he pulled out his phone. He opened the photo of Abigail's ring that they had shown to the police.

"He recently purchased this," Tony said. "I'd like to double what he paid. I want it for my own collection."

Hobbes took the phone and stared at it for a long moment. Then he spoke. "Mr. Doe has not been in town to take possession of this as of yet. And I'm pretty sure you're wasting your time. He often doesn't sell items from his collection."

"I see."

Hobbes handed the phone back to Tony. Tony closed the app and put the phone back in his pocket. "Okay. I'll try emailing him. Thank you."

Hobbes stiffly got up and shuffled back toward the door. There was another bookcase in the hall. It contained more knickknacks and a few rare books. Tony recognized a journal he had picked up for Doe on a job.

But something underneath it caught his eye. It was a small photograph of Doe standing next to a familiar-looking woman. She was younger in the photo and her hair was down, but he could swear it was Lulu Scott, Abigail's boss. He stopped to get a better look.

"Sir?" Hobbes questioned.

"This photo. Who is this?"

"That's Mr. Doe's one true love," the old man said. "But it is also his history. Long over."

"What happened?"

"What always happens," said the old man. "People make the wrong choices. They see a brighter bauble elsewhere and don't realize that the one they are holding is really the greatest treasure."

"I see."

The couple was standing in Montmartre, in front of Sacré-Cœur . Lulu was wearing a summer dress and smiling. The day was breezy, and the wind was pulling her skirt to the side. Her hair was loose and blowing away from her face. She looked radiantly happy.

He suddenly saw Ms. Scott in a new light and wondered what her story was. She wasn't much for sharing. He would have to tell Abigail and see if she knew. Tony turned back to Hobbes. "Thank you for your time."

"Of course, sir." The old man let him out.

Tony walked down the street, thinking. Doe didn't have the ring yet. That meant that Lena still had to have it. The texts they read hadn't actually said Doe had picked it up. He had just thanked her.

Tony looked at his watch. It was almost time to meet Lena. This would give him a chance to formulate a plan. Maybe while he talked to her, she'd give up clues to the ring's whereabouts.

He got there a few minutes early and found a nice spot to sit. There was a little table under a tree with four chairs around it. He really enjoyed the quaint spots like this in this city. Plus, it was away from other tables, so nobody would be able to overhear their conversation.

Lena arrived right on time and sat down across from him. She wasn't very tall, and he realized that it hadn't been Lena who had been following them those few times they saw someone lurking about, wearing a hooded sweatshirt. Nor had it been Lena snatching Abigail's purse, obviously. She definitely had an accomplice. Maybe a boyfriend? Or the woman who lived with her? But the voice on the other side of the door sounded young. Like a teen or pre-teen.

"So you decided to come," Lena said.

"Yes," Tony said. He leaned back in his chair.

"I want my phone back."

He pulled it out of his pocket and handed it to her.

"I need to see the ring before I agree to anything," he said.

"I told you, I sold it."

"You sold it, but you still have it in your possession. John Doe has been out of the country."

The look in her eyes told him he had surprised her with this bit of knowledge.

"You *are* good," she said.

"I just know the market well."

"I see."

"You said if I came today, you'd show me the ring," Tony reminded her.

She was quiet for a moment. "It's not on me," she said. "And the deal is once I get what I want, you'll get what *you* want. Not before."

Tony considered that. Maybe if he gave up some information, she'd give up some too.

But he had another burning question.

"What did you mean when you said I wasn't Antonio's only heir?"

Lena was quiet for a while. She watched him, as if weighing what to tell him. Finally, she spoke.

"Antonio had a daughter with his wife. The daughter had an illegitimate child when she was only sixteen. I'm from that line."

"You?" Tony sat up in his chair. "*You're* Antonio's other heir?" So his hunch had been correct! He looked across at this relative of his. His family. And also a thief. Was she lying to gain his sympathy? He leaned back and crossed his arms. "Prove it."

"I did the research. I have the proof."

Her word wasn't good enough for him. He raised an eyebrow, wanting more.

"A few years ago, when I was doing one of my first art history tours, I saw a photo of Antonio and his wife Gaia, with their daughter. I had seen it before, at least a dozen times, and the daughter's eyes always seemed familiar to me. But I didn't think much of it. Then a customer asked if the daughter had children, and when I said no, someone else, a local, told me there had been a rumor of a child given up for adoption. I had never heard that before."

Tony thought about that. So that would mean that Gaia and Antonio's daughter had a baby. There was no history of it. He had checked. She had died unmarried and childless.

"Why isn't there a record of it?"

"There is. It's just not public. She was only sixteen, and they kept it very secret."

Her story lined up with what Louis told him. But maybe it was just a local myth.

"Then how did you find out?"

Lena lowered her voice, even though no one was in earshot. "I asked a nice lady at the records department to open up the child's closed adoption file. Antonio and Gaia went through legal adoption procedures, and there it was."

"You just *asked*?" Tony snorted. "How much did it cost you?"

"The price of a diamond ring."

Tony whistled. But money talked and Lena was clever enough to find it. They were silent for a few moments as Tony pondered over what she said. "You said her eyes were familiar. A lot of people look familiar to me. How did you make the connection that you were related?"

"My grandma was adopted. She had Italian heritage. I just had a hunch."

Hunches. He had trusted them his entire life.

"Your grandma didn't know who her birth parents were," he said. "So you mom didn't know either. That's why you didn't know."

"Right. But now I do. So that ring belongs as much to me as it does to you."

"Oh, no," Tony said, suddenly feeling a little defensive. "He gave that ring to Laurel. Not to his wife."

"Still."

"No. And all you want it for is the money. I gave it to Abigail because it means something to us."

Lena's face fell, and she grew quiet.

Was she suddenly going all sentimental? Had he hit a nerve? "What's wrong?" Tony asked.

She looked back at him, her eyes flashing. "Nothing's wrong. You and your sappy stories."

And yet she was willing to sell out family heirlooms for money. *Family*. He was still in shock that he was actually related to this woman. She was his...what? His cousin? How many times removed?

But he'd have to think about that later. Right now, he needed to stay on his game. He began thinking over what he knew about her. Her rough background. "Why the Hestia symbols?"

"Obviously you do not know your mythology well."

She was a prickly one.

"Hestia symbolizes hearth and home and all that is good and cozy," he said. "Thus the table with flames on top." He crossed his arms and sat back, waiting for her to answer.

"You've done your research," Lena nodded. "You figure it out."

"I already have. You were part of a kind family, and all was well until you were ten years old. Then your father died, and your mother married a man named Albert Boucher. He was a jerk and mistreated you and your mom, and your life pretty much sucked after that."

Lena looked surprised and then angry again. Anger seemed to be her primary emotion. "You dug in to my personal life!"

"You dug in to mine first."

That stopped her. A little smile came to her lips. "I guess I did. Touché."

He had lost his father too. And his mother. He knew the pain of those losses, how deep they ran and how you didn't every really get over them. Being an orphan haunted you all the days of your life. When they found the *Laurel* painting, he was wishing his mom could be there to see him. When he turned from his life of crime, he imagined her as being proud of him. When he married Abigail, the side of the church that his parents would have occupied seemed a bit too empty.

He understood Lena. In a way, they were alike. Almost too alike. And she was on the same path as he had been until five months ago.

"Look," he said, softening his voice. "You don't want to do this. All of this breaking in to places, stealing rings, and who knows what else. I did. It's not worth it."

"It's very worth it," Lena said. "How do you think I finance an apartment in Paris? On my tour guide salary?"

"I lost friends," Tony said. "My best friend, George, in fact."

Lena smirked. "Well, I don't have any friends to lose."

He tried again. "I know what it's like to have money. And I know what it's like not to have much. You've seen our bank account." He raised an eyebrow. "We're definitely poor at the moment! But I'd rather be poor and have my integrity than rich and alone."

"That sounds like a lot of psychobabble. Or something I'd read on a poster."

He smiled at her sarcasm. Then, uncrossing his arms, he leaned forward on the table so he was closer to her.

"I thought being alone was okay until I met Abigail. She supports me. She believes in me."

"Lucky you."

"Yes. Lucky me."

"I've read about you," Lena said, locking eyes with him. "You don't deserve it."

"No, I don't," Tony said. "And that's the beauty of it. She loves me despite all of my flaws. She has chosen to forgive what I've done and looks forward to what I can be. I had this job, a legit one painting walls in houses and businesses. I always thought I'd do that and be a thief on the side. When I needed a new car or wanted a new television, I'd just steal something and sell it. It was easy, and it was fun. And I never really thought beyond the next day. I had a lot of one-night stands with women. It was just the way I lived. But Abigail changed all of that."

"Some of us don't have an Abigail," Lena said.

"Abigail is not all I had. I had God. And so do you." Tony said.

"Don't give me the God lecture. Where was God when Boucher was beating me? Huh? And no one was there to help me. Not my mom. Not my teachers. Not even my friends. I was alone. And I still am. I've learned it's better that way. Don't trust anyone. Just count on yourself."

She crossed her arms around her torso, as if in a hug. Her eyes were still angry.

"And you have me," Tony said.

He let the words hang in the air. She bit her lip, and her eyes filled with tears.

"We're family, right?" Tony said softly.

Lena dropped her eyes to the table. He could see her fighting back the tears. After a moment, she looked back up at him, the anger back in her eyes. "I *don't* have you. You're here until tomorrow, and then I'll never see you again. And all you want is your ring."

"Abigail and I can help you," he said. He had no idea how. But there had to be some way. His grandma would love to meet Lena, this distant cousin of his. And who else? Who was Lena living with? Was it her sister?

"No one has ever helped me," Lena said. "Why start now?"

"I know you've lost a lot. Your mother. Your little sister. But you can't pretend you don't care for anyone. Who's the girl staying in your apartment? I'm betting you care about her. You sure are going to great lengths to hide her from us."

"She's none of your business."

"She sounds young."

Lena uncrossed her arms and sat up in her chair. "Look. This discussion is supposed to be about you helping me get into the Louvre."

She wasn't going to change. At least not at this moment. Tony needed to quit feeling sentimental and get his game back on. He leaned back in his chair. "I need to see the ring first."

Lena glanced around. Their small table afforded them a lot of privacy. Tony couldn't hear the conversations of people nearby. He could only hear the wind whispering through the leaves in the tree above them.

There was a gold chain around her neck. It was long enough that the lower part was hidden inside her shirt. She pulled it out and held it up. The emerald in the ring caught the light and twinkled. She quickly slipped it back inside her shirt.

He thought of reaching across the table and grabbing it. If he pulled hard enough, he could probably break the chain.

But it would look like a physical struggle, and there were people around.

"You can't get it unless you're willing to reach your hand down the front of my shirt in broad daylight," Lena said.

"This *is* Paris," Tony said with a smirk.

"So how can you help me? All I need is the name of the security company they use. And a bit of info about their system."

"You need more than that," Tony said, an idea forming in his mind. "You need to know where the weak spots are. I'm heading over to the Louvre now. Come with me, and I'll give you a tour. I'll *show* you the weak spots."

Chapter Twenty-Five

Abigail was sitting outside of the lecture room when Tony showed up at the Louvre. He was early. And he had Lena with him.

Abigail didn't know what to say. Or to do. So she simply stared.

"Abigail, you remember our tour guide, Lena," Tony said, smooth as ever. There were, after all, people standing around.

"Um, yes," Abigail said. She came to her senses enough to shake Lena's hand.

"I thought I'd show her around the Louvre before your talk."

He seemed all confident and cocky. Abigail felt a sudden wave of butterflies in her stomach. What was he up to?

"I need to talk to you first," Abigail said, grabbing his hand. She led him down the hall out of earshot.

"*What are you doing?*" she hissed.

"I have a plan."

That's what worried her.

"What kind of plan?" She met his eyes. If he lied to her, she'd know it.

"I'm just going to show her around the Louvre," he whispered.

"Because...?"

"I want to help her," Tony said.

"Help her *break in?*"

"Abigail, she's my cousin."

She wasn't expecting that. It took her a moment to respond. "She's your *cousin?*" But it suddenly made sense. Tony wasn't the only heir. That's what Lena had said. "How do you know?"

"She told me."

Abigail frowned.

"I know it sounds crazy. But she says she has proof. And it makes sense."

Of course it did. Abigail knew how much Tony wanted it to. How much he wanted it to be true.

Tony explained to her about Lena's background and how she came from the line of Antonio's legitimate daughter. Tony's whole face lit up when he talked about it. "So she's my cousin. I have *family!*"

Abigail closed her eyes and took in a long, slow, deep breath. He had always wanted to have more than just his grandmother. He had wanted uncles and aunts coming over for the holiday. Cousins to play with. Big tables surrounded by people eating meals together. He talked about it often. She supposed that was the Italian in him.

"I know this is your big day," he said. "Don't let this stress you out."

"No. Of course not." She couldn't keep the sarcasm from creeping into her voice.

"She and I are just going to walk around the Louvre. So I can point out their weak spots."

"Tony..."

"No. I'm just going to *act* like I'm helping her. I'm hoping as we get to know each other more, trust each other, she'll give up the ring."

"You're going to *pretend* like you're thinking about helping her break in to the Louvre—"

"Shhhhh!!" Tony said, even though Abigail was whispering.

"—just to give you more time to build a relationship with her?"

"Kind of."

"You're going to *lie* to her. To build trust."

She could tell that part hadn't registered with him. He was quiet for a moment. She waited. He'd come back with something smart, she knew it. She was starting to get mad at him. This was her big day, and here he was ruining it. *Again.* Flashbacks of her last big talk came to mind. The one with

152

the stolen Vesconte. How six months of work she had put in to it ended abruptly and badly because Tony had—

"She is wearing the ring around her neck." Tony said.

Again, his words stopped her train of thought. "She's *what?* Grab it!"

"How? Reach my hand down her blouse?"

"I will!" Abigail turned to leave, but Tony grabbed her arm.

"Abigail, give me some time." He looked at his watch. "We have a few more hours before your talk. Let me build a relationship with her. I'm good at reading people. I'll know. And if it's true, please let me find out more about my family before I lose her. Then I'll get the ring back for you. I promise."

Abigail was skeptical. All she'd have to do is get Lena to show that ring in front of Ms. Scott, and she'd have a witness. Ms. Scott had seen the ring plenty of times. She would know it was Abigail's. Then they could shout for a security guard, and it would all be over.

But then she looked at Tony. He seemed small to her now, more like a little boy instead of the confident man she knew. And this is why they had wanted to come to Paris. To discover his roots. His family. And now that discovery was standing in this same building.

Wearing Abigail's ring.

Abigail sighed dramatically. "Okay. Go. Work your magic. And leave me alone to go do mine. My job is on the line, you know."

"I know. I haven't forgotten that." He kissed her on the lips. "I've been praying for you. You'll do fine. Dunning is a fool if he doesn't realize your value."

They looked over at Lena, who was standing there, looking small and unsure. Abigail gave her a reassuring smile.

"Abigail!" Ms. Scott was coming down the hall toward them.

"I'll see you later." Abigail said to Tony. "Coming!" she waved and went to meet her boss. She saw Tony walk over to Lena and say something to her. He grabbed a map of the Louvre from a kiosk nearby and opened it. Lena bent over to follow what he was pointing at in the brochure.

Abigail had spent the past two months rebuilding her feelings of trust toward Tony. She had once thought he had turned back to a life of crime when he was only trying to save her. And she thought he had cheated on her when he hadn't. She had always been able to trust him, she just hadn't realized it. His motives had always had her best interests at the center of them.

Now she'd have to trust him again and let him do his thing. Because she didn't have time to follow them around. Her job was on the line, and she had to go to work to save it.

"Abigail," said Ms. Scott, catching up to her. "I'm so glad I found you. We need to talk. It's about your job."

"Robert Dunning and Michael Benedict have been spending a lot of time together," Ms. Scott said. "They went out last night for dinner, just the two of them, and I saw them sitting in the commons this morning having coffee. I'm afraid you're going to have to think of something if you want to keep this job. It seems to me that Mr. Dunning already has his mind made up. Especially now that Mr. Coopersmith wants Michael on board before he donates any money."

Ms. Scott stood in front of her and clasped her hands together.

"I'm feeling confident about my closing talk," Abigail said. "I can't add anything to it to make it better."

"I don't mean that. I mean you need to come up with some funding, and quickly."

"You mean, I have to come up with a donor who says they'll give handsomely but only if the library keeps me on?"

To her credit, the color rose in Ms. Scott's cheeks. "Yes. Something like that."

"You know I can't do that. Not this late in the game!" Abigail was upset. But if she really thought about it, her job had been on the line since January, when Tony first dropped in to her library. She had been lying and keeping things from Ms. Scott since then.

"Either way, I want you and Tony to sit with us tonight at the closing dinner. You plan to, right?"

"Yes, of course," Abigail said.

"Okay, then."

"Okay."

The two women stared at each other for a moment. Ms. Scott seemed at a loss for words. She was looking at Abigail with what seemed like pity. And what else could Abigail say? Ms. Scott apparently had no control over any of this anymore.

Abigail gave a little nod. "I need to catch this next talk. It ties in to some of the things I want to say tonight."

She left Ms. Scott standing there, wringing her hands. Lena had messed with the wrong woman when she took Abigail's ring. And now Dunning, too, had picked the wrong person to mess with. Abigail wasn't going down without a fight.

———◇————————◇———

Abigail couldn't concentrate on the speaker's words. Her mind kept going back to Coopersmith and his haughty request that Michael be brought on with "all his fantastic ideas." Hmph. Abigail had already thought of those ideas, and had already *promoted* some of them within the past month. But Dunning didn't seem to care. He was determined to get rid of her.

She supposed he had probable cause. She had brought the wrong kind of notoriety to the library. But because their little library had made national news, it had rekindled new awareness in their program. That was how the Bulgarian museum heard of them. And some previous donors stepped forward to add additional funds. Small funds, to be sure. One hundred dollars here. One thousand dollars there. But still, people were taking interest.

She had done so much for that library in the seven years she had worked there. She's the one who had researched and begun the detailed preservation program that allowed them to bring in and store older and more delicate maps. And not just maps. Rare documents as well. Books. Manuscripts. A document signed by King Henry.

Now they had the Napoleonic map, which they had been allowed to keep after the trial with Mauvais. Not to mention hand-drawn maps from the beginnings of America.

Abigail was mad. She knew that anger clouded her judgement, so she tried taking slow, deep breaths, just like she did in yoga class. Yoga breathing was good. She closed her eyes so she could concentrate more.

"Are you okay?"

She jumped and opened her eyes, embarrassed. It was Julia. The woman sat down beside her. She had her usual large cup of coffee in hand.

"Yes," Abigail said. "I'm fine. Just trying to relax."

"I understand that. You're the closing speaker tonight. Wow. What a privilege! But what a stressor!"

Only that's not what was making her nervous. It was the *rest* of her life. She wondered where Tony was now.

"Yes. It is a privilege. I'm pretty excited about it."

"I really enjoyed your previous two talks," Julia said. "You're very good at what you do. Do you have children?"

"No. Not yet." The question took Abigail by surprise.

"Just wait. But I think you'll be excellent at balancing both your career and your kids. You look like the type." Julia took a sip of her coffee. "I couldn't survive without this stuff!"

"I imagine six kids would require a lot of coffee."

"Yes. As I said before, three are foster. My husband and I have fostered kids for about ten years. Mostly teens. They're the hardest to place. And I do a lot of volunteer work with the local foster agency."

"Which state do you live in?" Abigail asked. She could tell from Julia's accent that she was American.

"No, I live here in Paris. My husband has been here for work for twelve years. I'm American, but not really anymore!"

She took another sip of her coffee and focused on the talk. Abigail tried to do the same. But her mind kept wandering back to Coopersmith.

After a few minutes, Julia leaned toward her. "Have you seen all of the paintings left by the mystery artist?" she whispered.

"No. I hear he or she left one at the Musée de l'Orangerie, but I haven't seen that one yet." She and Tony had Googled it, but she didn't have a photo.

"Oh! I have it!" Julia brought out her phone and flicked through some photos. "Here."

She handed Abigail her phone. The painting was of a small, blond-haired girl sitting in a field of flowers. Her back was to them so her face didn't show. She had a basket beside her and was collecting wildflowers.

"I don't see Nemesis here but look at the swirling pattern in the clouds. And how some of the grass looks like spears."

"How'd you get this photo?" Abigail asked. "We couldn't find it in the papers."

"Since I'm a symbologist and I'm local, I was asked by the police to take a look at the paintings. The yellow flowers in this basket are celandine, which symbolize *joys to come* or *future joy*. I thought that was interesting. I think the artist is sending us a message in each painting. But what is even more interesting is this little blond girl. She's also in all of the other paintings."

"Really?" Abigail hadn't noticed her. Julia swiped to a photo of the carnival painting. Sure enough, there was the little girl. Her back was turned, but it was clear it was the same child. She was wearing the same dress.

"She has a flower tucked in her hair. Look." Julia pointed. It was one of the celandines.

"Wow," Abigail breathed.

Julia swiped over to a photo of the painting that Tony had seen in the Musée D'Orsay. "Here she is at the picnic."

The little girl, back turned, was sitting off to the side on a little checkered blanket. Her picnic basket was opened. It contained some food, and one of the yellow flowers.

"Joys to come," Abigail said.

"And here is Nemesis watching over her," Julia said, pointing.

Nemesis was sitting just up the hill, looking down toward the little girl. Her hand, which contained a closed parasol, was raised.

"This is amazing," said Abigail. "I never even saw the little girl. Tony and I have looked over these paintings, but I guess we were both fixated on the Nemesis figure—"

"Shhhhh!" A man in front of them turned around and hushed them.

"Sorry!" Abigail whispered. She and Julia giggled quietly. "I guess we'd better be quiet before we get into trouble. Can you text me that one photo?"

Julia nodded. She sent the text, and both women turned their attention back to the speaker.

Abigail wondered who the little girl was. Now that they knew Lena had made the paintings, she better understood the retribution symbology and the Hestia mark. Lena longed for the comfort of family and wanted to get back at the art world for shunning her. But the little girl? Who was she?

Her mind went back to the voice they heard coming from the room that Lena kept locked. It sounded young, but not this young. Not young enough to be, say, a daughter of Lena's. Right?

She wondered if the little girl in the painting represented the sister that Lena had lost. This was her way of saying she wished she had been there to protect her.

Or...maybe the little sister wasn't so lost after all.

Abigail looked at the time. She had a few hours this afternoon before the dinner. The next few talks weren't that exciting, and she was already prepared for her own so she didn't need to practice it.

If she wanted to know who was in that room, there was only one way to find out.

Chapter Twenty-Six

"See this spot here?" Tony pointed up to the small stone sculpture on the third shelf. "A person could reach up there and take whichever one they wanted. The cameras," he pointed up to where he knew they were located, "don't quite reach here. Now, there's a thin laser line here that's invisible to the naked eye." He pointed in the general area he knew it would be. "But you can find it by spraying some moisture in the air. I usually use hairspray. Of course, you don't want to get any on the artifact."

"That thing?" Lena scrunched up her face as she looked at the thimble-sized stone statuette. "That can't be worth the effort."

"Untrue," Tony said. He pulled out his phone and looked up similar items on an art collector's site. "At least five grand. If you steal four of them, that's a tidy profit. If you add that ancient bowl sitting next to them, it will easily fetch another twenty grand. There's your year's salary. Made in less than a day."

The two of them stared at the artifacts wistfully for a full minute.

"Tony?" Both of them jumped at the voice. It was Tony's boss.

"You need to finish up those few items today," the man said.

Tony looked at his watch. He was about to be late.

"I'm so sorry," he said to Lena. "I need to go to work." To his boss, he said, "This is my cousin, Lena. Can she tag along?"

"Of course," the man said.

They walked back to the locker where Tony stored his tools. He took them out, and his boss handed him some wiring they wanted installed. He headed off to the third floor to fix a few things. Lena followed him.

When they were alone, he briefly explained what he was doing, leaving out the details she would need to know if she actually *did* break in to the Louvre someday. She listened intently.

Then they were silent while he worked. Lena took a seat nearby on a bench. There was no one else in the room.

While keeping half his attention on Lena so she didn't wander and the other half on his job, Tony had time to think in the silence. How was he going to get the ring? He could back her into a corner now and take it. But knowing Lena, she'd yell and the cameras would catch him with his hands on her.

And that wasn't his way. He prided himself on being smoother than that. Suddenly, as he worked, an idea came to him.

"Lena, why don't you come to dinner with us tonight? Abigail is the closing speaker here. There's going to be a fancy dinner before she speaks, and there's room for one more at our table." He saw the hesitation in her face and quickly added, "It'll give you a chance to see all of the Louvre. There's a space in the banquet area where I think we can come in."

"We?"

"Yes. I'm not letting you do this alone."

"All I need from you is the security information."

She had played right into his hands. "I'm finished up here," he said, testing the wire. "Now I need to go into the computer room. Join me, and I'll show you firsthand." He put his tools in his bag.

"Seriously? They'll let you bring me in the security room?"

"Of course. They trust me." He winked at her.

She smiled. She was quite pretty when she let her guard down, he noticed. She should do that more often. She maybe even looked a little like his grandma.

"I'm so glad I found family," he said. He put his arm around her and gave her a sideways hug. She didn't feel him lift her phone out of her purse.

They took the elevator to the hub that ran the security system for one of the world's great museums. Tony used his badge to swipe them in. The room was cool and filled with a soft hum. There were six men, all checking computers and cameras. They each had their own separate workstation. Alfonzo swiveled in his chair.

"Tony," he said, giving him a nod.

"Alfonzo." Tony liked this man. He had been the one to train Tony on these very computers earlier this week. "I'd like for you to meet my cousin, Lena."

"Nice to meet you." Alfonzo stood up and shook her hand. Then to Tony he said, "It's time for my break. You got me covered?"

"Yes, I sure do," Tony said, sitting in his chair. "See you in thirty minutes. Oh, Alfonzo? Why don't you take my cousin here and find her something to drink? Do you mind?"

Alfonzo was young and single. And Lena was pretty. He knew Alfonzo wouldn't mind at all.

"I would be delighted," Alfonzo said.

"No, I'm fine," Lena protested.

"It's okay, Lena. Go with him," Tony insisted.

She gave him a look, meaning *You're supposed to be showing me the system.* He shrugged innocently. She glared at him as Alfonzo showed her out.

Tony swiveled his chair back toward the monitor. The other guys were busy at their own stations. Tony adjusted a few cameras so he looked busy and then quickly pulled Lena's phone out of his pocket. Thankfully, she hadn't had time to change her passwords since the last time he hacked in.

He scanned her apps and looked for the most innocuous ones. There was a game called "Colour." She didn't seem like the type to color on a virtual palette, but when he opened it, he was surprised to see some beautiful designs. Of course. She was an artist.

There was another app called "Feed the Bird." He opened it. There was food you could "buy" to give to the bird. Each time it ate, you got points. Stupid, but he knew it was a cover. He pulled a wire out of his tool kit and plugged her phone in to the Louvre's super computer.

161

He glanced around. Pierre, one of the men, was playing Solitaire on his own phone. Another guy was adjusting some cameras from his computer station while eating out of a bag of chips. Tony quickly typed in some code and soon was on the dark web. If he got caught linking the Louvre to the dark web... A thrill of adrenaline swept through him.

Lena's Feed the Bird app linked to a financial institution. Just as he had figured. Working quickly, he used the codes he had created to break in to Lena's bank account, the one she kept on the dark web. There was a recent transaction. John Doe had deposited $500,000 in it, but the transaction was still pending. It said "Upon receipt."

He almost whistled aloud. A half million for the ring! Lena would be set for years as soon as she handed the ring over.

He typed in a few more things. He set a timer to cancel the transaction and sent the money back to John Doe at 7:15 p.m. tonight.

"We're back," Alfonzo said.

Tony quickly pulled the phone out of the computer and hit a few keys before Alfonzo could see it. The screen went back to the cameras overlooking the third floor.

"Any action?" Alfonzo asked.

"Nothing," Tony said, as Alfonzo came around. "Lena really wanted to hang with you, so I'm dropping her back off. I'll go finish my break and see you in twenty."

"Oui," Tony said. He liked to throw out French words when he knew them.

Alfonzo chuckled as he left.

"You said you would show me what you do," Lena said. Her voice was pleasant for the benefit of the other men in the room, but her eyes were daggers.

"And I will. This is pretty cool. Look at that man there." Tony pointed to a middle-aged man near a life-size stone statue. "He's picking his nose. He doesn't think anybody is looking." Lena scowled at Tony. He put his arm around her shoulders. "I'm sorry," he whispered into her ear as he slipped her phone back into her purse. "I had to throw Alfonzo off our scent. That was the only way I could figure to do it."

Lena shrugged his arm off her. "Whatever," she said.

162

Tony smiled and spent the next twenty minutes showing her people behaving badly on camera.

When Alfonzo came back, Tony excused himself to the restroom while Lena waited in the hall. He went into a stall and closed the door. He pulled John Doe's card out and made a call. He let his caller ID go through.

"The infamous Tony Russo," said the voice.

"The infamous John Doe," Tony said in return. "I have a proposition for you."

"I'd love to hear it."

"I'm in a public place. I'll text you."

Tony hung up. He rapidly typed his message on his phone, inviting John Doe to the dinner tonight. He'd save him a seat at the table. Tony promised to make it worth his while.

Tony had worked with John Doe before. They had only met once in person. Their other dealings had been over the internet. Tony sold him the stolen journal of a famous German music composer. And a manuscript written but never published by the best-selling author Anika Benting. He got quite a price for that one.

I wouldn't miss it, John Doe texted back.

Tony smiled and deleted his texts. Then he hurried back out to join Lena, who thankfully was waiting for him. But it would have been okay if she weren't. He had added a tracker to her phone so he could find her at all times.

Feeling only a little guilty, and mostly highly pleased with himself, he offered to take Lena out to buy a dress for tonight.

"We only have a few hours," she said.

"We'll be quick. I have to stop by the hotel and change in to a suit, as well."

Outside, he hailed a cab and asked Lena to take them to her favorite place to shop. He hoped it wasn't expensive. Buying dresses for cousins was not in the Paris vacation budget.

While Lena was trying on clothes, Tony took a seat in a chair outside the dressing room. He pulled out his phone and did a Google search on Lulu Scott in Paris. About twenty years ago, she was in the city to oversee the presentation of some rare documents to the Louvre. It was a big deal, and there were several articles about them and what a treasure they were to the museum. There were some photos of her during the ceremonies. She had her hair pulled back and was dressed primly, but she looked radiant.

He enlarged them one by one and scanned the other people in the photos. Sure enough, there was John Doe. Here he was called Reginald Phipps, and he was standing next to Ms. Scott in one of the photos.

Using Google Translate, he was able to read one of the articles. John Doe—or Reginald Phipps—was writing a check to the Louvre to help with the preservation and storage of the documents Ms. Scott had with her. As well as others.

So they had originally met in the work world. Interesting.

"I'm all set," Lena said, coming out of the dressing room with a skirt in hand. "I hope you can afford this."

"It's not Gucci or Prada or something, is it?"

"Coco Chanel, darling. We are in Paris."

Tony must have paled because Lena smiled. "No, cousin. I got it off the sales rack. Really. I've seen your bank account."

Tony paid and looked at his watch. It was going to be an interesting evening. Gathered around the dinner table would be Lena and the ring. John Doe and his money. And of course, Ms. Scott, who was about to be reunited with her former lover. He didn't quite have a plan yet, but with that much ammunition in one place, he should be able to come up with one. He'd mix it all up and see what happened.

Chapter Twenty-Seven

Abigail took a cab to Lena's apartment. She knew Lena was with Tony, so she was hoping to catch the mysterious houseguest home alone. She knocked on the door and waited. Nothing happened. She knocked again.

After a few minutes, she pulled a large paper clip out of her purse and picked the lock. Tony wasn't the only one who knew these tricks.

She turned the handle and was pleased to find that Lena hadn't had time to repair the deadbolt yet.

She cautiously entered, looking around. There didn't seem to be anyone home. She closed the door behind her.

"Hello?" She didn't want to startle the girl, just in case.

No answer.

Abigail went to the room where the girl had been and tried the handle. Locked. "If you're in there, it's okay. Lena knows me." Taking her paper clip, she worked at it until she heard the click. She turned the handle and carefully pushed the door open.

Sunlight streamed in from a window on the other side of the room, covering a bed made up of yellow linens. Above the bed was a painting of daisies. There was a dresser next to the bed with a hairbrush and some books on it. This was obviously the room of a girl, but judging by the length of the dirty jeans on the floor, it was a tall girl. So a teen?

The room seemed empty, but Abigail had learned not to trust everything she saw. She gently pushed the bedroom door back against the wall, but just as she suspected, it stopped short. There was someone hiding behind it

Suddenly, that someone pushed back with a force that almost knocked Abigail down. Thankfully, she was prepared for it. She sidestepped into the room, pushing the door closed behind her and praying the girl didn't have a weapon. She flung her hands into the air and said, "I'm not here to hurt you!"

The girl's long blond hair was disheveled, and she put her hand on the door, about to flee.

"Wait! Please! I only want to talk!" Abigail said.

The girl hesitated. Her blue eyes were wide with fear. She looked like she was about seventeen years old. She was taller than Lena, with long, thin legs poured into skinny jeans. She had on a soft blue T-shirt that brought out the color in her eyes. She wasn't wearing any makeup. Her young, startled face was beautiful.

"I saw you in the paintings," Abigail said, wanting to pique the girl's interest so she'd stay. "Lena is an exceptional artist." She had planned what she would say in the cab ride on her way over. "I'm Abigail."

"I know who you are," the girl said. Her English was more accented with French than Lena's.

"What's your name? Can we talk? Please?"

The girl took her hand off the doorknob. "Lena will not be happy that you're here."

"Lena is with Tony right now. He's showing her around the Louvre."

"Fine. Let's talk." The girl motioned for Abigail to sit on the bed. She did.

"I'm Giselle," the girl said.

"Tony and I want to help," Abigail said.

Giselle crossed her arms in front of her chest. "Help put the painting into the Louvre?" She looked skeptical.

"Well, I do want my ring back," Abigail said. "And Tony is very good at breaking in to places."

"Apparently, so are you, oui?"

Abigail laughed. She looked over at the stack of books on the dresser. She wanted to connect with Giselle somehow. "I love *The Little Princess*. I read it at least once a year."

"Me too," Giselle said, glancing at the paperback on her stack.

"May I?" Abigail nodded toward the books.

Giselle nodded and Abigail scooted over and looked through the titles. *The Little Princess* was on top. She had recognized the title even in French. She looked at the book under it. "What's this one? Can you translate the title for me?" She held it up.

"*How to Be Your Best You*," Giselle said, her cheeks coloring,

"Perfect. And this one?"

"*The Broken Chalice*."

"A fantasy. I've read it in English!"

Giselle was relaxing. "Books aren't what you came here to discuss," she said as she pulled out the chair by her makeup table. She sat.

"No. I just want to know who you are to Lena. That little girl in all of the pictures is you, isn't it?"

Giselle hesitated and then nodded.

"Why is Lena hiding you? Who is she protecting you from?"

Giselle didn't answer.

Who was Lena most afraid of? Boucher had entered Lena's life when she was ten. She was in her late twenties right now. Abigail did the math. That was about seventeen years ago.

"Are you Lena's half-sister Dana?"

Giselle dropped her eyes but remained silent.

"You *are*," Abigail said, her voice nearly a whisper. "Albert Boucher is your father. He's the jerk she's protecting you from."

Giselle looked up. "Yes."

So that explained it. Lena kidnapped Giselle from Boucher and was keeping her here.

"Giselle isn't your real name."

The girl shook her head. "Lena gave me a new identity. She's been sending me to a private school under that name, and I just graduated. Now she's going to send me to college." Even though she was sharing information with Abigail that she probably shouldn't, her words came out in a gush. She spoke as if all of this had been bottled up for too long. "Lena would do anything for me. She has done too much."

"She's financing all of this with stealing, isn't she?"

Giselle nodded, and her eyes filled with tears. "At first, it was just little things. Jewelry from tourists. Or she'd pick pockets and we'd use the credit cards to buy groceries. After that, she stole a few larger items from some of the local tourist shops around here and started selling them on the dark web. That got scary, but I helped her because she worked so hard to help *me*. We were just trying to survive."

Abigail had a thought forming. *The dark web.* A person had to be pretty computer savvy to tap in to that. "What do you want to go to college for?"

Giselle's eyes lit up. "Computer science. I'm really good at—"

She stopped, finally realizing she was saying too much.

"Ahhhhh," Abigail said, as the pieces came together. "So you're the hacker in the family."

Giselle didn't respond.

"But now she has stolen my ring." Abigail held up her finger, which had a slight tan line on it where the ring used to sit.

"I'm so sorry," Giselle said. "I told her not to, but she made me do all of this research on the two of you. It's worth so much, and she said if we sold that, we'd be all set. She promised me she'd quit stealing once we had it. That we could live a normal life. She said nobody would get hurt. I mean, it's just a ring."

"It *is* just a ring," Abigail said. A ring that could finance this girl's college career. But would Lena really give up stealing?

"I don't like the man she is going to sell it to," Giselle said. "He buys a lot on the dark web. His name is quite famous in the sales circles, really, and he is powerful, from what I can tell. He scares me. I've never met him, but anyone with that much money is scary. He's going to give us half a million Euros for your ring."

"What?" Abigail said. She had no idea it would fetch that much. That was *over* half a million US dollars. "Wow. I can see how that would change your life."

But stealing wasn't the answer. And it wasn't a way for this girl to start off her life.

"But it's not right," Abigail said. "There are other ways to get you through college. Tony and I will help you. You can do it a legal way, and Lena will be safe and not go to jail."

"Lena doesn't trust anyone. She said Tony offered to help her but she doesn't trust him."

With her past, Lena had a right not to trust anybody. Abigail's heart went out to both her and Giselle.

"Did Boucher hurt you?"

Giselle shook her head. "Lena got me out before he could."

"How long have you been with her?"

"Since I was thirteen."

"Wow."

Lena had been raising this girl for four years, asking her to hide her true identity when they simply could have gone to the authorities. But sometimes the system didn't help kids of abusive homes until it was too late. Lena probably didn't want to take that chance. And from what Abigail knew of Boucher's temper, Giselle would definitely have been a target for him if she stayed around.

What Giselle needed was a decent chance at starting over. What Lena needed was a break. And some psychological counseling.

"I'll see what I can do," Abigail said aloud. "I'm sure I can help you."

"What? No. Please don't tell Lena you were here! She'll be angry if she knew I talked to you."

Abigail stood, smoothing down her skirt. "I need to get back to the Louvre. My talk is coming up. Lena won't know I've been here. She's scoping out the Louvre's weak points with Tony. Trust me, when he wants to be interesting, he doesn't disappoint."

Giselle stood. "He's not going to let her break in to the Louvre, is he?" Her blue eyes were frightened again.

"Tony? He'd better not!" Abigail gave Giselle a reassuring smile. "I'll be back. If you need to get hold of me, here's my cell phone number." She pulled a business card out of her purse and gave it to Giselle.

"Thank you, Abigail."

"I'll come back, and we'll figure something out for your college," she said. "I promise."

She knew of at least a few ways to get Giselle some money for college. She had done it for herself. And if Giselle had good grades... She and Tony would come back tomorrow to get more information before they left the country.

One last thought occurred to her.

"Giselle? There's something I'd like to borrow from you, if you have it," Abigail said. "It would mean a lot to both Tony and I. Will you help me?"

Abigail arrived back at the Louvre just ten minutes before the dinner started. She had enough time to change in to the purple spaghetti strap dress she brought and put her hair up. Tony was waiting for her in the lobby, wearing his dark blue suit with a white shirt underneath. He looked amazing.

Lena was standing next to him. She had on the same blouse she had worn earlier, but it was paired with a sequined skirt instead of the slacks she had been wearing. And a pair of heels instead of her sandals. Abigail raised her eyebrows.

"She's joining us," Tony said, giving Abigail a kiss. "Let's go off and pray before your event."

Before she could respond, Tony pulled Abigail down the hallway and over by the drinking fountains. "Bow your head," he said.

"What?"

"I need to tell you stuff, quickly. This is our cover. By the way, where were you?"

Abigail bowed her head and closed her eyes. "It's a long story, but I met Lena's half-sister."

"The girl in the locked room. I figured it out. Dana Boucher from the birth certificate I saw. She'd be seventeen now. She disappeared when she was thirteen."

"Yes. Lena has her. She's called Giselle now."

Tony grasped Abigail's hands and kept his head bowed. She peeked up.

"People are staring," Abigail said.

Tony ignored that. "I've invited someone else to the dinner. You're not going to like it."

"Who?" Her stomach did a flip-flop.

"John Doe. His real name is Reginald Phipps. I told him I had something for him."

"Like what?"

"Like Ms. Scott?"

"What?"

"I'll explain later. And like the ring Lena is wearing around her neck."

"How does that get me my ring back?" Abigail asked.

"I'm improvising. I'll figure it out. But I hacked in to the dark web here at the Louvre—"

"Now I'm praying for real."

"—and put a hold on his transaction for the ring. His funds will be back in his account at 7:15 p.m."

"All half million?" Abigail said.

"What?" Tony looked up at her. "How'd you know? That amazing number was going to be my finale!"

Abigail laughed and kissed him. "Thanks for the prayers. Ms. Scott is staring at me. Let's go." *And please Lord, give us wisdom*, Abigail prayed.

Chapter Twenty-Eight

The dinner looked amazing. Tony never let stress interfere with his eating. Beef bourguignon, seared swordfish, and glazed chicken breast were the headliners. Servers were slicing and laying out food on the buffet. Tony was going to try it all when their table was called up.

Dunning was sitting across from him, bragging about Michael Benedict's talents to Ms. Scott. Tony raised his eyebrows ever so slightly and yawned in a mocking display of boredom for Abigail's sake and then glanced at his watch. He looked toward the door for the tenth time. This time, he wasn't disappointed. John Doe—a.k.a. Reginald Phipps—walked through. He was wearing a flashy gray suit in high-gloss silk with a pink handkerchief fluttering out of his pocket.

Tony glanced at Ms. Scott, who was still deep in conversation with Dunning. She hadn't noticed Phipps' entrance. Tony stood, and Phipps made his way across the room. Lena was looking intently at her dinner program. He hadn't told her that Phipps was joining them, and he had no idea if she'd recognize him by his face. She probably only knew him as John Doe and had never seen a photo. As far as he could tell, all of their interactions had been on the dark web.

"Nice to see you again, Phipps," Tony said, shaking his hand.

"Tony! What a pleasure!" Phipps was tall, very thin, and a dapper dresser. He was in his early sixties now, but rumor was he had been a runway model in his younger days. He gave that up years ago. Tony knew he was far more passionate about his collecting than his physique.

The men shook hands, and Tony introduced him to the others at the table. Ms. Scott looked up and saw him at the same time Phipps' eyes found her. She turned pale.

"Reggie?" she said, her voice a whisper.

"Lulu?"

"Do you two know each other?" Tony asked innocently.

"We…met…before. When I was here on a work assignment," Ms. Scott said. "I was chosen to carry some rare documents to the Louvre, and Mr. Phipps here was financially supporting them."

"Reggie." Abigail said softly, recognizing the connection. Tony glanced at Abigail and gave her a little smile to let her know he knew about this strange liaison.

"Yes," Phipps agreed, his expression neutral. "A long time ago."

"Very long." Lulu politely shook his hand and nothing more was said. Tony couldn't tell if Ms. Scott was happy to see Phipps or upset. She hid her emotions well.

When Tony came to Lena and introduced her as his cousin, the two didn't seem to recognize each other. So far, so good.

The head of the symposium got up and briefly talked about how successful the week had been. He shared a few highlights and promised they'd all be thrilled by the closing speaker, Abigail Russo.

Tony looked proudly over at her.

Their table was called up to the buffet. Tony piled food on his plate. "Eat up," he said to Lena, was too skinny in his opinion. She put small portions on her plate and seemed ill at ease in the room. He was pretty sure she wasn't used to fancy dinner parties.

"If you'll excuse me, I want to go wash up," Phipps said when they got back to the table. "After handling all of those shared utensils on the buffet…you never know." He left through the double doors.

"I should do that too," Abigail said suddenly. "I've been shaking a lot of hands."

She disappeared through the double doors also.

The food was delicious. Tony was trying to work out in his head what his next step was. He had Phipps here. He had canceled Phipps' transaction to Lena so she no longer had any hold on the ring. And she was wearing it. That alone should cause a stir.

He wasn't sure what he could do with that information quite yet. And he was running out of time. Plus, he had told Phipps that he had something for him. Well, he did. He had the ring. But he wasn't planning to give it to him.

And he had Ms. Scott. But neither of them seemed to care they had been reunited. Or at least they weren't showing it.

Maybe he had gotten himself in a pickle.

Tony took another bite of the beef. He would let slip that Phipps' money wasn't in the account, and Lena would have a fit. If there was one thing Tony could count on, it was Lena's anger. Then she'd try to work something out with Phipps. Tony would suggest she show Phipps the ring, and when she took it out, he'd grab it.

And promise Phipps something better in return.

But what? He didn't know, but that would give him time to think.

He glanced at his watch. Abigail had been gone a long time. Just as he was about to go check on her, she returned and sat down. Her cheeks were flushed. She gave him a little smile.

Phipps came back shortly after she did. He looked uncomfortable. He tugged at his tie and took a sip of his beverage.

"I was just telling Mr. Phipps here about my lovely ring," Abigail said.

Lena's eyebrows shot up.

The game was on! Tony leaned over and whispered in Lena's ear. "Phipps is John Doe."

Lena choked. She coughed so long and hard Tony was beginning to fear for her. "Are you okay?" he asked and handed her water glass to her. She took a few sips and wiped her mouth with her napkin.

"I think so," she said in a strangled voice.

"What ring?" Dunning asked.

"Her wedding ring, I'll bet," Ms. Scott said, shaking her head. "Abigail lo—"

"Loaned it to Lena," Tony said quickly before Ms. Scott could get the word 'lost" out.

"Lena?" Ms. Scott said. All eyes turned toward the poor girl. Lena shrank down in her seat but tried to smile.

"Lena is a *huge* fan of the painter Antonio Russo," Abigail said. "*Huge*. She has her own historic tour guide company and gives these wonderful tours telling all about the artists. Her Russo stories are especially interesting. That's how Tony and I met her."

"Are you Lena *Martin*?" Phipps asked. Tony hadn't give out last names when he introduced people. Phipps was catching on.

"You met her on a tour?" Ms. Scott said. "I thought you introduced her as your cousin."

"It's a long story," Tony said, meeting Ms. Scott's eyes. "You'll have to *trust* me to tell you the whole thing later." He gave her a meaningful look.

She glanced at Abigail, who gave her a sight nod. "Of course," Ms. Scott said.

Tony was impressed with how well Ms. Scott was handling Phipps being seated at their table. Perhaps they had ended their relationship amicably. He had been hoping that Phipps would miss his lost love and Tony could score points for bringing them back together. He assumed the man still had a thing for her, since the photo was prominently displayed. Maybe he was wrong.

"So, Lena, why don't you show the ring to us?" Abigail said. "Actually, I'd like to have it back to wear up on stage."

Lena turned a few interesting shades of red. She glanced at Tony, and he knew she had a lot she'd like to say to him right now. He felt kind of bad she had been set up. With a shaking hand, she pulled the chain up out of her blouse. There it was.

Abigail held her hand out, and Lena lifted the chain over her head and gave it to Abigail. With everyone watching, she had no choice.

"Brilliant," Tony said. "I do hope you enjoyed wearing it." He glanced at Phipps, whose eyes had gone steely.

"So, I don't get why her being an Antonio Russo fan has anything to do with your ring," Dunning said.

"It's the ring from the painting," Abigail said, taking it off the chain. She offered Tony an apologetic look. The truth of its value was out there now.

"The ring from the painting *Laurel*?" Dunning said. "You mean a replica?"

"He means the real thing," Phipps said. They turned to him. "That is the ring that Antonio Russo gave to his lover, Laurel, to bind their love. She was wearing it when he painted that portrait of her. It was lost. Until now."

Phipps turned to Tony. "You said you had something for me. Is this what you wanted to show me?"

"Well," Tony said, struggling to come up with a plan as he went along. "Actually, yes. But I have other things as well." He looked to Abigail for help.

"Why Tony wanted Mr. Phipps to join us tonight," Abigail said, slipping her ring on, "is that Mr. Phipps offered to buy this ring from us. But I told him it wasn't for sale. Mr. Phipps is appreciative of old things, things of value, and so I told him about our library and the wonderful maps and documents we store there." Abigail looked straight at Dunning. "Mr. Phipps has $500,000 earmarked to give us if I'm allowed to stay on board and continue to run the department," she said.

Brilliant! Tony wanted to clap. But he kept his poker face on as he watched Phipps turn a deeper shade of red.

"He was going to use it to buy my ring but instead decided to use it for something that he could share with the world. Which is the work we do at the library." She held up her hand with the ring on it. The light caught the emerald, and it sparkled. "He would have kept this in his home, but the work that will get done with that money, the things we can share with the public," Abigail raised her eyebrows at Mr. Dunning, "will affect a much broader audience. Mr. Phipps was delighted at the opportunity."

Abigail turned her attention to Ms. Scott. "He had passed up an opportunity with Ms. Scott many years ago, and I believe his heart has told him that now's the time to donate to her library."

Phipps glanced at Ms. Scott and then cast his eyes down to his plate. When he spoke, his words were harsh, even though his tone was not. "I said I'd think about it."

"That's not what you said in your emails," Abigail said to him sweetly. She wasn't finished applying pressure.

"Which we have copies of," Tony added, smiling broadly at him. "And the money is sitting there in your account. You can look for yourself. You were kind to let me in to see it."

Phipps gave him a dark look but played along. "Of course."

Lena picked up her phone and began furiously tapping on it.

"Five hundred thousand dollars?" Ms. Scott had gone white. "A half million? To our library?"

"That's right," Abigail said, laying her hand gently on Phipps' shoulder. "He's such a generous person. Over the years, he has learned to appreciate the value of treasures over money. Those things you hold dear. He's a collector, not a seller. Right, Mr. Phipps?"

Ms. Scott's excitement had turned to a look of quiet satisfaction.

Abigail smiled and picked up her fork. "What's good?" she asked Tony.

"Everything," he said, still smiling. "Everything is good."

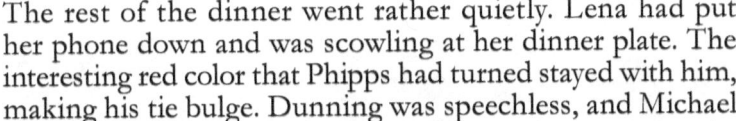

The rest of the dinner went rather quietly. Lena had put her phone down and was scowling at her dinner plate. The interesting red color that Phipps had turned stayed with him, making his tie bulge. Dunning was speechless, and Michael Benedict seemed to have given up on trying to please the board member. Michael was texting and eating, alternately.

Ms. Scott was beaming. Tony looked across the table at her, and she gave him a big smile, not the tight-lipped little grin she usually offered.

"Mr. Phipps, we'd love to dedicate a plaque in your name," Ms. Scott said as the plates were cleared away. "We often give larger gifts to such generous donors, but I know from past experience how much you like to keep a low profile."

177

"I'd like that," Phipps said. "I'd like that very much." He picked up his phone and sent a text.

Tony felt his phone beep. He pulled it out of the pocket of his suit coat and read the text under the table.

You've made an enemy today, Russo.

He put it back in his coat pocket and looked across the table at Phipps. He gave him a nod.

The grandmaster of ceremonies walked up on stage and began to introduce the closing speaker. He gave all of Abigail's credentials, which were amazing. Some of them even Tony didn't know about. When he was finished talking, the crowd erupted in applause, and Abigail stood.

Tony reached over and gave Abigail's hand a squeeze.

"They're all clapping for *you*," he whispered. She smiled at him and squeezed his hand back. He watched his wife walk up on the stage like she owned it. And she did. Her talk kept the room interested for the thirty minutes she was up there. Afterward, she could hardly make her way back to him because so many people wanted her to stop and talk with them.

He was so proud of her.

Now that people were getting up and moving about, he figured he should apologize to Lena and figure out what they could do to help her and Giselle. He turned to speak to her, but she was gone. She had left the hall and was nowhere in sight.

Chapter Twenty-Nine

Abigail scooted closer to Tony so she could feel his comforting warmth against her side. "We did it," she whispered. "We got my ring back."

They were sitting in the lobby of the Louvre, watching the people file out. Some were taking their week's worth of stuff with them, pulling dollies loaded with boxes. Others would clear out their booths tomorrow morning.

"You double-crossed John Doe," Tony said.

"How dangerous is this guy?" Abigail looked at her ring. Now that she knew somebody would pay a half million, she wasn't sure how she felt about it. It had gone from sentimental to dangerous. This wasn't the first time somebody had wanted it.

"Not dangerous as in he'll stab us while we sleep. I think he's more likely to degrade my name in the world of art, and I'll never thieve again."

"Well, that's not a problem."

"Not really."

But Tony looked doubtful. Abigail decided not to dwell on that.

"That was brilliant, by the way," Tony said. "The way you figured it all out. I had no idea what I was going to do once I got them there together."

"Teamwork!" she said, kissing him on the cheek. She looked at her ring again. "I missed this little treasure."

Ms. Scott approached them. Tony stood.

"Thank you for trusting me in there," he said.

"I guess it paid off," Ms. Scott said. She was still smiling. "Abigail, it looks like you will have a job for quite a while. And tenure, most likely. Dunning can't seem to figure out what hit him back there. Oh, and Michael Benedict has decided to stay where he's at."

Abigail gave Ms. Scott a light hug. The director stiffly accepted it.

"Was that your Reggie?" Abigail asked softly.

"Yes." Ms. Scott didn't offer more. Abigail waited quietly.

The director cleared her throat. "He...we might go out for drinks later." She cast a glance at Tony. "How did you know?"

"I was at his house and saw a picture of the two of you together. He has it sitting on his bookshelf."

"He does?" Ms. Scott's face took on a glow, but she didn't smile. "Well. We shall see. I'm sure we'll just talk about the library, and he will write out his check."

"Um...I'm not sure he's quite on the up and up," Tony said. "Just so you know."

Ms. Scott nodded. "I'll keep that in mind."

"Thank you," Abigail said. "Thank you for everything."

"You two go back to your hotel and get some rest," Ms. Scott said. "We don't have much to take home, so no worries about cleaning up. I can do that myself. We gave out most of our brochures and information. I'll see you tomorrow night at the airport. I have some sightseeing to do tomorrow. I've been too busy this week to enjoy the city."

Tony reached for Abigail's hand. "You ready to go?"

Abigail looked around at the Louvre, taking in the beauty of it one last time. She had been invited to the World Maps Symposium. An *world-wide* event. She had been the closing speaker. And she had done well.

She closed her eyes for a moment, soaking it all in. Then she put her hand in her husband's. "Yes, I'm ready," she said. "Let's go."

Outside in the darkness of the courtyard, Phipps stepped out of the shadows. Abigail caught her breath.

"Mr. Phipps, you scared me," she said.

Phipps came closer to them until he was right up in their faces. "I should kill you," he said, his voice low. He was looking at Tony.

"That's not your style," Tony said lightly.

"You took something from me," Phipps said. "I won't forget that."

"But didn't you notice that I also *gave* you something?" Tony asked. "Her picture still sits on your bookshelf for Hobbes to dust. She must still mean something to you. Maybe she can forgive you. Why don't you ask?"

Phipps was silent. Abigail could feel her heart pounding in her chest and wondered if the men could hear it. Finally, he spoke.

"Very well. But stay out of my way, Tony Russo."

Tony nodded, and then he and Abigail walked quietly through the night back to their hotel room, taking the long way for one last moonlight stroll along the Seine. The lights played off the water, much like in Lena's painting. Abigail thought about her and Giselle. She and Tony had decided to go over in the morning and discuss what they could do to help Lena climb out of her financial problems. And when she got back home, Abigail was going to look in to college options for Giselle. Since the girl was being supported by her sister and was not under the legal care of a guardian, she would qualify for a lot of financial support in the States.

She smiled happily and leaned her head against Tony's shoulder as they walked. This was turning out to be the perfect ending to a beautiful honeymoon. If all went according to her plan, there was one last thing to make it even better.

Abigail couldn't hold back a smile as they stopped outside their hotel room door. Tony was about to swipe the key when she stopped him.

"I have a surprise for you," she said. "Inside."

Tony glanced at the door and back at Abigail. "Inside there?" He waggled his eyebrows.

She laughed. "Yes, silly. But not *that*. Something else. You are always one step ahead of me, always the romantic, always sweeping me off my feet. I wanted a chance to romance *you* a little bit."

"You did when you surprised me with the ticket to Paris," he said.

She remembered. She took him to see the painting of the Laurel and said "Let's go see where your great-grandfather's studio used to be. Together." And handed him the ticket.

"Think of this as bringing it full circle." She took the key from him and swiped it in the door. She swung it open to reveal small twinkle lights hung across one of the walls.

"This would have been better if we had a balcony," she said, pulling him into the room. She was glad to see that room service had their table set up with a single candle on it and some flowers, as she had asked. Standing next to it was a tall man with a violin. He was dressed in a tux. As soon as he saw them he put the instrument up on his shoulder and started playing.

She looked at Tony. A smile spread across his face as he listened.

"It's Rachmaninov," Abigail said. "It's supposed to be one of the most romantic pieces ever written."

"It's beautiful."

They sat at the little table, their chairs scooted close together, listening to the music. It filled their tiny room, and for a moment, Abigail forgot their stressors and was transported away. Tony's hand was warm in hers, and when she looked at him, he was listening intently to the music.

He noticed her watching him and he turned. "This is amazing," he whispered. "When did you set this up?"

She had made a call in the taxi when she was leaving Giselle's. It had seemed like the perfect ending to their week.

"I don't give away my secrets," she said. "But I have a present for you."

"For moi?" Tony pointed to his chest. He was so much fun.

"Oui," Abigail said. She opened her purse and pulled out the envelope that Giselle gave her. "Open it."

Tony took a pocket knife out of his suit coat and carefully cut along the sealed lip. Then he pulled out the paper and opened it. It was Lena's birth certificate, which Giselle had been so kind to loan to her.

"It's real," Abigail said. "It's embossed. Look at the other papers."

He did. Her grandma's official birth certificate was there too. As well as papers from her adoption. Her birth mother was listed. It was Antonio's daughter.

Tony stared at it. He was quiet for a moment, which was unusual for him. She saw him swallow a few times.

"You have family," she said quietly.

"I have family," he repeated. When he looked at her again, there were tears in his eyes. "I have always wanted..." his voice trailed off as emotion caught.

"I know," she said, and pulled him against her. He roughly wiped the tears away with the back of his hand and leaned his head on her shoulder. The violinist had moved on to another song, this one light and cheery. The music slowly lifted up and carried across the room, as if spreading their joy. "I know."

Abigail was full and sleepy. Neither of them had any desire to go out on the town this late, even to see the Eiffel Tower, so she changed in to her nightgown and crawled in to bed. It was past 11 p.m. She still felt a little jet-lagged and was feeling Paris's six-hour time difference. They had tomorrow to sightsee.

Tony put his arm around her, and she spooned her back up against his chest.

"Happy honeymoon," he whispered.

"It was perfect," she mumbled and drifted off into a dreamless sleep.

A loud beeping awoke her. It sounded like an Amber alert.

"Is that your phone?"

Tony's arms were still around her, and the hotel room was dark. "I think so," he said sleepily and turned over. He looked at it. "Darn that girl!"

"What?" Abigail turned over as Tony sat up. He had shut off the beeping sound and was punching some keys on his phone.

"I put a tracker on Lena and set my phone to let me know if she went anywhere near the Louvre," he said. "And she is. She's actually going to try to go in."

Abigail sat up and brushed her hair away from her eyes. She had been in a deep sleep, and it was taking her a moment to wake up. "What?" she said again. Then she remembered. "Did you give her the security information? Giselle is the hacker. Not Lena."

"Not all of it." Tony got up and went to the desk. He opened his laptop and plugged his phone in to it.

Abigail got out of bed, pulling her robe around her against the chill in the room. The air conditioner had been on too high. She went and stood behind Tony, watching him type.

"Look," he said eventually. "That's her." He pointed to a red dot moving around the outside of the Louvre. "She's near the north side. That's where I told her to go in. But I was just making conversation. I have no idea if that's a good spot or not!"

He sounded stressed, something Abigail didn't often hear in his voice.

"She's going to get caught!" he said.

He switched to a different screen and logged on to the dark web. After some typing, he said, "The security at the Louvre is still up. How on earth does she think she's going to get in?"

Abigail's phone rang. She looked at the unknown number, and answered.

"Abigail!" It was Giselle. The girl's voice was frantic. "Lena told me to knock out the security at the Louvre, and I thought I did, but it seems like it's back up. And she's there, Abigail! She's going to get caught!"

"Calm down, Giselle," Abigail said, putting the phone on speaker so Tony could hear. "Tell us what Lena's up to."

"She is going to put that painting in the Louvre," Giselle said. She sounded like she was crying. "She left me with instructions on how to shut down the security at the Louvre. Stuff Tony had shown her. I tried it, and I thought it worked. But as soon as she left, it all turned back to green on my computer screen. It's still up, and she thinks she has an hour!"

"You can't just take out the security," Tony said, frustrated. "If it simply goes down, the whole world will be there trying to figure out *why*. You'd need to disguise it with a camera loop so it gives the appearance of still being active."

"Help her!" Giselle was crying. "Can you do that?"

"Not from here," Tony said. His fingers were still flying along the keyboard as he talked. "Which way is she going in? Do you know where she wants to put the painting?"

"I don't know where she's going in, but she wants to put in in the room with the Russos. She came home from the dinner really upset. She said my entire future had gone up in smoke, and that she didn't have anything for me. Nothing. She told me to forget college. Then she grabbed the painting and gave me the specs you showed her." Giselle was crying so hard she hiccupped. "She told me she was breaking in and that I needed to give her an hour, like I did at the other museums."

"I didn't even give her the right information," Tony mumbled under his breath. He ran his hand through his hair, a gesture that Abigail noticed he did when he was upset. "Crap."

Tony shut his laptop. "Call her, Giselle. Tell her to stop."

"I've been trying. She won't answer her phone!"

Tony pulled his black bag from under the bed. Then he grabbed his black cat-burglar suit from his suitcase and started changing into it.

"*What* are you doing?" Abigail said, even though she already knew.

"I'm going to go stop my cousin before she gets herself arrested," Tony said.

"You'll get caught," Abigail said, but she was already pulling out her own black spandex outfit. "Giselle, I'll call you back after I have Lena." She ended the call.

"Did you bring yours too?" Tony asked.

"You told me you might need me to cover for you someday, remember?" She smiled. "You trained me to do this."

"You are absolutely *not* coming."

"You are absolutely *not* telling me what I can and can't do," Abigail said, putting her hair back in a ponytail. "Are *you* coming?" She headed for the door.

"Um, yeah."

She heard Tony behind her. Her heart was pounding frantically in her chest. *What was she doing?* She had no idea, but she figured if they got there before Lena broke in, all would be well. They'd get her and talk some sense into her. She could take the painting back to her apartment and hide it. They could calm Giselle down.

It would all work out.

"Hurry!" Abigail said, opening the stairwell door to go out the back way of their hotel. This exit, behind the hotel, would help them avoid going through the lobby at 1 a.m.

In their cat-burglar suits.

Once they were outside, Tony grabbed her hand and stopped her.

"Abigail, no. The line, remember?"

"Tony, we've already crossed that line so many times..."

"That doesn't mean we should again. Or that you should."

"You are."

"She's my family. She and Giselle are the only family I have outside of Grandma," Tony said.

"You have me," Abigail said. "And we stick together. That's what family does." She tugged on his hand, and they started running toward the Louvre.

Abigail saw her first. She was at the north window, just as Tony's phone showed. She had a huge package with her, wrapped in canvas. The painting.

They ran toward her. "Lena!" Tony said as loud as he dared.

Lena froze and turned to look at them. She was dressed in black, making her look smaller than she was. She had a ski mask on her face and blended in nicely with the shrubs around her. If it hadn't been for Tony's tracker, they would never have seen her.

"Get out of here!" she hissed at them. "You've already ruined everything else!"

She had a ladder propped up against the side of the building. She was halfway up it, heading toward the window.

"The alarm is still on!" Abigail said as they arrived at the base of the ladder. "Tony gave you the wrong specs. Giselle was just smart enough to figure it out anyway, but she only bypassed the first system."

Lena paused and looked down at them. "I don't believe you. All you want to do is stop me. Giselle is brilliant, and she turned them off. I saw her. The whole system is shut down for an hour."

"They have a backup system," Tony said. "It came on when the original went down. And they will be looking in to why the first system failed. Trust me. I have some experience with this."

"Well, so do I!" Lena said. She continued the climb.

"This is no way to raise Giselle!" Abigail said. "Think of *her*. What will happen to her if you go to jail?"

Lena had reached the window. She pulled out some masking tape and taped up a spot near the edge of the glass. "Leave me alone," she said down to them. "You have no idea what you're talking about. I won't go to jail. I'm good at what I do. Maybe even better than Tony."

With that, she took a rock and smashed at the tape. Abigail saw the glass shatter. The pieces stuck to the tape.

"Don't," Tony said, as her hand started to reach for the taped-up glass. "There's an alarm running around the entire perimeter of the window. Once your hand goes through, it'll catch you."

Lena paused for a moment. She looked below. "You promised to help me," she said.

"We will!" Abigail said. She glanced around to be sure nobody was coming. They were still alone.

"Then help me now!" Lena said. "All I want to do is put my painting in the Russo room." The canvas package was large. She was balancing it on top of her knee, barely keeping it on the ladder. "And maybe take a little something extra. Which I would not have to do if I had sold the ring."

"*My* ring," Abigail reminded her.

"Don't do it, Lena," Tony said.

Abigail could tell they weren't getting through to Lena. The girl was peeling away the taped-up glass, leaving a hole big enough for her hand. She'd reach through in seconds and trigger the alarm.

"Don't be stupid!" Abigail said. "We will help you! Just come down!" But Lena wasn't listening.

Abigail grabbed Tony's hand. "Come on!" she said and pulled him with her. She'd run around to the front and cause a distraction of some sort. Maybe that would give Lena time to run after the alarms started up.

Chapter Thirty

Tony stopped in the courtyard near the giant pyramid. Its golden glow softened its edges, making it even more beautiful at night.

"What now?" Abigail asked him.

Tony looked around, and the only thing he could think was the front door. Sometimes being out in the open was the best hiding place.

He pulled Abigail to the large double doors and knocked loudly.

In what seemed like an eternity, but in reality was only about twenty seconds, a guard appeared behind the glass door.

"Tony?"

"Gerard!" Tony said, glad somebody he knew had answered. Gerard worked the afternoon shift, coming in around 4 p.m. and working twelve hours until morning.

Gerard cautiously opened the door. "What's up?"

"Someone is about to break in to your museum. I want to stop them."

Gerard stared at them. Only then did Tony remember he was dressed in black and carrying a black bag of tools.

"Not us," he added.

Gerard was about to say something when alarms went off. "Voleur!" shouted a man from somewhere inside the museum. Gerard swore and took off running. Tony deftly caught the door and slipped in, with Abigail right behind him.

"This way," he said. They ducked behind the ticket booth while guards ran past. Then Tony took Abigail's hand, and they made their way through the lobby and into the elevator. Tony swiped his card, and they went down.

"You still have your ID?" Abigail asked.

"I might have kept it by accident."

The doors opened, and they were in the basement. Tony zipped up his hoodie, hoping it concealed some of the spandex of his climbing suit and made him look less like a thief.

"Follow my lead," Tony whispered. They walked up to the security room. Tony took a deep breath and walked inside. Two men were busy scanning cameras around the museum. They were talking excitedly in French.

"Richard!" Tony said. Both men looked at him. "They called me in to help. What's up?"

Richard was on the phone. Just then, Tony's phone rang. His caller ID said it was the Louvre. He answered.

"Hello?"

Richard locked eyes with Tony.

"Break-in," Richard said into the phone. "I was calling you in to help."

"Great timing," Tony said, closing his phone and spreading his arms wide. "Here I am!"

"How—" Richard began, but Tony moved over and took a look at the screen.

"I saw her first," Tony said. "Outside. I just reported it to Gerard, and he let me in."

"We were out…sightseeing," added Abigail.

Tony saw Lena's shape just inside the north window.

"Looks like it's just the one," Richard said. "They'll have her in about thirty seconds." He pointed to another screen where two men were advancing down the hall. They were almost to the room Lena was in. One had a gun pulled.

Tony walked over to his own workstation. "Let me see," he said, and sat down. He swiped his own card in the computer, and it opened up to allow him access. Quickly, so no one saw him, he pulled up some film from an hour ago and replaced it with the current running film. Nobody saw him.

"Where did she go?" Richard asked as his screen suddenly showed an empty room.

Next, Tony shut down the inside system and silenced the alarms. The perimeter was still up, but as Lena moved through the museum, the internal security wouldn't pick her up. He had spent several hours this week running this system and knew the ins and outs of it. That, and years of hacking in to places he wasn't supposed to be, had left him skilled in this illegal craft. It was paying off now.

He hoped he wouldn't spend a lifetime in jail paying for it later.

"I'll go check it out," he said, standing.

Abigail followed him into the hallway. He pulled out his phone and saw Lena on his tracker. A map of the Louvre overlaid the grid she was on. "She's smart," he whispered. "Looks like she figured out where they were coming and slipped into this side room here. Some sort of office, if I remember correctly. We need to distract those two men so she can get out."

"Tony," Abigail whispered. "This is definitely crossing the line now. We're playing both sides here. Maybe we should just let them catch her. They think we're here to help. So far, we're not in trouble."

Tony looked at his wife. If they continued, Abigail would go down with him. But if they didn't, Lena would get caught. There was still a chance he could save her. She was his family. But then again, so was Abigail.

Uncertainty stabbed at Tony, an emotion he wasn't familiar with. In the past, he would have done what needed to be done, despite the law. But now those actions could hurt the one woman he loved more than life itself. If Abigail ended up in jail because he tricked the guards, he would never be able to live with himself.

He looked at where Lena was on the grid. The guards were just about on her. "You're right," he said, sighing. "You're right. Of course." He looked up into the eyes of his wife and shrugged. "We'll let her go."

But Abigail's eyes were filled with empathy. She reached up and pressed her palm against his cheek.

"I love you," she said, and she threw her flashlight into a side room. There was a crash.

Tony hoped she hadn't just broken something priceless.

"Here!" Abigail said. "I see the thief here!"

Her distraction worked. The two men rounded the corner, and Abigail pointed into the room toward the noise she had just created.

"Tony?" one of them said.

"They called me in for backup," he said, still recovering from Abigail's actions.

They nodded. "Richard?" said the man into his headpiece. "Do you have the thief on film?"

"Negative. I've lost her," Tony heard Richard reply over the coms.

The two men turned to look at Abigail and Tony. "Stay here. We have a gun." And they went into the room.

Tony faced Abigail. "What have you done?" he whispered.

"Sometimes to do a great right, you must do a little wrong," Abigail said. It was a quote from *The Merchant of Venice*.

Tony kissed Abigail and grabbed her hand. "Come on!" They ran along the hallway the men had just come from and found the room Lena's tracker said she was in. But she was moving, heading toward them. When they reached the door to the room, which was an office, she was just coming through. They all stopped, and Lena drew in her breath. They had startled each other.

"Lena! It's us!" Tony whispered. "This way!"

He made his way quickly to the window and ran his hands along the sill. Finding a wire, he pulled it. Then, with some effort, he slid the window open. They were on the second floor.

"Abigail, get my rope."

"Got it," she said, handing him the rope so they could rappel down the side of the building.

"Lena, you go first," Tony said, turning to hand her the harness. But she was gone.

"Where did she go?" he asked. Abigail looked around and shrugged. He pulled out his phone and looked for her tracker. She was moving east, along the hallway. Working her way toward the Impressionists and the Russo Room. Unfortunately, it would take her right across the paths of the two men they had just escaped.

"Darn it!" he said, coiling his rope up and stuffing it back in his bag. Abigail shut the window, and they ran after Lena. "She's more trouble than she's worth," he mumbled.

They heard footsteps. Abigail grabbed his hand and pulled him back against a wall. They flattened out, and Tony willed his breathing to quiet down.

The footsteps turned down a hall, missing them. Once they were gone, Abigail whispered in his ear. "Where is she?"

He looked at his phone. "Here," he said. "Follow me." He headed toward the Seine side of the museum. "She's headed toward the paintings."

They heard the footsteps of the men heading back. Tony pulled Abigail behind a large statue. They huddled there and saw shadowy figures pass them across the room. The men entered a stairwell.

"They're going downstairs," he said. "This way."

They scurried across the floor. Tony was glad for the low auxiliary lighting so he could see his way around. He was also glad that the cameras were on a loop so no one else could see *them*.

"There!" Abigail said, pointing to a sign that led to a room of paintings containing some Russos Most of his impressionistic work was in the Musée D'Orsay, but his portraits and other paintings still hung here.

As they rounded the corner, Tony fully expected to see Lena. Instead, the room was empty. He turned on his penlight and swept it around in the corners. No Lena.

"Where is she?"

"Look." Abigail was pointing to the wall. Tony turned his light on the large, dark painting hanging in the center of it. A painting had been removed from its original spot on the wall. Hanging in its place was Lena's original work.

The auxiliary lamps in the room cast a soft glow on it, illuminating the play of light on the puddles. The two figures walked hand in hand in a world far kinder than their reality.

"Incredible," Tony said.

"It really is." Abigail whispered.

Tony looked at his phone app again. It said Lena was right in front of him. He walked over to the bench that was set up in front of the painting on the wall so a patron could sit and admire it. On the bench lay Lena's phone. He picked it up. A button on the screen said "Push me." He pushed on it, and the phone sent a text. His own phone buzzed.

He looked at his phone. Abigail peeked at it as he opened the text.

I'm smarter than you think, Sucker. Now you're the one who's gonna get caught.

He closed the app.

"She's gone. Let's get out of here."

They saw a light sweeping along the hallway. "I think they're on their way here," Tony said.

"Sit." Abigail grabbed Tony's hand and pulled him down on the bench. "Play it cool."

The two men entered the room. Tony's back was to the door, but he felt them behind him. "We're too late," Tony said. "They mystery artist has struck."

The two guards walked over to them and stared at the painting. "Richard," the tall man said into his mic, speaking in English for Tony's benefit. "Do you see her?"

"Where are *you*?" Richard's voice came across the mic. "I don't see anybody."

Now we're in for it, Tony thought. *Richard will guess that I created the camera loop.* He looked around. There was no way out of this room except the hallway behind them.

"I think someone has tampered with the system," Richard said. "I think the video feed is looping."

"Really?" said the tall man. He switched over to French, and the three men had a rapid, quiet conversation.

"What's up?" Tony said, standing and turning to face them.

"Someone tampered with the system. It came from your workstation. Tell me again, what exactly are you doing here?"

"I told you, they called me in for backup," Tony said. Beside him, he could feel Abigail's breath quickening. "But I showed up before that because I saw someone breaking in."

"And her?" The tall man nodded toward Abigail.

"We were sightseeing. She's my wife."

"I see. But——"

Richard interrupted him on the coms. "I see the thief! She's going out the window she came in. Vite!"

"Allons-y!" the tall guy said, and the two men took off.

As soon as they were through the door, Tony and Abigail made a run down the hall in the opposite direction and into the office. Abigail shimmied the window open while Tony pulled out his rope. He didn't wait to put a harness on either of them. Grabbing her around the waist, he slid through the window, one arm around Abigail and one arm on the rope. They slid down quickly. As soon as their feet landed, he gave a quick tug on the rope and it fell, coiling at his feet. He heard the blast of alarms behind him. They had triggered the perimeter alarms.

"Let's go," he said, ducking behind some bushes. They made their way along the wall until they came to the edge of the shrubbery and then casually began walking along the street. It wasn't until they had turned a few corners and were well away from the museum that Tony turned to Abigail.

"I think we made it."

"You mean until they find us," she said.

"They weren't ever really after us. I mean, I was there to *help*. Right?" He grinned at her. "I have to admit, I have always wanted to break in to the Louvre."

He tried to keep the mood light, but Abigail's hands were shaking. They walked a few more minutes and then sat on a park bench.

"What do you think happened to Lena?" Abigail asked.

Tony had her phone now, so there was no way to track her. "I don't know. Maybe she escaped when we did. I was hoping the diversion we created would be enough cover for her."

He was unsure where to go next. Were they fugitives? If they went back to their hotel room, would someone be looking for them? Or did the men at the Louvre buy his story that he had come to help? After all, he had used his official name badge to scan in. He had reported a break-in. And Richard had been on the phone to call him.

"I can't believe Ms. Scott has finally put her trust back in us and we're going to end up in jail," Abigail said.

Tony laughed. "That's what your concern is right now? What Ms. Scott thinks?"

"Yes," Abigail said. "And Jimmy. Jimmy will be so disappointed." She sniffed.

"Are you crying?" Tony turned and tried to see her face in the dark.

"No. Of course not!" But she sniffed again.

He sighed and leaned against the back of the bench. He reached for Abigail's hand and found it in the darkness. It was cold.

"I guess Pauline will take care of Cocoa. But her husband is allergic to cats."

"Abigail, stop it," Tony said. "You're being morbid. We're fine."

She turned to him. "How do you know that exactly? *We just broke in to the Louvre!*"

"No. We were *let in to* the Louvre by a guard who knows me. There's a difference."

"Your version of reality has always been a little twisted."

"What does that mean?"

"Exactly what I said."

She pulled her hand out of his. He sighed. She was angry with him now. And why not? She had every right to be. Although he had told her not to come.

"I told you to stay behind."

"And let you go to jail alone?"

"It's not like we'll be bunkmates," he said.

"Maybe we won't make it that far. Bonnie and Clyde were ambushed and died together. Somebody will write a book about us. Death in the Louvre. Death Along the Seine."

"Death in the Park."

They both jumped at the voice behind them. "You two make enough noise to wake the dead," Lena said, coming around the bench and sitting next to them.

"Lena," Tony said, scooting closer to the edge so Abigail could move in and make more room for Lena.

"Can I have my phone back?"

Tony dug in his pocket and handed it to her.

"Take the tracker off."

He took it back, and Lena watched as he signed in to the app and removed it. He handed it back to her.

"Do the guards at the Louvre know who I am?" Lena asked. "Did you give them my name?"

"What? No!" Tony said. "Heck, they might be after us too."

There were sirens in the distance. They were quiet and listened. The sirens grew more distant, moving away from them.

"You lied to me," Lena said to Tony. Her voice was steely. "You said you would help me, and you led me to believe you were. You gave me information which didn't work and nearly got me caught when I went through the window."

"I tried to tell you that," Tony said.

"That's why we followed you!" Abigail said. "We wanted to warn you!"

"You said you were helping me," Lena said again. "And then you turned on me. Both of you did. I thought I had finally found someone who was different. Someone who cared!" Her voice was rising with her emotions. "You invited me to that dinner, bought me a nice skirt. I thought, for a moment, that maybe I could be part of your little family. That us being cousins might really matter to you!"

"It does!" Tony said. But she interrupted him.

"And then you sold me out right there at the dinner table. John Doe texted me and said I will never work in the underground world again because I can't be trusted to deliver."

Lena stood and looked down at Tony. "All you really care about is yourself. You're more interested in making sure you survive than anything else. You look out for number one."

Tony was quiet. It was true. He had spent most of his life looking out for himself.

"You're right," he said quietly. "I see what I can do to stay out of trouble, even if it means sacrificing others. But I'm trying to change."

"People can't change," Lena said.

"Yes, they can. Just not overnight. I'm learning that it's a process."

"Lena," Abigail said gently. "Let us help you."

197

"No!" Lena said, her voice rising again. They heard police sirens in the distance. "Your help has been nothing but trouble. My life was going well until the two of you stepped into it."

"We didn't exactly do that on our own," Abigail reminded her. "You pulled us in."

"I'm usually a better judge of character," Lena growled, as the sirens came closer. "Go home, Tony Russo. You make a mess of every life you touch."

"Hey!" Abigail said, angrily, but Lena walked around the bench. The girl stepped back behind some bushes and slipped off into the darkness.

"Let her go," Tony said, reaching for Abigail's hand again.

She gave it a squeeze. "It's not true, what she said."

"It has some truth to it," Tony replied. "Still no regrets?"

Abigail sighed and leaned back, looking up at the stars in the night sky. "I have plenty of regrets. But none of them involve marrying you, if that's what you mean."

Tony looked up at the stars too. The police sirens disappeared again, moving away from them.

"I really messed her life up," he said.

"We both did. We'll find a way to fix it."

The night was quiet except for the slight rustle of the leaves overhead. A small mouse darted out onto the sidewalk, saw them, and then ran back under a bush.

"I guess we should move," Tony said. "Let's go back to the hotel. They'll either be waiting for us there or not. If not, let's go to bed. Grandma always told me things are easier with a good night's sleep."

He stood, and holding the hand of his bride, they walked through the darkness back to their hotel. Just as they were about to go upstairs, Abigail's phone rang. It was Giselle.

Chapter Thirty-One

"Abigail, it's Giselle!" the girl said, unnecessarily. "I need your help!" She was sobbing again. Abigail put the phone on speaker so Tony could hear. "Lena sent me a text. She is being chased by the police. They've figured out that she was the one who hung the painting in the Louvre! They're here at our apartment. What should I do? Should I let them in?"

"Do they have a warrant?" Abigail asked.

"A warrant?"

"Can you leave through your bedroom window?" Tony asked.

"Um, maybe. I think so?" They heard some sounds like a chair scraping across the floor and a window sliding up. "Yes. I can get down."

"Okay. Be careful," Abigail said. "Find a place to hide. We'll try to find Lena. Do you know where she is?"

But Tony had pulled out his phone. There it was, the blinking red light of Lena's tracker. "I didn't really delete it. I thought it might come in handy," he said.

"Never mind," Abigail said to Giselle. "Just go. We'll call you later and tell you where to meet us." She ended the call.

Lena was headed north, toward the center of town. They heard police sirens in the distance again.

"Giselle says they found her," Abigail said. "Do you think those are the police who are after her? They're certainly headed in the right direction."

"Maybe if we get there first, we can talk her in to surrendering," Tony said. "She hasn't done anything too bad so far. Just breaking and entering."

They were running along the sidewalk in the general direction of where Lena was heading.

"And stealing," Abigail said.

"But they might not have records for that. I didn't see any police records for Lena under either of her names when I was snooping."

Abigail was worried about Giselle. Where would the girl go if Lena went to prison? Maybe she should have told her to let the police in. What if they broke the door down? But no, it was best Giselle stayed out of this. Best if she wasn't there when they showed up. She was afraid the girl would get hurt, and the girl was obviously afraid of the police and what they might do to her and Lena, judging by her frantic phone call.

She needed someone she could trust. Abigail wanted to be that person. She swore to herself that before this trip was over, she'd figure out a way to help Giselle. She hoped it wasn't too late for Lena, as well.

"She's headed toward the Eiffel Tower, I think," Tony said.

"We shouldn't flag a cab," Abigail said, jogging along with Tony. She was glad she did cardio at home on the treadmill. "We don't want to leave a trail."

"Correct thinking, Mrs. Cat Burglar."

The streets were nearly empty, but it was a Friday in Paris. Or actually, close to 2 a.m. Some of the pubs were still open, and Abigail could see people through the windows, sitting in groups, drinking.

They turned a corner, and there was the Eiffel Tower, lit up in all its glory. Abigail caught her breath. It was incredible at night, and she believed if she lived in this city she'd never get tired of looking at it.

The festival was up ahead, and people were still milling about. Abigail saw a crowd gathered around the base of the Eiffel Tower. There were musicians playing some punk rock and several people dancing to their music. To her left, she saw some acrobats building a human pyramid. The man on top was tossing a flaming sword. To her right, there were three clowns, swaying together comically to the beat of the music. One reached into his hat and pulled out a handkerchief, which he waved around. The handkerchief seemed to disappear into

200

thin air. Because of the hour, the clown faces seemed almost ghoulish to Abigail. She found herself uttering a prayer for God to keep her and Tony safe.

They stopped to catch their breath. Tony's phone indicated that Lena was somewhere in the crowd. Police cars were circling the area. Their lights were on, but their sirens were now turned off. One stopped, and two officers with dogs got out.

"There!" Tony said, nodding to his right. Abigail squinted into the crowd, near the area he indicated. The music was loud. There were so many people in the crowd that she was having trouble picking out individuals. But then she saw Lena. The small, hooded figure was slightly bent over as if she carried a weight on her shoulders.

She does, Abigail thought. The weight of the world.

They followed her. The police were closing in on Lena, with some to her right and some to her left. Lena looked around, frightened. Abigail was close enough now that she could see the panicked look on her face.

Suddenly, Lena blended in with a crowd who was heading into an elevator to go up to the top of the Eiffel Tower. The doors shut just as the police shouted for them to stop. But it was too late. Lena was on her way up.

"Let's go!" Abigail said. Suddenly, she could only think of stopping Lena, of saving her. She had to, for Giselle. The girl's face came to mind, so young, so frightened. She needed to come out of hiding and live. Abigail was determined that she find a normal life.

"Tickets are sold out," a middle-aged man next to her said. He seemed a bit intoxicated. He swayed, sloshing some of his beer on Abigail's arm.

"No problem," Tony said to her. "We have some, remember?"

He pulled out his wallet, and to Abigail's relief, there were the tickets he had bought earlier.

He showed them to the lobby guard, who let them get in line for the next elevator up.

It came quickly. Despite the desperate nature of their visit, Abigail was still enthralled with the view. As the glass-encased elevator carried her up, she watched the City of Light expand beneath her. It was exhilarating.

Before the doors opened, an announcement came over the microphone, first in French, then in English, and then in what sounded like Chinese. It was about rules and safety. Abigail hardly listened.

They stepped out onto the observation deck. The wind was harsh, and she zipped her hooded jacket closed. The stars above her seemed closer than ever, and people around her were taking photos of the city lit up below. The crowd was thick and smelled of beer and perfume.

She saw Lena across the way from her. There was an area with caution tape and boards across it, blocked off for repair. Lena headed toward it, ducked under the tape and kicked down the boards.

Another elevator door opened, and several police officers poured out, including the two with the dogs.

"Arret!" one shouted, which Abigail knew meant "stop" in French.

Lena froze and then began to slowly back up toward the railing. Because of the construction, there was no protective caging above it.

"Wait!" Abigail said, pushing through the crowd. "Wait!" The wind carried her words off. She didn't know if she was shouting to the police to wait or to Lena. She just knew she had to get between them. Tony was right by her side.

But Lena was grasping the railing, her hands on it, ready to boost herself up.

The police shouted something in French. Lena responded by climbing fully onto the rail. She was now sitting on the railing, with an eighty-one-story drop behind her. Her hood blew back, and her hair came loose from its ponytail. Her hair whipped around her face, blowing across her eyes.

"Oh, dear God." Abigail stopped so fast, Tony bumped in to her. "Dear God, no. No Lena," she prayed.

"Lena!" Tony shouted. Lena heard his voice and turned toward them.

"Get back!" Lena shouted. "Everybody get back!" By now, the people in the crowd had noticed what was happening.

Their reactions varied. Some of them were horrified, holding hands against their chest or in front of their mouths. Some of them had pulled out their phones and were videotaping.

Guards appeared and started pushing them back. Someone turned on a walkie-talkie and said something. Probably letting the people down below know what was happening.

The police reached them and began pushing them back.

"We know her," Tony said. "She's my cousin. Please let us stay."

A policeman shouted something in French to Lena. She nodded.

Abigail wasn't sure what just transpired, but he let Tony and Abigail stay. Maybe if Lena had acknowledged that they were relatives, there was hope. Abigail and Tony ducked under the tape as the police were removing it.

"Lena," Abigail shouted against the wind. The gusts were powerful and cold. "You can't jump. Think of Giselle. She needs you!"

"There's nothing left for me here," Lena said. Tears were now running down her face. She could neither brush them away, nor push the hair out of her eyes. If she let go of the railing with either hand, Abigail was sure the girl would fall.

"She'll jump," Tony said, so that only Abigail could hear. "We've taken everything from her."

"Not Giselle. She still has Giselle."

The police had formed a semi-circle around Lena, reaching hands out toward her. One of them, ironically, had pulled his gun. They were shouting for her to come down.

The staff was slowly clearing the crowd out, sending them back down in the elevators.

"Lena, please. Let's talk," Abigail said.

"Stay away!" Lena shouted to the police. They had frozen and weren't advancing any closer. The one officer had put his gun away. An older one, probably in his fifties, was speaking calmly to Lena in French. He reminded Abigail a little bit of Jimmy, her dear cop friend back home. She would give anything to have him here with her right now. Jimmy would know what to do.

The wind beat harder around them, a gust picking up some loose paper and swirling it around the deck. It blew over the railing and disappeared in the space below them.

"Lena, let's talk, please," Abigail said.

"You have ruined *everything!*" Lena shouted to Abigail and Tony. "Everything I have worked so hard for!" She turned to the police. "I am *not* going to jail!" Then she said something to them in French, probably repeating the same thing.

"You won't go to jail," Tony said, making promises he couldn't keep. "We will help you."

"You lie!" Lena shouted. "That's all you are. A liar! Just like the rest of them!"

Abigail didn't have to ask who "the rest of them" meant. Lena had been betrayed by a lot of people. The people who should have cared for her.

The wind blew Lena's long, dark hair, and it stood out around her, reminding Abigail of the wings of Nemesis, like in Lena's paintings. She thought of the small, blond-haired girl in the paintings and how Nemesis stood guard over her. Protecting her. Wanting her to be safe, while reminding the world of all she herself had lost. Retribution.

And then the signature. A symbol of hearth and home. Happiness. Warmth.

Safety.

"Lena, we will keep you safe," Abigail said, taking a step closer. "Give me your hand, and I'll help you. I'll keep you safe. I will."

Out of the corner of her eye, she saw one of the police officers circling around closer to the side. It looked like he was heading for the rail and was going to come up alongside Lena. Abigail locked eyes with Lena, trying to distract her so the officer could grab her.

"Give me your hand," Abigail said, taking another step.

"Don't come closer," Lena said. But Abigail was close enough now that she could hear her above the wind without shouting. Tony slowly walked up beside Abigail. They were just out of reach of Lena.

Lena was crying harder now. "I've ruined everything, Abigail. Everything," Lena said. "There's no way I'll get out of this. They'll know what I've done. They have found the paintings by now. I'm sure they are searching my apartment. Giselle said that they were trying to get in. I'm lost. It's too late."

Lena turned to look down. She wobbled on the rail and almost fell backward. Her seat was precarious, and the wind wasn't helping. It kept rocking her. Her hair and her clothes were blowing wildly.

"You're Tony's cousin," Abigail pleaded. "He has been looking for family for his entire life. He can't lose you now."

She was trying to think of anything to keep the girl from jumping. Lena still had both legs on this side of the railing. But if she leaned back, even a little, she'd lose her balance and fall backward.

Lena was sobbing now. "It's too late," she said. "Too late."

"It's not too late," Tony said. "It's never too late."

The cop was almost on her, but he was not close enough to reach her yet. Lena saw him.

"Don't touch me!" Lena screamed and jerked her arm away. She lost her balance, and her hand flailed wildly. She was going over.

Chapter Thirty-Two

Tony's heart jumped in his chest as he watched Lena almost fall backward, but she caught herself. She had strong core muscles and was good at climbing. Her balance was intact.

"Don't anybody move," she said, between sobs. "You all just go away and leave me alone."

The deck was cleared out by now. Just Abigail and Tony remained, along with five police officers. The police stood in a semi-circle around Abigail and Tony, who were closest to Lena. The young officer along the railing had retreated a few steps back to his line.

"It's never too late," Tony repeated.

"I've done things," Lena said. "I've messed my life up. And things have been done to me." She was still crying, choking the words out.

"We know," Tony said. "But you're safe now. Giselle will be safe. We need to go home and get her."

Lena didn't seem to hear him. Her eyes were still on Abigail.

"You have the ring," Lena said. "All you have to do is sell it, and you'll be set for life. All you ever wanted."

"I have *him*," Abigail said, pointing to Tony. "He's all I ever wanted. This ring is a symbol of that. I love this ring because Tony gave it to me. And I can trust him. That's worth more than money. And Lena, you can have that too. You're smart, beautiful, resourceful. There are people out there who love you."

"Like who?"

"Like us," Tony said. "You're my family."

Lena turned her gaze to Tony. She gave him a wry smile. "That would be nice," she said, her voice quieter. "I could come to Sunday dinners and make small talk. We could all pretend. But you know that will never happen. I'm a thief. I've broken rules and hurt people. It's too late for me, Tony."

Lena turned and swung one leg over the railing so she was straddling it. Tony's heart jumped again in his chest.

"I thought that about me, too," he said. "I thought it was too late for me. Nobody would ever love me, not like I was. Not with what I did. How could anybody ever trust me? And then someone did."

He looked at Abigail. Tears were running down his wife's face. "Abigail believed in me, and it changed my world."

"But I don't have an Abigail. Or a Tony," Lena said. "I won't even have a Giselle after tonight. They'll take her from me. I don't have anybody to believe in me, and therefore I am nothing. I can't change. It's too late for that." She swung her other leg over. Now she was sitting facing out, her legs dangling over the side of the Eiffel Tower. She was going to jump.

"Abigail cut a quote out of the paper and put it on our fridge," Tony said, looking at Lena and inching closer to her. "It says, 'You can't go back and change the beginning, but you can start where you are and change the ending.'" I have a lot of regrets, Lena. Probably more than you do. I've hurt a lot of people, including you. But I am trying to change. And I have changed."

"Is that why you lied to me?"

"I was trying to protect you!" Tony said. "I'm not perfect, but I know someone who will never, ever let you down. God."

Lena laughed up at the sky. "God? God will send me to hell. But what's that matter? Life here has been hell too."

"Redemption is possible," Tony said. "God not only forgives, He forgets. All you have to do is ask. Jesus took your place on the cross, Lena. Don't put yourself up there too. Take His gift. He will forgive you completely, and you can start over. That's what I did. I started over."

Tony's cheeks were cold, and he brushed his hand against them, realizing he was crying. Lena was swinging her legs now. He wasn't about to stand here and watch his cousin die.

He took another step closer, as did Abigail.

Suddenly Abigail pointed. "There's Giselle! Oh my gosh, Lena, don't jump. Don't let her see you die. She's been through enough!"

Lena looked down. So did Tony. He could see the blond hair and a pale face looking up. Abigail was pushing buttons on her phone. "I have her on the line, Lena," she said, holding the phone out. "Talk to her."

Abigail was reaching the phone toward Lena when the Lena cried out, "Boucher! That's Boucher, and he has Giselle!"

Tony saw a large man down below grab the girl. How did he find her? There's no way Boucher could know where they were. The girls hadn't been in contact with him. Then Tony remembered how Boucher had brushed up against him in the stairwell. The ink pen. It was still in his jacket pocket. Boucher had put a tracker on him.

"Save her! He will hurt her!" Lena shouted. She jerked her head around to look to the police for help and lost her balance again. This time, as she flailed her arms, Tony knew she wouldn't be able to save herself. As he saw her slipping, he lunged toward her, grabbing her wrist. Then she disappeared over the side.

The jerk on his arm was enormous as she fell, but he caught her, nearly taking him with her. His ribcage hit the railing, stopping him, and pain tore through his shoulder. He had a grip on her wrist. She wasn't heavy, but he didn't have a good hold.

"Abigail!" he said, trying to talk through the pain. "My bag. Get my rope."

Abigail unzipped his bag and dug in to it, as two of the officers ran up to them. They tried to help Tony, but Lena was so far over none of them could get a grip on her.

"Lena, look at me," Tony said, half hanging over the edge. Lena's wide eyes were looking up at him. "Don't look down," he said, between clenched teeth. He felt an officer grab him around the waist, holding on.

Abigail tried to loop the rope around Lena, but it she couldn't reach. "You'll have to make a slip knot," Tony said, grateful he had taught her the different knots. She worked quickly and slipped it down.

"How do I get it around her wrist? Your arm's in the way!"

That was a problem. All Tony knew was that his fingers were slipping. He was losing his grip on Lena's wrist.

Abigail grabbed the other end of the rope and flung it downward. She leaned far over the railing herself, while an officer hugged her around the waist. The wind tore her own hair from its ribbon, and it blew around her face, getting in her eyes. She managed to wrap the rope around Lena's wrist anyway. She tied a knot, hoping it was a good one.

Tony's hand slipped, and Lena screamed.

Chapter Thirty-Three

Abigail felt the rope slipping fast through her hands. Tony grabbed hold with his good hand, and both of the officers grabbed hold. There was a jerk.

The knot held.

Abigail took a deep breath and peeked over the side. Lena was dangling from the rope, swinging back and forth, hanging nearly a thousand feet above the ground. She was screaming.

The four of them pulled her up, hand over hand, and hauled her over the side. Abigail reached for the knot, untying it. Lena's wrist was broken. Tony quickly embraced Lena with his left arm. The girl was sobbing.

"You're okay," he said, holding her against his chest with one arm. "You're okay."

Abigail brushed the tears away from her own eyes. "Are *you* okay?" she asked her husband. His arm was hanging limply from the socket.

He nodded. "But I'm pretty sure it's dislocated."

Lena pulled away. "We have to save Giselle! Boucher has her! How did he find her?" Her voice was a wail. Her hands were shaking, and her whole body was trembling. She was cold, and it looked like she was going in to shock.

"Shhhhh," he said. "You're okay. We're going to find her." She saw Tony put his good arm around Lena again, trying to warm her. He reached his bad arm out toward Abigail. "Pull," he said. He clenched his teeth together, and his face was contorted in pain.

"You mean…?" Her stomach clenched.

"Yes." He closed his eyes.

210

She had once seen Jimmy reset someone's arm on a patrol. She didn't have time to think it through. Giselle needed them. She reached for Tony's arm, lifted it to a ninety-degree angle, and gave it a yank.

Tony yelled a loud, primitive noise and then opened his watering eyes. He lifted his arm up. "Thanks."

"Yep."

"Back in place." But he looked like he could use a strong painkiller.

Abigail had lost the phone connection when Boucher grabbed Giselle. She dialed several times as she waited for the elevator but got nothing.

"How did he find her?" Lena kept saying over and over, like a mantra, trying to pull away from Tony.

"We'll get her," Tony said. "I promise. Give me your phone. Do you have Find Friends or something so we can find her?"

The officers took Lena. One put a handcuff around her good wrist, which Abigail was somewhat glad about. It would keep her from hurting herself. Lena sunk to her knees in a defeated heap, her shoulders heaving.

"We'll take her to the station and get her some help," one of the officers told Abigail. Thankfully, he spoke English. "These two here will help you find the other girl. They speak some English."

"This is my fault," Tony said as they waited for the elevator.

"What is? Lena?"

"Boucher. I'm the way he found us. I think he put a tracker on me." Tony pulled the pen out of his pocket. "Here." He unscrewed it and sure enough, there it was. He dropped the small device on the floor and crushed it under his heel.

"Why?"

"I guess he was suspicious. He saw me on the stairs, leaving. I could tell by the look in his eyes he didn't believe my story that I was there looking for a hookup with a woman."

His eyes were full of grief.

She didn't have time to deal with this now. She turned and briefly explained to the police what she knew about Giselle on the trip down to the lobby. When the elevator doors opened, Abigail rushed outside and looked frantically about. "I don't see them," she said. But how could you in this crowd? And in the dark?

"Call her again," Tony said.

Abigail tried Giselle's number again. It rang about six times and then went to voice mail. "I'm hoping that Lena has her on the Find Friends app," he said. He pulled her phone out of his pocket. "I figured this was the best way to trace her." He opened it.

"There," Abigail said, pointing. Lena had loaded Giselle's number into the app.

"She's at Boucher's apartment," Tony said.

Abigail grabbed the phone and took off running. All she could think about was Boucher and the horrible things Tony had described to her from the medical records. Lena beaten. Lena's mom dead, most likely at the hand of Boucher. And now Giselle. What would he do to her in his angry state?

"Abigail, wait!" Tony said, but he was a few strides behind her. The police were behind him.

She flagged down a taxi. It had taken a while to get Lena up over the wall, and for them to get down here. Boucher had quite a lead on them.

Abigail jumped in the taxi and shouted the address to the driver. She saw Tony running after her but didn't have time to wait for him.

The driver pulled away from the curb and was there in less than five minutes.

Abigail handed him some bills and jumped out. She remembered Tony saying that Boucher was in 2C. She ran up the stairs, not caring that she was making noise.

"Giselle!" she said when she reached the door. "Giselle! Let me in!"

The logical part of her mind told her that stealth would have been better. That it would have been wiser to wait for Tony and try to break in with him. That now Boucher knew Dana's name was Giselle.

Nobody answered. There was silence from inside.

Abigail rifled through her bag for the paperclip. She quickly picked the lock on the door and turned the handle. No deadbolt. She pushed the door open.

"Hey!" Boucher said as he came walking toward her. He was a big hulk of a man. Bits of something, maybe crumbs, stuck to the stubble on his face. He smelled of sweat and booze.

"You're breaking in to my place! What do you want?"

But as his eyes traveled up and down Abigail, a predatory grin came to his face. "You want to come in, little lady?"

"Where's the girl?" she said.

"What girl?"

"Don't play dumb with me!" Abigail said. "I know you have her!"

"Why don't you come in, and I'll let you see?"

Abigail hesitated. She didn't hear any sound from within to let her know Giselle was actually with him. She knew Tony and the police must be right behind her.

"I think I'll wait here," she said, but Boucher was quick. He reached out and grabbed her around the wrist, pulling her inside. He shut the door quickly behind them and pulled the deadbolt across. Apparently, the door had one after all.

"Hey!" Abigail said.

Boucher let her go, but he was now between her and the door. She knew she was no match for him in size.

"Show me the girl," she said, trying not to sound as scared as she was.

He laughed.

"Giselle!" she yelled. There was no answer.

Boucher walked toward her, and she slowly backed up, which was pushing her further inside his apartment. She passed a coffee table, which had a stack of porn magazines on top of it with a spilled can of beer soaking through some of them. An empty pizza box sat next to it.

Boucher grabbed her wrist again. Jimmy had taught her plenty of self-defense, but her mind had gone blank. Where was Tony? Where were the police officers?

She swallowed. He pushed her past the coffee table and up against the couch.

"What do you want with the girl?" he growled. "Why are you and that guy snooping around?"

"Why do *you* want her?" Abigail asked.

"She's my daughter. And she's worth something. Lena accidently told me that, when she left here one day in an angry tirade. Said they're related to a famous painter named Russo. And that means money. So I looked up this Antonio Russo guy. And then I saw that there was another Russo living in America and running a security company. Claiming to also be a relative of this painter. And apparently a former thief."

Tony.

"Nice photo of him on his website. Imagine my surprise when I met him on the stairwell. What was he looking for in my apartment? If it's proof that the girls are related to Russo, it ain't here, or I'd be rich by now."

Abigail remembered something Jimmy had taught her. She head-butted him hard, hitting his nose, hopefully enough to break it. While he howled in pain, she brought her knee up and hit him between the legs.

Boucher doubled over but regained himself quickly. He swore in French, took hold of her wrist again, harder this time, and threw her down on the couch.

"I'll teach you to mess with me," he said, bringing his hand across her face. The slap stung, and her eyes swam with tears. She tasted blood.

"Tony!" she called, knowing he couldn't hear her.

She would never be able to save Giselle now. Boucher had both of her wrists pinned above her head, pushing her down on the couch. Pressing his knee across her thighs, he held her so was now unable to kick at him. She was trapped. He raised his free hand to slap her again. Abigail closed her eyes, waiting for the pain to come.

Chapter Thirty-Four

Tony's hands were shaking as he used his tool to laser through the dead bolt on Boucher's door. Why did they all have to have deadbolts?

He couldn't believe Abigail had left him. It took him and the two officers a few minutes to get to the police car after she sped away in the taxi. She was stubborn and strong-willed.

On the ride here, he was swearing under his breath, both in English and in French. He had even thrown in the few Italian curse words he knew.

He alternated that with praying.

"Please God, let her be okay," he kept repeating. Fear gripped his heart as he thought of life without Abigail. He had almost lost her, just a few months ago. This felt like déjà vu.

The metal deadbolt finally snapped in two, and he threw his body against the door. The force carried him inside. The two police officers followed.

He saw Abigail on the couch, and Boucher's arm coming down at her face.

"Freeze!" one of the policemen shouted, pulling his gun, but Tony had already launched himself at Boucher. He hit him full force and took him down, knocking him away from Abigail onto the floor. He landed a punch in the man's face.

Boucher roared and sat up, practically flinging Tony off. But Tony came back at him, elbowing him in the side of the head. Boucher rocked for a moment, about to lose consciousness. But then he grabbed Tony's leg, pulling him down.

"Freeze!" the policeman shouted again.

Boucher ignored the policeman and punched at Tony. Tony's arm was still sore, and with every movement, he felt a searing pain in his shoulder socket. Boucher was suddenly on top of him, and he saw the man's beefy fist rise for a blow to his face.

This was gonna hurt.

But someone kicked Boucher in the ribs. It was Abigail. Then a police officer jumped Boucher and hit him across the head with something hard. Boucher's eyes rolled into the back of his head, but he regained himself. Tony jumped up.

What would it take to down this man?

Boucher flung both arms wide, knocking Tony and the officer down, and barreled his way into the hallway towards the bedrooms. He disappeared into a room and slammed the door closed. Tony heard it lock.

"Where's Giselle?" Tony asked. Abigail shook her head. He saw another room at the end of the hall and ran toward it.

The girl was tied to a chair, her wrists bound behind her. There was duct tape across her mouth. Her blond hair was a mess, falling across her face and sticking to her cheeks, which were wet with tears.

"Giselle!" Abigail said. But she was shoved from behind and landed hard on her knees. It was Boucher. In his hands was a Glock, and he pointed it at Giselle.

"Freeze!" one of the officers shouted.

"Put the gun down or the girl dies!" Boucher shouted back.

Everything stopped for a moment. Tony was about two feet from Giselle. He had his hands in the air. Abigail was still on her knees and had crawled over to the side of the room, out of Boucher's way. The police officer was behind Boucher, in the hallway, his gun pointing at Boucher' back. Behind him was the second policeman.

And Boucher was pointing the gun right at Giselle.

"Take it easy," Tony said.

"Don't move!" Boucher roared. "She's my daughter, and I have custody of her. Everyone needs to leave. Now!"

"People don't normally tie up their daughters," Tony said quietly.

Boucher swung the gun across to Tony. He heard Abigail gasp.

"You want to die tonight?" Boucher spat at him.

"Not particularly," Tony said. "But maybe we can make a deal." As he talked, he moved. Slowly. Boucher's gun followed him. He flicked the safety off the gun.

"Tony, no," Abigail said.

"Put the gun down or I shoot," the police officer said to Boucher.

Tony was now squarely between Boucher and Giselle.

"Looks like tonight's your night," Boucher said and started to squeeze the trigger. Tony heard a loud gunshot, and Abigail screamed.

He was waiting for the pain in his chest. For the blood. Then, as if in slow motion, he saw Boucher crumple and fall to the floor. A large red spot on the back of the man's shirt began to spread, and blood pooled on the dirty carpet.

The officer ran to Boucher and checked his pulse.

"He's dead."

Tony turned around to Giselle, who was shaking and crying. He carefully removed the duct tape from her mouth. His arm hurt something awful.

"You're safe now," he said.

Abigail was there beside him. She had pulled his knife out of his tool bag and was sawing at the duct tape around Giselle's wrists. Then the girl was free.

Giselle crumpled in the chair, shaking and sobbing. Abigail put her arms around her. "Shhh. You're okay now. You're safe. And Lena is safe. It's all over."

Tony turned to look at the man lying on the floor. The puddle of blood had grown larger. One of the officers was on his phone, making a call. Tony heard sirens in the distance.

"You're okay," he heard Abigail say to Giselle again. His arm was throbbing. It felt wet. He sank down in a chair.

"Tony? Are you hit?" It was Abigail's voice. It seemed far away. He rubbed his good hand across his forehead, trying to clear his thoughts. Then everything faded to black.

Chapter Thirty-Five

Abigail watched as the ambulance driver waved smelling salts in front of Tony's nose. His eyes fluttered open.

"Thank God," Abigail breathed.

Her husband looked up at her. It was those dark eyes and long lashes that she had first fallen in love with when he had broken in to her library just six months ago.

"What happened?" He tried to sit up.

She put a firm hand on his chest. "Lie still. You're okay. Apparently, Boucher shot at you. But the officer's gun hit him first, throwing his aim off. Still, it grazed your shoulder. The pain of that and your dislocation was apparently too much."

Tony was quiet, considering that for a moment. "You mean, I was *shot?*"

"Yes." She brushed his hair off his forehead.

"Cool," he said, giving her a weak smile.

She couldn't stop the tears that came. One fell on his cheek.

"Hey, beautiful," he said. "I'm fine." He pushed himself up on the elbow of his good arm.

"This will help the pain," the EMT said, and handed Tony some tablets and a glass of water.

Tony hesitated. "What's this? Where's Giselle?"

"It's just ibuprofen," Abigail said. "Take it. And she's fine. She's in the other ambulance."

"There's more than one ambulance?"

Abigail laughed. "We don't do anything small-scale."

There was a lot of paperwork. First at the hospital and then at the police station. Abigail called Julia, who agreed to meet them there to discuss the foster care system in France.

"I'll talk to some people this morning and see where I can place her," Julia said. "Until I find a place, she can stay with me."

"She'll come back to the hotel with us for a few hours first," Abigail said. She was sitting next to Giselle on a hard metal bench at the station. "We're in our hotel room until noon."

Tony was talking to the police. There was a lot to tell, starting with Boucher and his abusive background. He was trying to see if they could pin the murder of Lena and Giselle's mom on him. Not that it really mattered now. Boucher was dead.

Then there was Lena. Tony was trying to get her out on bail. He and Abigail had agreed to pay the bail when it was set, but it looked like that wouldn't be until Monday morning. The police had searched her apartment and knew she was the mystery artist. They had her on charges of breaking and entering, but so far, nothing else. She had been careful, and none of her past career moves as a thief were showing up. She didn't even have a police record in the system. She was clean, as far as the world knew, except for the crime of putting paintings *in to* a museum. Abigail and Tony dropped the search on the ring, claiming they had found it themselves. They explained that it had rolled under the bed at the hotel.

Giselle was holding Abigail's hand tightly. She was scared to death.

Abigail gave her a smile. "You can see Lena soon," she said.

At the hospital, while they waited for Tony to be checked out, Giselle had confessed to Abigail that she was the one who put the smoke bombs in the culinary school, and the one who had stolen her purse. She was also the one who followed them, feeding information to Lena such as when Tony got his job at the Louvre. Giselle was not a suspect in anything, and Abigail wanted to keep it that way.

Tony finally came over and sat next to Abigail.

"Well?" she asked.

"It looks like we're all free to go," Tony said. He looked meaningfully at Giselle. "*All* of us. We can't see Lena now. They are still booking her, and they want her to talk with a psychiatrist. We can see her in the morning." Abigail looked at her phone. Morning was practically here.

"What about the Louvre?"

"I was called in to help out, so we're okay. I told them we jumped out of the window to look for Lena. Which is true," Tony said.

"And how did Boucher find us? The pen had a tracker?"

"Yeah," Tony said. "He stuck it in my jacket pocket. They found several in his house. Looks like he has been looking for Giselle for a while. I probably looked suspicious to him so he thought he'd give it a shot that I was a lead to her. People are under the impression that we Russos are worth a lot of money. I don't know why, since my grandfather died penniless."

"Maybe he was going to try to lay claim to the *Laurel* painting."

"Maybe."

"I've called our lawyer," Abigail said. Stewart was going to see what he could do for Lena. "He'll try to find her a good attorney over here."

"What about Giselle?" Tony said.

Abigail met Tony's eyes. She couldn't imagine leaving her here. He understood and nodded.

"Giselle? Do you want to come back to the States with us?" he said. "We can get you enrolled in college. You could live with us or with my Grandma. She'd love you."

Giselle shook her head. "No. I have to stay here. France is my home. I love my country, and I love Lena. I need to be here for my sister."

"I'll make sure she's okay," Julia said.

"The paperwork is all filled out," Abigail told Tony. "Giselle will be in the foster system until she turns eighteen next month. Julia says they'll find her a place to stay until she starts college in the fall. They'll help her get enrolled. And of course, if Lena gets to come home, Giselle can stay with her." Abigail squeezed Giselle's hand again. "It'll be okay."

"Let's go get some rest," Tony said.

220

They took a cab back to the hotel. The sun was rising as they got out and walked into their hotel lobby. Upstairs, Abigail closed the curtains and tucked Giselle into the bed opposite of theirs. The girl was asleep in minutes.

She turned to Tony and threw her arms around his neck. She was careful how she hugged him. His arm was bandaged from the bullet wound and was in a sling so his shoulder could heal from the dislocation.

"I was so scared you were going to die," she whispered into his neck.

"And leave you? Never." But he pressed her against him with his good arm and held her there. "When I knew that Boucher had you..." He didn't finish the sentence. He couldn't. She felt his shoulders shaking. "It was *my* fault he found us."

"Oh, honey, I'm okay," she said quietly, holding him tighter.

He sniffed a few times and kept his face hidden in her hair. When he had composed himself, he pulled back and met her eyes. His own were red and watery.

"He hurt you," he said. "I wasn't fast enough." He tenderly traced the cut on her lip from where Boucher had hit her. "And we almost lost Lena. *I* almost lost Lena. She was going to jump."

He closed his eyes. Abigail pulled him to her again.

"But she didn't. She's alive, and so is Giselle. And they both have a new future now," she said. "Because of you."

"Because of *us*," he said.

"And now you have two cousins to help fill up those empty spots at the Thanksgiving table." Abigail smiled. Then she yawned.

"I do," Tony said, also yawning. "Maybe we can invite them this November."

"Grandma would love that," Abigail said. "Now, let's get some sleep."

They didn't bother to undress or shower. They just crawled into bed. Tony put his arm around Abigail, and she scooted closer to him until they were spooning. She could hear Giselle breathing softly in the bed next to theirs.

"*Sleep, oh sleep,*" Tony mumbled. "*Nature's soft nurse...*"

221

"Macbeth?"

"King Henry. My point."

Abigail went to sleep with a smile on her face.

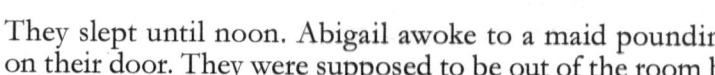

They slept until noon. Abigail awoke to a maid pounding on their door. They were supposed to be out of the room by now. Tony had to go downstairs to beg the manager to add an extra hour before they checked out.

They took turns showering. Abigail gave Giselle one of her dresses to wear, a light blue cotton one that brought out the color in her eyes.

She herself put on her favorite jeans and a T-shirt and tied her hair back with a ribbon.

Tony was the last to shower. He came out with his hair still damp and curly.

"Hey, beautiful," he said, pulling her to him with his good arm.

Giselle was sitting on the bed, waiting for them. Her face was pinched with worry.

"Let's tell her," Abigail said.

Giselle looked up at them expectantly. "Tony and I were talking while you were in the shower," Abigail said. "About this ring." She held out her hand. A beam of sunlight coming in through the window caught the stone, and it sparkled.

"It's beautiful," Giselle said. "I'm so glad you got it back. It's a symbol of love. I know now that means more than money."

"It *is* a symbol of love," said Abigail. "Which is why we're giving it to you." Without hesitating, she slid it off her finger and held it out to Giselle.

"Abigail and I want you to have it," Tony said. "It may be a family heirloom, but it's also worth a lot of money. There are a lot of legitimate collectors out there who will buy it from you."

"It could pay for college tuition and for a place to stay. It will give you and Lena time to make a fresh start," Abigail said.

Giselle was staring at the ring, not making a move to take it.

"I couldn't. It means too much to you," she said. "I mean...
you knew all along that it was valuable, and yet you didn't
sell it."

Abigail sat down on the bed next to Giselle and took the
girl's right hand. She slid the ring onto her fourth finger. It
fit perfectly. She closed Giselle's fingers around it.

"It's yours," she said.

"No."

"Please accept it," Tony said. "We want to leave you with
something. And I know my grandma would want you to
have it."

Tony's phone beeped. "Our cab is out front," he said.

Giselle was quiet as they gathered their suitcases and left
them with the desk clerk, for pickup later. They took a cab
to the police station. Julia was going to meet them there, and
they had promised Giselle she could see Lena.

A police officer took them back. Lena was behind bars,
sitting on a cot.

"Giselle!" She jumped to her feet. The sisters embraced
through the bars. Lena said something in French.

"English, please. For them," Giselle said. She turned and
smiled at Tony and Abigail. Lena followed her gaze. She hadn't
noticed them there before.

"They saved me," Giselle said.

Lena hugged her again. "Oh, Giselle, the police told me
you were safe, but I didn't believe it until now!"

Tony and Abigail lingered back. Abigail blinked rapidly,
trying not to cry.

After a few moments, Lena reluctantly let Giselle go. She
touched the ring on Giselle's finger. They said a few words
quietly to each other. Then Lena turned her attention to Tony
and Abigail. "Thank you," she said. "Thank you for saving
my sister."

Tony nodded.

"We love her too," Abigail said. "She's related to us also,
you know." Lena gave her a small smile.

"Why did you do it?" Lena asked. "Why didn't you tell
them I stole your ring? All they have on me is breaking in to

a few museums to leave my artwork. I put you through so much. I was so mean to you both."

"We've received a lot of grace," Abigail said. "Grace received. Grace given."

Lena pondered that for a moment. Then she said, "And I have been told that somebody is paying my bail. I don't have a 'somebody.'"

"You do now," Tony said. He was holding Abigail's hand. She wrapped her fingers tighter into his. She was never going to let him go.

Lena's eyes teared up. "I...I don't know what to say."

"Say it's not too late," Tony said.

Lena looked at Giselle. Then her eyes met theirs again. "It's not too late."

Julia met them in the lobby and told Giselle she had found her a nice home to live in, with an older couple who had been taking in teens for decades. Right now, they didn't have any foster kids. Giselle would live with them until the college year begun. Then she could live on campus.

"We'll get you in a college around here," Julia said, "so you can be close to Lena. Unless the two of you want to move out of the city."

Giselle turned to Abigail and Tony. She slipped the ring off her finger.

"Here," she said. "Lena and I want you to keep it. We'll be okay. Lena has a small savings. And you can help me figure out ways to pay for college."

"Giselle, please..." Abigail said. "I don't want to leave you with nothing."

"You aren't," Giselle said. "You are leaving me with a lot. We're safe from my father now and no longer have to hide. And you both have given me family. *Real* family. That's more important than anything." She took Abigail's hand and slipped the ring back onto her ring finger.

Abigail hugged Giselle. "Promise you'll call me," she said. "Or text. Or Snapchat. Whatever. I just want to know you are okay."

"I promise."

Giselle then turned to Tony and gave him a hug. "Cousin. Thank you. And I expect to get an invitation to visit for the holidays!" Abigail watched as his whole face lit up.

"You can count on it!" Tony said.

Chapter Thirty-Six

Tony was holding Abigail's hand in his good one. It was tough not being able to use his right arm. He wouldn't be climbing into any tricky places for a few weeks. He'd probably be stuck at his office doing paperwork.

With his non-dominant hand.

But that was a good thing. He was ready for some quiet. He was also ready to go home. But there was one last place they needed to visit before they went to the airport.

The afternoon sun was warm on their backs as they made their way across town to the storefronts where Antonio Russo's studio used to be. They arrived early, and the old man wasn't there yet. Tony ordered them both iced teas, and they took a seat at one of the tables outside.

"A slice of lime," Abigail said, sipping her tea. "Yum."

"That's what I thought," Tony said. "By the way, whatever happened to those pastries you were baking? Lena promised you'd bring some home."

Abigail laughed. "I'm sure they burned up along with everything else in the fake fire."

He loved it when she laughed. Her eyes sparkled, and her nose crinkled, bouncing her couple of freckles up and down. She claimed she didn't have any freckles, but he had found a few. And he adored them. Actually, he adored everything about her.

"It has been an interesting honeymoon," Abigail said.

"Interesting is a good way to describe it," Tony said.

"I'm glad I shared it with you." She reached across the table and took his hand.

"Bonjour!" A deep voice called out.

They turned to see Louis walking toward them. He pulled out a chair and sat. He had a paper sack. He opened it and reached in for a burger.

"My nightly meal," he said, unwrapping it and taking a bite. "The wife says it's going to be the death of me."

"It very well might," Abigail said.

"But it's so good." He chewed a few bites. "Très bien!" Finally, he picked up his napkin and wiped his mouth. "How is your honeymoon going?"

"It has been interesting," Tony said. Abigail laughed.

"Well," Louis dismissed that. "I won't keep you in suspense any longer. I know what you came for." He dug in his pocket for an envelope and pulled out a four- by six-inch, black and white photo. "Here."

He handed it to Tony. Abigail leaned in so she could see it too.

There were two young women, both younger than Abigail and Tony were now. Margaret would have been nineteen. They were wearing dresses and leaning against a railing, with the Seine behind them. Both women were laughing and looked incredibly happy.

"Turn it over," Louis said.

"Margaret and Lydia. 1944," Tony read.

"That's Margaret's handwriting," Louis said. He watched them for a moment.

"This is incredible," Tony said when he could speak again. "Thank you. My grandma will be so…I mean…this is her *mother*."

Louis smiled, the corners of his eyes crinkling up. "Oui. Then my wife got to digging through some old photos. I have one that I think you'll like even more. One that Lydia took."

Carefully, and with some flourish, he took it out of the envelope. He handed it to Tony. "You may want to keep this one out of the public eye. I think it's probably worth something."

It was of Margaret, wearing the same dress and smiling. Next to her was a handsome Italian man with dark, wavy hair. He was wearing trousers and a loose hanging white dress shirt, with the top three buttons unbuttoned. He was smiling too, and his dark eyes were sparkling. He had his arm around Margaret, and she leaned in to him in a casual, familiar way. On her finger was the ring.

"That's…" Tony couldn't speak.

"Yes." The old man's voice was solemn. "Yes, it is."

"You look so much like him," Abigail said to Tony.

Tony continued to stare at the photograph. He had seen photos of his great-grandfather before, while searching the internet. Some of the museums had them. But he had never, ever seen one with his great-grandmother in it. No public photos of the two of them together had ever been found. "Laurel," his mysterious lover, was only seen in the one painting. Which had been lost until a few months ago.

Tony finally tore his gaze away and looked at the old man. "May I keep it?"

He smiled. "Of course."

Tony looked across at Abigail. She was smiling.

"Looks like you did find your family on this trip," she said. "All of them."

They stood in the airport, looking at the display board of departures.

"It's leaving on time," Ms. Scott said. "Thank goodness. And wow, did I have a good time sightseeing today."

"Did Reggie come with you?" Abigail asked.

"No," Ms. Scott said, but she had a twinkle in her eye that Tony hadn't seen before. "We had a nice dinner Friday evening, and I'm bringing home a big check. But that's all. He wanted to see me again, and I said no. For now. I need time to think about it." The color rose in her cheeks, and she changed the subject. "Did you get rested after the symposium?"

Tony smiled. "Not really."

"We were up most of the night," Abigail said. "There was this festival going on near the Eiffel Tower."

"Oh my. Was it good?"

"It was…interesting," Abigail said.

Tony snorted.

"Well, what did I miss by not attending?" Ms. Scott asked. She was unusually talkative today. While Abigail tried to describe the acrobats and the clowns, Tony's mind wandered. He looked beyond them to the newspaper stand, thinking he should buy something to read on the plane.

"I'm so proud of you two," Ms. Scott said. "How you saved your job, Abigail. And Tony, our very own security guy, snagged a job at the Louvre!"

Snagged? Ms. Scott was in a fine mood this evening if she was using words like snagged. Tony squinted at the newspaper. There were two editions, one in French and one in English. From here, it looked like there was an article on the events of last night with Lena.

"So how do you think she did it?" Ms. Scott said.

"What?" Tony turned his attention back to the director.

"I was asking if you heard about the mystery artist who has been putting paintings into museums. Surely, you know about the attempt at the Louvre last night? It's all over the news."

"We...um...were busy," Abigail said.

"Of course! It's your honeymoon!" Ms. Scott gave them a knowing smile. "I'm off to get a bottle of water. I should buy a newspaper so we can read about it on the plane."

Tony put his hand on her shoulder and gently turned her in the opposite direction of the newsstand. "There's a great beverage bar down that way. Can you pick up an iced tea for me?"

Ms. Scott narrowed her eyes. "Sure," she said, subtly removing her shoulder from Tony's hand. "How did you say you hurt that arm?"

"We didn't say," Tony said. "It's a long story. I'll explain it all on the plane."

"The truthful version?"

He suppressed a smile and met her eyes. "The truthful version might have to wait until we're at home."

"In private," Abigail added. "Some stories shouldn't see the light of day. Especially for a recovering thief."

Ms. Scott eyed them both suspiciously but then smiled. "Good enough. I'm off to get that water. And your tea. I'll see you in a bit."

"She's in a good mood," Abigail said after Ms. Scott left.

"Of course she is. The library is getting half a million dollars, thanks to you. And she found her lost love and was finally able get some closure. The monetary kind. Wait here. I'll be right back."

Tony walked over to the newsstand. He read the headline and laughed aloud. He bought a paper.

"You're never going to believe this," he said when he got back to Abigail. He held up the paper so she could see it. A large headline across Paris's top English newspaper read:

Reformed Thief Solves Mystery Artist, Saves Lives

He started to read to her. "American cat burglar Tony Russo and his wife together solved the mystery of the artist who has haunted museums in Paris with her incredible paintings. Instead of breaking in to museums to *steal* paintings, this talented young lady was breaking in to museums to *leave* them."

"Give me that," Abigail said, snatching the paper from him. "What do they mean Tony Russo and his *wife?* Where's my name?"

She kept reading aloud.

"The internationally known thief, now a legitimate security guard with Black Cat Security—"

"*Internationally* known?" Tony interrupted. "Wow! I'm famous!" He waggled his eyebrows. Abigail scowled and read some more.

"The internationally known (and vain) thief—"

"Wait a minute. Did you throw that word 'vain' in there? Or did they write that?"

"—showed up right in the nick of time at the Louvre, just as the mystery artist left her painting." Abigail scanned the article.

"Read it to me!" Tony said, trying to peer over her shoulder.

"Why isn't my name mentioned? Who wrote this article?" She flipped it back to the front page. "A man. Of course. "'His *wife,*'" she added sarcastically. "I did just as much as you! Heck, I'm the one who figured out it was Lena!"

"Well..." Tony said. Then shut his mouth.

"Well, *what*?" Abigail looked him in the eyes.

"Well, I'm an internationally known cat burglar," Tony said. "And you're..."

Her eyes narrowed. "I'm what?"

Tony swallowed. "A librarian."

She whacked him with the paper. On the good arm, fortunately.

"Next comment like that, and I'm going for the bad shoulder. I did procure the library a half million dollars."

"You should have just given them the ring to sell. Ow." He braced for a second swipe, but she opened the paper again.

"Let's read on, shall we? Blah, blah blah...here we go. Russo saved her life by grabbing her arm just as she fell over the edge of the Eiffel Tower. Both suffered minor injuries, as his shoulder was pulled from its socket and her wrist was broken."

Tony grabbed the paper. "It has to say something about you. Here...'his *wife* assisted in the rescue.'"

He looked up at her and then quickly dropped his eyes back to the print and continued to read. "They were taken to the hospital and treated. More details as the police release them."

He dared to raise his eyes again. "Nope. I guess they didn't mention your name after all. But here's a lovely photo of you."

There was a blurry black and white photo of Tony leaving the Eiffel Tower, his good hand gripping his shoulder. His face looked frantic. He had been looking for Giselle then. Abigail's back was turned as she searched for the girl behind them. All you could see was her hair. He gave her a weak smile. "I love you, *wife*."

Abigail frowned.

"Really. I do." Tony racked his brain for something to say. He couldn't tell if she was really angry or not. He thought he'd try a quote. "*Kiss me, Kate, Shall we be married o'Sunday?*"

He saw her angry stare falter ever so slightly. She was thinking. Had he stumped her with the quote?

"We're already married, you goof," she said, finally. "And I will definitely kiss you."

She landed a kiss on his lips, long and lingering. The lavender shampoo of her hair enveloped him, and he felt her arms circle his waist. If he had both good arms, he would have taken her and waltzed across the walkway toward the gates. Instead, he stuck the newspaper in his pocket and pulled her closer to him. It was so good to have her in his arms, safe.

They heard the boarding call for their plane. They broke apart and took hold of their carry-on bags.

"I'm boarding first," Ms. Scott said when they saw her. She looked a little flushed with excitement. "They overbooked our section of the plane, so they moved me up to first class! This is the best trip ever!" She handed Tony his iced tea. "But that means we won't be sitting together."

Tony smiled and thanked her for the tea. Then he pulled the newspaper out of his pocket and handed it to her.

"Read this when you get settled," he said. "There's a great article in there that I think you'll find interesting." He winked at her.

Ms. Scott looked confused but nodded. Then she hurried off for early seating.

Abigail laughed. "That will give her something to think about."

"Yes, it will," Tony said. "So, did you figure it out?"

"Figure what out?" Abigail said, pulling her boarding pass out and not meeting his eyes.

"Where the 'Kiss me, Kate' quote was from. *Your* kiss only distracted me for so long. The game's back on."

"Oh, that," Abigail said. "It doesn't matter."

"Oh, but it does. I think we're tied."

She met his eyes. "Okay, then," she said. He could see her struggling. She hated to lose.

"*Love's Labor Lost*," she said. It was a good guess. There were lots of women in that play. And it was about romance. But she was wrong.

"*The Taming of the Shrew!*" Tony said, possibly a little too vigorously. "My point. I win." He raised his fist into the air and pumped it.

Abigail shook her head. "Unbelievable. You're so immature." But he saw her crack a smile. Then she took his hand. Together they boarded the plane for home.

THE END

What happens when the honeymoon's over? Follow Tony and Abigail's further adventures as they get tangled up in the mystery of a stolen violin! *If music be the food of love, play on!*

Author's Note

I took French in college, but that was a long time ago. Thanks to Google translate I was able to (hopefully) capture the language without too many grammatical errors. I can edit in English, but not so well in French. All errors are mine.

Same thing goes for the setting and atmosphere. I wrote from what I remembered, but I visited Paris quite a while ago. The landmarks are real. I may have taken some creative license on the details. Forgive me.

The food, the romance, the ancient beauty—there's no other city quite like it. I love Paris and hope I captured the romance and beauty of this great city for you.

Mangez bien, riez souvent, aimez beaucoup!

Acknowledgments

I am forever indebted to my readers. Because of your support, I can continue to do what I love. Thank you for reading my books, for emailing me, and for your wonderful reviews. I am grateful for you all. I'll try my best to continue to give you a quality product, and I pray that the magic of storytelling offers you a pleasant respite from the real world.

Once again to XP2, the most awesome critique group a girl could possibly have. Xanthe and Other Pam, you make this job so much easier and a heck of a lot more fun!

To my sister-in-law Peggy, who was my first beta-reader. Your comments are more valuable than you can possibly know. Thank you for your time and attention to detail, when you'd probably rather be out on the boat in the sun!

Erin, my editor. Thank you for making me sound competent, for dotting my i's, and crossing my t's. Your enthusiasm and prayers keep me going! Lyndsey, my cover artist. You work miracles with color. I love the way you've made Abigail and Tony come alive. Dallas, for your reliability and speed, and a solid formatting job. The three of you are the best.

Duane, Zack, Logan, Mom and Dad. Thank you for your love and support. It's because of you that I can do what I do.

Thank you to God, my savior and creator, for life and the chance to write. To Him be the Glory.

About the Author

Pamela Gossiaux is the author of the Russo Romantic Mystery series, and the romantic comedy *Good Enough*, as well as the inspirational books, *Why Is There a Lemon in My Fruit Salad? How to Stay Sweet When Life Turns Sour*, and *A Kid at Heart*. She is also a Christian speaker, writing instructor, and freelancer. She lives and writes in Michigan near a wonderful university town with her husband, two sons, and three cats. Visit her website at PamelaGossiaux.com to learn more or to sign up for her newsletter.

Other Books by
Pamela Gossiaux

Meet Amy Summers, a big-hearted heroine whose simple life gets turned upside down when she finds a winning lottery ticket worth millions...but should she cash it?

Amy Summers has it all: the world's best job, an awesome boyfriend, and a happily-ever-after in sight. Then, in one very bad day that involves burnt toast and a police arrest, she loses everything – except for a winning lottery ticket her ex left behind.

Afraid to cash it, she decides to give up men and become a Bohemian novelist. She takes her laptop to Starbucks and literally bumps into caffeine-free, easy-going Josh Gray, a life coach and very handsome man. (Not that she's noticing.) When he offers to help Amy get back on her feet, she decides to hire him.

Her heart is telling her that he's the man for her, but Josh is big on honesty and Amy has a huge secret that could push him away if he ever finds out.

"Richly meaningful while wildly entertaining, GOOD ENOUGH is a major new book by an exceptionally talented author."
– Grady Harp, Amazon Hall of Fame Top 100 Reviewer

"This story is such a fun read, it is impossible once you have opened it not to be thoroughly captivated by Amy's escapades."
– Susan Keefe, *Midwest Book Review*

"GOOD ENOUGH touches a nerve every woman faces. Are we ever going to be good enough? Gossiaux has written a funny, revenge romance that will have you cheering on the heroine, Amy, until the very end."
—Diana Lesire Brandmeyer, author of CBA Best Seller *Mind of Her Own*

Available at PamelaGossiaux.com

www.ingramcontent.com/pod-product-compliance
Lightning Source LLC
Chambersburg PA
CBHW031235120726
47905CB00002B/609